L E A P

Z Egloff

Ann Arbor

Bywater Books

Copyright © 2013 Z Egloff

Bywater Books First Edition: March 2013

Printed in the United States of America on acid-free paper.

Cover designer: Bonnie Liss (Phoenix Graphics)
Cover photo: Barbara Hadden
Author photo on back cover: Sassy Stafford

Bywater Books
PO Box 3671
Ann Arbor MI 48106-3671
www.bywaterbooks.com

ISBN: 978-1-61294-023-6

This book is for Melissa

Ball

Rowan stands behind the counter, assessing the situation. Everyone's eating, which is good. It gives her a minute to think. The whir of the ice cream cooler at her knees provides an anchor, a pivot point, for the knots of frustration traveling through her awareness. From her feet to her head. Snap. Back down.

It's not that she doesn't want to be here. She does. Sherry at the grill, a roomful of bellies stuffed with burgers and hot fudge, a glaze of satisfaction rambling through the place like a smile. She's just got her nerves packed close to the bone, is all. What with everything around the bend.

"Girl, you got that look on your face again. I swear, sometimes I don't know where the hell you go." Sherry blows a bleached curl off her forehead and wedges her bra strap under her tank top. She's only thirty-four years old but looks forty, years of smoking and hard living battering her into an always older version of herself.

"Me?" Rowan presses against the counter. "Where would I go?"

"Beats me. But I know you ain't always here. Like one of them pod people, dilly-dallying around the universe, leaving only the crust behind."

Rowan shivers. "You're onto me, Sher. Crust and all. I thought I could—"

"Load me up some ice in this cup here, will ya?" Sherry extends a bronze arm, brushed with blonde. "The sweat's pouring off me like spit."

Rowan scoops the cup into the ice bucket next to her and hands it back to her boss. "Yeah, you look a little wiped out today."

"Don't get me started. I was up late last night, waiting for Jerry to come home. Not that he ever *did* come home." Sherry drops

1

an ice cube in her mouth and rolls it around inside. "I'm telling you, Ro—don't pop out any munchkins of your own. You'll regret it the rest of your life."

"If you say so."

"I'm not kidding, girl. They're way too much trouble. Both those boys. You're almost an adult now—you need to know these things."

Rowan pulls a hand through her hair—black, thick, straight as rain. "No kids. I'll remember that."

"Don't let that Danny get all slippery between the sheets, is what I'm saying. I'll kick his ass if he does. You can tell him that, too." Sherry removes another ice cube from the cup and plops it down her shirt. "Brrrr." She shudders heartily and her breasts follow along. "Now that's more like it."

"You don't have to worry about me, Sher. Seriously."

"I know that, girl. What with all them smarts you got crammed in your head."

Rowan winds her arms around her torso. *Smart.* She's been affiliated with this label since before she can remember and still doesn't know what it means, really, or how to answer to people impressed or intimidated by her intelligence. She especially hates when Sherry tags her with it, as the older woman holds things Rowan doesn't even begin to understand. Things she wants. Sherry's experience and intensity alone never fail to knock Rowan forward, toward the future.

"Of course." Rowan slips out the syllables with a shy drawl. "You know I'm being careful."

"Good." Sherry grins and reaches inside her cup. "How 'bout you, Ro? You want a little pick-me-up? I'm telling ya, it's just the thing."

"No thanks. I have to go. Baseball, remember? I told you."

"Baseball." Sherry clucks it out. "What a waste of precious male flesh. You can send some of the finer specimens over here, if they get tired of bats and balls."

Rowan rolls her eyes. "Will do, Sher." She lifts the pink and hite striped apron off her tall, narrow frame and drops it on the stool behind her. "Hey, when's that franchise guy coming? I thought it was supposed to be today."

"Nah. He switched it to next week sometime. I tell you, I can't wait. This place is gonna start hauling in some real money now. Cashola, dripping from my fingers. We'll go year-round and everything. I may even be able to buy me one of them—what do they call 'em?" Sherry pauses for effect. "Houses. Yeah, one of them." Her eyes are glowing from the inside out and the flesh on her cheeks is shining—from sweat, but from something else as well.

Rowan catches a taste—anticipation, fat with hope—and looks away. She can't join Sherry in her glee. She wouldn't know how. "Sure," Rowan says, her gaze fixed at her feet. Sherry laughs. "Liar. I know you're happy for me. But you don't gotta pretend you're not all bunched up about something. What is it?"

"Nothing."

"Like hell." Sherry shakes her cup. "I got ice and I'm not afraid to use it. Down your shorts, what do you think?"

"It's nothing." Rowan's foot shuffles to the side, then back to center. Sun is pouring onto the floor, slapping the color out of the tiles. "I was just thinking about how things are going to be changing soon and all that. You know . . ." Her hand flitters between them to make up for what her mouth won't say.

"Is that all?" Sherry reaches out and shoves Rowan in the shoulder. "Girl," she laughs, "you'll be having so much fun, you won't even remember my name. 'Who was that lady I worked for back in Ohio? Lady Gorgeous? I can't recall.'"

"'I can't recall.'" Rowan tries it on. "Yeah, maybe. That's probably what I'll say." She digs her car keys out of her front pocket. "I have to go."

"I know."

❧   ❧   ❧

Five minutes later she's lounging outside Art's Gas 'N' Go, Wakefield's version of a Texaco station. Her car, a Chevy wagon that's been in the Marks family since Rowan was a baby, sits beside her, drinking gas.

3

It's another muggy evening, dark clouds low in the western sky suggesting rain. Green takes over the town this time of the year, as the grass and trees and shrubs bloom in the heat and the water. Rowan searches the quiet leaves of a huge oak on the corner across from the station, losing herself for a moment in the empty green. It's the perfect time for Invisible Girl.

She's been playing this game since before she can remember and she's excellent at it. The goal is to make herself as small as possible, so that if someone were to pass by, they wouldn't even see her. Of course it's not true that she's actually invisible, but she can still pretend. Like a superhero in a movie, the kind who can slip past criminals without detection. Rowan breathes in the sights and smells around her—the ripe tang of petroleum and pop; the call of crows over streets and houses; the steady green of the oak, parked smack in the middle of summer—and feels herself shrinking from all of it. She's a speck, a mere smidgen of existence. She's nothing, really. Nothing at all.

Until the gas handle surrounded by her grip bucks back, signaling the end of her little game.

"Nice." Rowan salutes the giant tree, iridescent in the aftermath of Invisible. Then grabs her cash and runs it in to Art, the main man on the premises.

"If it ain't my old pal Rowan." Art Giretti is a big guy, round everywhere you look. "Where you been hiding yourself?"

"Out at the Sugar Shack. Sherry's keeping me out of trouble."

"I'll bet she is." Art chuckles, a big round shake.

Rowan plucks a candy bar off the rack in front of the register and slams her cash on the counter. "Once this chocolate hits my bloodstream, though. Watch out. I can't be held responsible."

"You and them Rocket Bars." Art clucks. "How many cavities you got in that mouth of yours, anyway?"

"Cavities are good luck. Didn't you hear?" Rowan tears the wrapper off her candy and takes a large bite. "Something about the metal. It attracts coins."

Art rubs his chin, fat fingers soothing day-old stubble. "Is that so?"

4

"It is."

"Speaking of luck, what's this I hear about you and Massachusetts?" Art volleys the ball into her court, commencing a set of Tell Me About Your Future Plans. A game Rowan hates.

"What do you mean?" she says.

"I hear you're going to some fancy college out there."

"Not that fancy. Just a regular one. Rollins, in Boston."

Art's belly bounces against the register. "Still fancier than anything I've ever done."

"Yeah, well. It's not that big a deal."

"Says you. When are you going to—"

"Shit." Rowan spits this out in reaction to the revelation that, according to the clock behind Art's head, it's 7:15 already and she has yet to find herself playing ball. She's aware of the other motive as well, the one about sidestepping her least favorite game, but hopes Art didn't notice. "Sorry," she says.

"No problem." He eyes her curiously. "It's hard to offend me."

"Hey, I got worse words than that. That's nothing."

"I'm sure you—"

"Oh, and can I get some cigarettes? They're for Ben. We're playing baseball. You know how he is, Art. Just pretend he's buying them."

Art shakes his head, smiling, and turns to grab a pack of Marlboros off the top shelf. Rowan takes this opportunity to slip a few Fireball penny candies into her front pocket, then places her hands on her hips so by the time Art turns around, he'll know there was no funny business going on behind his back. She understands she's way too old to be pulling a stunt like this, but it's a little habit she just can't seem to break. As hard as she may try and as much as it goes against her Up And Up approach to life, occasionally borrowing a few things here and there from the shopkeepers of Wakefield, Ohio seems to be something that Rowan is, if nothing else, extremely good at doing without getting caught.

That is, until today. It's as Art is handing her the pack of Marlboros, still shaking his head, that Rowan realizes they're not alone. There's a man in the frozen food section, one she's never seen before. It's rare in a town the size of Wakefield to encounter someone she doesn't know, and even rarer to have them stare at her like this guy is doing. He's leering, his eyes sliding from her face to her pocket, a tiny trail that tells her everything.

He saw her take the candy. He saw her do it and he's basking in his awareness. Will he tell Art? And who the hell is he? He's her father's age or thereabouts, but taller and more stylish. And he's witnessed a side of Rowan she thought was hers, and hers alone.

Rowan coughs, checks Art's face. He's oblivious, or appears to be. Rowan grips the pack of cigarettes in her hand. "I better get to the ball field," she says. Her mouth tastes like sand. "Don't want Ben to have another one of his nicotine fits."

Art rolls his eyes. "God forbid."

"Yeah," Rowan says. She peeks over at the frozen food section. The guy is still there, still watching her. Doesn't he have anything better to do?

Rowan gulps. Without a goodbye to Art—because she can't speak, not even a little—she shoves herself out of the Gas 'N' Go and back into the muggy evening. Her body feels like someone else's. Light, shaky, barely there. What the hell just happened?

Rowan slips into the Chevy, her fingers curling around the Fireballs in her pocket. Maybe the tall man wasn't real. Rowan's got a hefty imagination, after all. Maybe her guilt about her stealing habit caught up with her, manufactured a stranger in frozen foods with jeering eyes. Rowan blinks, cranks up the ignition. She's got a game. Ben and the boys are depending on her. Whatever just happened, she needs to pretend it didn't.

❧   ❧   ❧

"Hey, Ro. You made it." Ben salutes his sister with an open can of Budweiser and motions for her to join him and the boys at home plate. "We were waiting for you."

"I can see that." She approaches the group slowly, wondering if ball is even what's happening here. The smell of reefer is in the air, mixing with the beer and the recently mowed field to invoke a sense of both blush and decline.

Ben has a roach pinned between thumb and forefinger and tucked inside his palm. "You want a little pregame buzz?" He squints underneath the patch of curly blond locks he's had since childhood and offers up what's left of the joint that, from the looks of those assembled, has already been passed around more than once.

Rowan tosses Ben his cigarettes and shakes her head. "No thanks. You guys haven't started yet?"

"Nah. We're working up to it. Right, boys?"

"Mmm." A grunt rises from the crowd, the usual mix of Ben's friends from the neighborhood and a few other guys who have latched onto the pack over the years. The crew is low on motion tonight—an occasional cough, flicks of ash, hocks of spit. Mostly they're all just staring at Ben, waiting for something to happen.

Rowan's brother is the leader of this particular gang of boys and always has been. For whatever reason, Maple Street and its surrounding blocks were littered with boy children in the sixties, when Ben and Rowan were young. Ben, with his full-steam spirit and irreverent inclinations, was a natural for provoking trouble and perpetuating fun. Everyone idolized him back then, including Rowan. She was four years younger than her brother, but endowed with honorary older-boy status due to her coveted spot in his heart. She played kickball, rode bikes, and swam in the creek alongside every boy in the neighborhood and, always, her brother Ben.

Not much has changed since then. The boys are all grown, of course, hitting their twenties with the speed that dominates rural Ohio. Slowly. Almost backwards. Even the few that went away to college, like Ben, seem to be utterly untouched by the experience once they set foot back in Wakefield. The town has a way of spitting out everything that's not simple and accommodating. Bordering on comatose.

7

Most of the boys have real jobs nowadays—construction, retail, auto sales. The kinds of occupations that allow them to plant themselves in the pace of this place where they were born and now raised. Ben's attempt at the same includes a summer job painting houses with the Conner brothers and some side work in the distribution of marijuana. And a smooth step back into his old role as Chief Boy, seasoned by the years into a just as rowdy but touch more cynical leader of good times and fun for all.

"Check it out." Ben lifts his head to drain the rest of his beer and rubs a palm across his soft, stocky belly. "There's something I got to say. Before we play. I got some news."

"News?" Rowan jabs a hand in her mitt and pounds it with the other one, now in a fist. "What kind of news? You didn't tell me about any—"

"I'm thinking about going back to school. Get a Masters maybe. Or a PhD."

"Really?" Rowan says.

"Really," says Ben. "There's a new university for sexual studies opening up. It's gonna be in Cleveland, I think."

"Far *out*!" Someone yelps and Rowan turns. Ben's best friend Lyle stands away from the crowd, swinging a bat around his head in wild, erratic loops. He's sporting a pair of brand new baseball pants—tight, bright white. He grins. "You better sign me up for *that*."

"Wait." Ben staggers, rights himself. "You got to hear the name of the place. It's the best part." He finds Rowan with a wobbly glance. "Fuck U. Ever heard of it? Fuck U?"

She laughs. This is why. This is why she loves her brother.

"Fuck me?" Lyle throws down his bat and stumbles toward Ben like he's failing a police sobriety test. "You want to say that to my face?"

Ben crashes to the ground, howling. "I already did. Fuck U. Get it? Like, the University of Fuck?"

"Huh?" Lyle arrives at home plate perplexed, then amused. "Ohhh. Good one." He slams on top of Ben and the two begin a wrestling match, rolling on the ground like puppies.

8

"Shit," Rowan says. "Not again. Ben! Cut it out, Ben."

But it's too late for that. The wrestling match inspires the others, in various stages of consciousness, to either join in the rumble at home plate or drop in place, overcome by the substance use or laughter or a combination of the two.

Rowan slumps onto the bench. "C'mon, Ben. You always do this. We never get to play."

"Wuuump." Her brother's voice emerges from the heap.

Rowan yanks off her mitt, flings it onto the ground. "It always gets messed up. I really wanted to play tonight. Hey, Ben!"

The pile creaks and shifts to the left. Deep inside, somebody belches.

"Man." Rowan sighs. The tall man's face storms back into her awareness. She can still see his shiny eyes, lit up with the evilness of her actions. What the hell is wrong with her? And why did someone have to see it?

Rowan picks up her mitt and flattens it between her hands. She should tell Ben. He'd know what to do, how to handle it. Though she knows, the minute she thinks this, that she can't. Ever since he got back from college last month, Ben has been troubled, strange. She never used to worry about her brother, it was always the other way around, but lately she feels like someone who's missing half an arm and is on constant lookout for the other half. He won't tell her what's wrong, or even admit there's a wrong to discuss. Not that their family ever talks about anything anyway.

The pile starts to pick apart, dusty bodies and bleary faces. The upper half of Ben pops up from the earth like a body with no bones, then flops back on the ground. Rowan slips her hand into her mitt.

"Look alive, boys," she says. "We'll choose teams. Ben and Lyle as captains. How about it? Ben? Let's go."

❧   ❧   ❧

Rowan releases the knob to the back door of her house, trying for an unobtrusive entrance. It's late and she doesn't want to wake her father, who should be asleep by now. She opens the door and sees a low blue glow shining from the center of the refrigerator—a reflection of the television in the adjoining room. Her father may not be awake, but the TV is.

Television is a new habit for Rowan's father. She finds it perplexing that a man of his distinction and intelligence has taken to watching movies from the fifties on the UHF stations and, worse, primetime network fare on occasion. Rowan came home a few weeks ago to discover him nursing a glass of brandy and watching *Quincy, M.E.* Her father was laughing out loud at the wacky situation Dr. Quincy had gotten himself into. This is all vaguely disconcerting, as far as Rowan is concerned. Her father was the one who would always shut off the television when she and Ben were little. Proclaimed it would turn their minds to jelly. Now it's his turn to wobble. The recent addition of two glasses of brandy a night, up from the time-honored one, seems to aid in his enjoyment of all that television has to offer.

"Dad?" She rounds the kitchen into the family room on the other side of the counter.

"Rowan?" Dr. Marks turns his head to capture a look at his daughter. His face is tired, ragged.

Rowan freezes. What? Does he know about the stealing? He must. Should she say something first, prove that she has a semblance of honor, of responsibility? She drops her jaw, thinking some words might tumble out, but nothing comes.

"How was your game?" her father says.

"Uh," Rowan stammers. "You know. Uh, fine. They're still going. Ben said he wants to play till tomorrow."

"Ah." Her father clears his throat. His face is still tired. But that's all. He knows nothing.

Rowan takes a step toward the TV. "What are you watching?" she says.

Her father sighs. "*The Avengers.*"

"Oh yeah. I know that one." Rowan's voice comes out small, tinny. She studies her father's hand, curving round a glass on the table beside him. It's a calm hand, a composed hand. He can't be mad, right? If he knew something, he would have said it by now.

"Well?" he says. He peers up at her. His eyes blink—once, twice.

"What?" Rowan flinches.

"Do you want to watch with me?"

"No." She swallows. "I mean, no thanks. I have to go to bed."

"Ah." Her father's attention flickers back to the tube. "Sleep well, my dear."

"Sure." Rowan shudders, turns toward bed.

She rounds the corner of the first set of stairs and attacks the second, a last wave of energy before sleep. Rowan took possession of the third-story bedroom of this seventy-year-old house when she was fourteen, the year Ben left for college. It was more like Ben bequeathed the room to her; the possession followed. This has allowed her four years of sitting on top of a house that's been in her father's family for three generations, Rowan and her siblings being the third. She finds the experience to be like floating on top of history, hiding from and being sustained by it at the same time.

Rowan enters her bedroom and catches the red-fingered signal of the clock by her bed: almost midnight. She should brush her teeth and put on proper nightclothes, but she doesn't want to. She slips off her shorts and sneakers and slides under the covers in her T-shirt and underwear, draping her body with a cool sheet and releasing her head to the pillow. Rowan closes her eyes as if expecting sleep, though she knows it won't capture her quickly. She's grown accustomed to this dance her brain does before going under, an enthusiastic resistance to the inevitability of unconsciousness.

Tonight it is her mother's face that emerges first and Rowan brightens at the image, gliding easily into the rich array of feelings her mother always evokes in her. Rowan's ongoing fantasy is that if her mother had lived, if Helen had made it past the car crash that claimed her when her youngest child was only three months old, life would be altogether different. For starters, she imagines her mother would have armed her family with the ability to converse in the language of normalcy and emotion. The one

11

everyone else seems to speak. Everyone but anyone in the Marks family.

She also imagines that everything that's good about her—everything pure, everything true—came from her mother. This keeps her connected to Helen with a grip as real to Rowan as her link to the living others in her life. As clear and constant as the steps she follows down through the center of the house every morning after a night of dreaming. As real as the hands fastened to her arms or the feet to her legs. This bond with her mother is one that nobody can take from her, no one can break.

Except for those times when Rowan breaks it herself, flipping the maternal affiliation on its ass, the dark side matted with mold and uncertainty from lack of air and too much time passed. That's when everything gets to be Helen's fault—Rowan's lack of direction, her emotional isolation and ineptitude, her penchant for petty theft. In the same way her mother lives behind her skin, always ready to grace her daughter with redemption, so does Helen's real-life absence threaten to pull Rowan into the unformed and less desirable shades of who she undoubtedly is. Rowan's sense of self is, if nothing else, a mystery. Her mother's death confirms and confounds this lack of clarity every day of her life. Even in sleep.

Rowan rolls onto her stomach, a sure way to nudge herself beyond consciousness and into absolute nothing that much quicker. Thoughts of her mother gradually give way to other images from the day. Ben collapsing at home plate, cigarette dangling from his lips. The sweat on Sherry's face, the light deep in her eyes. The fat green leaves on the tree across from the Gas 'N' Go, so sure of their purpose and place in the world. This last picture takes Rowan deeper in, first to pure green, then somewhere beyond that. Her slow, steady breathing begins and elsewhere is all she can see.

Boom

Rowan frowns at the scraps of paper scattered around the desk in front of her. She's camped out in the back of the Sugar Shack, attempting to work magic with Sherry's loose understanding of the term "bookkeeping." It's hard to focus, though, because of the storm: torches of lightning flashing through the windows, rain streaming onto the roof, claps of thunder joining the party like a brigade of rowdy, arrhythmic drummers.

And it's not only that. It's the thunder inside. Usually it's just clips of conversations and the cash register slamming shut that make their way into the office. Today, with the storm, she shouldn't even be able to hear that. But there's something going on in the front of the Shack—a human growl, a clatter, an upset of sorts, combined with shots of laughter. Which is weird, as no one comes out for ice cream when it's raining. At least, no one regular. No one human. Maybe today's the day that an army of aliens decided to take over the Sugar Shack once and for all.

Rowan gathers up a clump of receipts and drops them into the shoebox at her feet. The books can wait.

She enters the main room of the Shack through the kitchen. Sherry has her back turned but Rowan can tell by her posture that she's nervous. She has her arms wrapped around herself and she's massaging her waist with hot pink-fingernailed hands. Her voice is strained, like there's a threat to remove it. But by whom? The man in front of her, the one she's talking to?

Rowan peeks around Sherry to get a look. Her throat closes like she's being strangled. It's the tall guy, the one from the store. What is he doing here? Did he come to tell Sherry about Rowan's misdeeds? How did he find out where she worked?

"An inspiration," he's saying. "A true life, honest to God in-spiration. You can feel it, out here. The corn fields, the open sky. It's a great country, America, one that AmeriBurger is proud to serve from coast to coast."

Rowan shakes her head. The franchise guy. The tall guy is the franchise guy, the one Sherry's pinning all her hopes on. He looks different than the other day, fancier. He's got on a suit and a tie, with a shiny grin to match. His hair is thick and brown, sweeping over his brow with an air of satisfaction. Or maybe it's just his face that's satisfied. Whatever it is, he sure looks happy. Or confident. Or something.

"I have to say, our Midwest franchises are my favorite," he says. "No bullshit, you know what I'm saying, Sherry? You can take people at their word. Solid work with solid folks. It doesn't get any better than that."

Rowan continues to stand behind the group of two, unsure what to do. The tall guy doesn't appear to have noticed her yet, and neither has Sherry. She should go, sneak away before she gets caught. Again. But it's too late.

"I see we have a visitor. Is this your daughter?" Mr. Happy punches the vowels into the air like he's taking a victory lap. Rowan has never heard anyone with a volume of happiness set so high. He's probably trying to compete with the thunder. "She sure looks like you," he says. "Just as pretty."

Sherry turns to Rowan and her face rises with joy. "No, this is Rowan. My best girl. Ro, come and meet Mr. Lowell from Chicago. He's gonna help us get legit."

"We've met, actually," Mr. Lowell says. "Rowan and I. It was just the other day."

Though standing completely upright, Rowan feels the floor underneath her tilt. She tries not to fall. "I guess," she says. "I mean, I don't remember."

"Of course you do," Mr. Lowell says. "It was at the bank, downtown. You were making a deposit. Or was it a withdrawal? We didn't meet officially, of course. But I remember. I never forget a face. The salesman's gift." He winks.

14

"Well, how about that?" Sherry clucks. "Small ass world."

"Sure," says Rowan. Her shoes feel tight, like she put them on backwards. At least she's still standing.

"And this is my daughter, Catherine." Mr. Lowell gestures to his right. "She's part of our team. Right, hon?" Rowan peers around Sherry to take a look. The girl is nodding, slow and precise. Rowan gets the sense that the younger Lowell is not quite with them. Like she borrowed a body to be here but has plans to return it immediately after her departure. She is shorter than her father, with a mass of red-brown curls sprouting from her head and dropping just below her shoulders. Her face has been sprayed lightly with freckles, so lightly that on first glance they look like flecks of sand. It certainly is an attractive body she's acquired for the occasion, sturdy and compact, but one that also seems to be causing her a specific share of discomfort. For a second, Rowan wonders if the girl's discomfort is a result of knowing about Rowan and the stolen Fireballs. But how would she know that? She wasn't there, was she?

"Nice to meet you," Rowan says.

The girl blinks.

Sherry's hands drop to her sides, fingers flexing. She grins. "AmeriBurger's gonna put us on the map, Ro. Mike's company sent him out to fix us up with our Dairy Barn gig. He'll be popping by, on and off, for the next month or so."

"Well . . ." Mike rubs his palms together and leans over them ever so slightly, like a Boy Scout trying to make fire. "That's not exactly it. How it'll be. We have a—"

"What do you mean?" Sherry says. Down the road somewhere, thunder growls, then cracks. "That's what they told me on the phone. As far as how you people work these things out. Evaluating the place and all."

Mike and his daughter have a brief visual meeting. He inhales a quick breath, exhales a statement. "Actually, it will be my daughter Catherine who will be doing most of the book work and evaluation, as well as eventual orientation into AmeriBurger policies and procedures. She's just graduated from college and wants to get herself into the business field."

"No shit," Sherry says.

"We'll be traveling around a radius of towns this summer, setting up a variety of folks with a variety of business opportunities. And you're right about the frequent visits, Sherry." Mike shortens the distance between them in an apparent attempt to shift the sudden pale on Sherry's face. "Catherine will be here once or twice a week for the next few weeks or so."

Catherine nods, quick and tight. Rowan wonders if this odd girl is incapable of speech. Perhaps her body came without a voice box. "It's an exciting time for all concerned," Mike says. "We're looking forward to this opportunity to assess your prospects in becoming a member of the AmeriBurger family."

"Are you?" Sherry squints.

"You betcha," says Mike. "There's no other company as committed to excellence. All of our franchises have to pass strict standards of business and professional ethics, as well as fiscal solvency and structural capacity. Only the best for AmeriBurger."

"So why is your big fancy corporation sending a *college* student to evaluate my store?" Sherry pronounces "college" like it's a swear word. Something a kid says to get a rise out of the folks. Rowan wants to laugh but decides against it.

"She's not a college student per se." Mike blanches. "She's actually a college *graduate*."

Sherry peers over at Rowan, then back at Mike. "Right," she says. "You know, Rowan is going to college." Sherry's voice acquires the sharp sound she usually reserves for lecturing her boys. Cheese-grater sharp. "She's been doing our books for over a year now. I don't see any difference between that and your daughter here."

Rowan shrinks, reestablishing her visual connection with her feet.

Sherry huffs. "I thought you all were the real deal. With your snazzy-ass promotions, your stacks of cash. Now you're telling me your kid is going to take our company to the big leagues? I don't think so." She snaps out this last line like she's spitting on the AmeriBurger logo itself. The echo crackles in the air.

"Perhaps you would be willing to give it a chance." Catherine steps in front of her father. It's her first foray into speech, her voice surprisingly assured. "I actually have a fair amount of experience in the business field, not to mention coursework in accounting and business techniques. And all my work will, of course, be supervised by my father and the AmeriBurger corporate staff. We have no intention of shortchanging you or your opportunity for a franchise." The technique is similar to that of her father, the drive and obsequiousness of a salesman's pitch, but there's another quality as well. Like she doesn't care one way or the other what effect she has on the outcome. The game is all.

"I didn't say you were stupid," Sherry says. "I assume they're not going to send a moron to check this shit out. But I got a lot riding on this, see? It's not like I—"

"So do I," Catherine says. "I've got a lot riding on this as well. You're not going to meet anyone more passionate about this job than I am. No offense, Dad."

Mike smirks. "None taken."

"I'm going to work harder for you because I want this more than anyone else. The veteran staff, they do a great job, but they're not as hungry as I am. So in this case, you get my hard work and passionate commitment combined with my father's experience. You couldn't be in better hands, Sherry. Honestly." Catherine opens her palm, as if offering evidence.

Sherry glances away. "Maybe not," she says.

Catherine's hand slips behind her back. She's wearing the same colors as her father, light blue shirt and dark gray suit, except she's sporting the junior, feminized version of his outfit. "What do you say, Sherry?" she says. "What if you give me a chance? Give *us* a chance. You won't be disappointed."

"A try is maybe all you'll get." Sherry wedges her palms against the counter. She looks weak, weary. "I guess we could *try* that."

The tail end of this sentence gets swallowed up in hurt and pride, and Rowan can sense her boss floating away, her faith in the future and a chance at her own house drooping in the wind of a successful sales pitch. Like always with Sherry, Rowan wants to smooth away the threat of possible hurt, shape it into an easier edition of Sherry's hard life. But how can she do that? In this case, AmeriBurger seems like the best shot, the best way for Sherry's shaky life to get a little more solid. And maybe it's crazy, but all Rowan can think is that they need to keep the ball rolling. For Sherry.

"Hey, so how about this?" Rowan bounces forward, next to her boss. "Why don't I show Catherine the current facts and figures? I was just working on this month's receipts." Rowan flushes. She keeps her eyes off Mike, off his invasive gaze and hearty smile.

Sherry's face fans open, relaxes. "Sure," she says. "I guess it couldn't hurt."

"Sounds like a plan." Mike beams.

"Cool," Rowan says. She nods at Catherine with a glance she hopes exudes competence and self-assurance. "It's back this way," she says. She turns to follow the trail of her entrance, her gait hopefully oozing a similar competence and self-assurance. Catherine follows behind at a distance that is unnecessarily polite. Or perhaps just distant.

"Here we go." Rowan enters the office, sidles up to the cluttered desk, and opens her arms, hands spread. The "ta-da" remains unspoken.

Catherine eyes her companion expectantly, as if Rowan was planning on producing a more magnificent item. A rabbit from a hat. Smoke from her ears. She glances away and takes a small notebook out of her pocket.

"Yes," she says. "I'll take a look at these. It might take a while. You don't need to—"

"I've got my own system, but hopefully you can make sense of the figures." Rowan stands near the desk, shifting her weight from one foot to the other, kneading her anxiety through the floorboards. "This place does pretty well, financially speaking. We're only open in the summers, though."

Catherine flips the pages of her notebook. "That would have

to change." Her speech is clipped, like she could slice onions with the sound alone. "AmeriBurger only sponsors year-round operations."

Rowan nods seriously, though serious is not what she is. She's thinking that the office feels entirely too small for someone as entitled as Catherine. Entitled people need floats, not offices. Rowan can see it now: a tropical theme, perhaps. Palm trees and men in outfits made of colorful cloth, serving AmeriBurger's newest employee with tasty fruits and fanning her fair skin with large leaves pulled from exotic plants. While the crowd cheers, transfixed by her alluring, yet obnoxious, aura.

"And it continues to be unclear what will happen."

"What?" Rowan has a hard time prying herself from the float. The noise of the crowd intersects with the patter of rain hitting the roof, creating a peculiar blur of motion and stillness.

"I said we don't know what will happen here." Catherine enunciates the words as if she is speaking to a two-year-old. "As far as the Dairy Barn. Do you understand me?"

Rowan is flattened by this remark. Water pounds on the roof and she is dry. Fallen. "I understand," she says.

"Perhaps I could have some privacy so I could start to examine these numbers?" Catherine speaks quietly, addressing the random pattern of papers on the desk. Her lips roll into what passes as a smile, but all Rowan can think is that Catherine has no interest in smiling, and even less in spending another minute with Rowan. Rowan squints, locks her arms across her torso. *Very well, then, Miss Priss, I'll leave you to it. Make sure the love slaves on that float of yours don't choke you with their mangos. On account of your winner attitude.* Rowan smirks. "Okay, then. You have fun, Miss Lowell."

Catherine shudders almost imperceptibly at this last statement, but Rowan notices. She guesses the college graduate is one of those gals who like to be called "Ms." and not "Miss." Rowan actually agrees with this wholeheartedly but can't resist the impulse to aggravate the entitled one.

"Thank you," Catherine says. She maintains her condition

19

of mild distress. They probably put her body on too tight, Rowan muses. Whatever it is, Miss Lowell is in need of a serious personality transplant.

"No problem," Rowan says. "You know how it is with us folks out here in the country. We aim to please. It's the fresh air. And the corn. It makes us more . . . accommodating. That's the right word, isn't it? Miss Lowell?"

Catherine doesn't answer. She's already hard at work, arranging Rowan's papers into frighteningly orderly piles. Rowan closes the door behind her.

She wanders back into the main room, mostly on account of having nowhere else to go. She hears a surge of laughter and understands that there has been a change. Sherry and Mike are sitting in the empty dining area, side by side in front of what appears to be an AmeriBurger scrapbook. Or maybe it's Mike's wedding album and he's interviewing Sherry for bride number two. Or three.

"That's an attractive-looking building there." Sherry taps a glossy photo with her glossy pink nail.

"Very attractive." Mike appears to have the ability to see the building in Sherry's chest.

Sherry twists the photo album for a better look. "Would we be getting a facility like this one?"

"That's possible." The building inspection continues.

Sherry nods and flips the pages of her future. "Possible is good."

Rowan coughs to announce her presence. Sherry turns and finds her through a glaze of happy. It's more than Rowan can bear. She's relieved to see the shift in Sherry's spirits, but something's off. The whole thing feels shaky, wrong. Rowan takes a breath. "I have to get over to Danny's," she says. "I told him I'd stop by when I was finished here."

Sherry kicks the air with her platform-sandaled foot, perpetuating the levity. "You better get on down the road, then."

"Hold on there, Rowan." Mike jumps from his seat. "Let me see you out." He hops to her side, a firm hand plopped on her

20

shoulder. As they walk to the door, she can smell his breath, which is like hamburgers and coffee.

Mike says nothing as they head to his car. He keeps his hand on Rowan's shoulder, though. When they reach the car, he lifts his hand off her shoulder and puts it in his pocket.

"I'm only going to say this once, because I know you'll hear me," he says.

The hard rain has turned to drizzle, the water clinging to their skin and clothes like little bugs. Mike appears unfazed—his posture hearty, his voice firm. "AmeriBurger is a corporation," he says. "You know what a corporation is, don't you, Rowan?"

She nods, buries her gaze in the gravel.

"We pride ourselves on integrity. Integrity all around. From management down to the line staff. Even the janitors. If that chain of integrity gets broken, no matter where, it hurts everyone. *Everyone*. You see what I'm saying, Rowan?"

She nods again. Then slouches her shoulders to avoid the drizzle.

"As long as we're clear," he says. He brushes a crop of raindrops from his sleeve. "I'm willing to leave Sherry out of this. For now. Everyone deserves a second chance. But only one. I'm sure you understand."

"Yes," Rowan says. Her mouth tastes like lard. "Thanks."

"Okee doke." Mike claps his hands. "I'm glad we had this little powwow. I think you'll find us easy to work with. My daughter and I."

Rowan sees herself on the float, poking Catherine with a palm frond. "Easy," she says. "Yeah."

Happy Times

"Here's the question. Fresh or frozen?" Rowan stands in her sister's kitchen, one hand on the refrigerator, her other in midair. "What do you want, Janie?"

"Do you have to ask?" Years of family jokes about Jane's substandard cooking skills have led to a perpetual, if awkward, beat-'em-to-the-punch on her part. "Frozen, of course."

Rowan smirks and yanks open the freezer door. "Frozen ye shall have. I shall liberate the small green prisoners from the tyranny of their cage and present them to the world in all their glory." She tears at the plastic bag with her teeth and plops the pea block into a small saucepan on the stove, turning the gas to high.

Jane stares at this display of cooking finesse, apparently keeping the lid on a suggestion or two.

"What?" Rowan jabs at the peas with a wooden spoon.

"Aren't you going to add some water to those?" Jane speaks slowly. Although the statute of limitations on jokes about her cooking for the most part expired with Ben's exit to college, his recent reemergence on the landscape puts her in a precarious position. Not to mention that he is in the living room ingesting alcohol with her husband and father at this very moment.

"Nah." Rowan does her best to suppress a smile. "Water is for wussies."

"Okay," Jane says. "I guess it's not necessary. You know best." She draws her long black hair away from her face, flicking it behind her rounded shoulders. "I saw Ethan yesterday."

Rowan fills a glass from the sink and adds a swish of water to the pan. "So?"

"So, he's interested. It's not like you have to marry him. It's just a date."

"No, it's not."

"Yes, it is."

Rowan stabs her peas. "He's old."

Jane clucks. "He's twenty-one. Only three years older than you."

"I'm not eighteen yet."

Jane sighs. "You're almost eighteen. And he's a nice guy."

"I don't like nice."

"Yes, you do. Danny's nice. But he's not marriage material. Ethan's a much better—"

"You said it was just a date." Rowan shakes the pan of peas. "I'm not going, Jane. You can stop talking now."

"But I—"

"Stop. Talking."

Jane huffs. Except for the longer hair, and the fact that she's ten years older, everyone always says she and Rowan look like twins. Rowan can't see it. She views Jane's compressed, proper features—placid mouth, delicate nose, dark eyes that shroud worlds—and she sees a foreign entity. They have nothing in common, except for blood. Which is a lot, actually, but given the absence of their mother, and their father's inconsistent accessibility, blood doesn't seem to count for much. At least for Rowan. Jane tries to reach out, but the reaching always seems to involve an agenda, like this Ethan scheme. So Jane reaches and Rowan rejects. And then feels bad. Like now—with Jane pouting at the kitchen table and Rowan accosting the hapless peas in an inept attempt to make her sister feel better.

"Hey, what about this?" Rowan says. She bounds over to the kitchen table and plops onto the seat next to Jane. "Tell me about Mom."

Jane flushes, taps on the tabletop. "I thought you didn't want me to talk."

"I do. Tell me about Mom. Tell me about her singing." Rowan leans forward, arms on legs, hands dangling between them. "When you would sit on her lap."

23

"I told you already."

"Tell me again."

"But it doesn't—"

"Please?" Rowan spins it with just the right amount of insistence—steady, pressing.

"Well . . ." Jane softens, the girl she was peering shyly through the eyes of her older body. "It was like the best chair in the world, comfy in all the right places, holding me up. And she would sing the most beautiful songs. I've never heard any of those songs since then. Ever. She must have made them up." Jane hesitates, swallows. "She would sing about me, and how pretty she thought I was. And how special. I'd be embarrassed by it now, I'm sure, but then, back then . . ." She studies her hands as if her voice dropped inside them and she is considering whether or not she can retrieve it.

The white circle on Rowan's ankle says "Converse All Star" in big red letters. She traces it with a finger. This is a difficult subject for Jane, she knows this. She should stop. But she can't. She's not sure why, but she can't. "What about the breakfast thing," she says. "How does that go again?"

Jane shifts her view from her hands to the face of her sister. "She smelled like breakfast. She always did. Like pancakes or toast, like that. Like everything was being taken care of."

Rowan sits in this notion like a pocket—sure, content. Until she surveys her sister and understands that this confidence has come at a price. Jane is all but gone, burrowed inside herself like vanished time. Rowan wonders if this is what she looks like when she slips into Invisible Girl. A shiver passes from her knees up to her elbows, carrying a curious sensation along with it. It's like she's afraid, but of what?

"Sweetie? Do you need any help in here?" Jane's husband Hank pokes his head through the swinging door that divides the kitchen from the living room.

"No," says Jane.

"Are you sure?"

Jane sighs. "Hank."

24

"I don't mean anything by it, sweetie. I just wanted to help."

"Oh fine." Jane waves him in. "We're about ready anyway."

Hank grins. "See? I knew you needed me." He enters the room head first. Rowan's brother-in-law, she can't help but always notice, bears an extreme resemblance to a beaver. It's not just his stout build and lumbering movements, or the brush of thick black hair that stands off his scalp like a salute. It's his demeanor—bright, industrious. As he kisses his wife on the lips with a soft peck, Rowan ponders the possibilities of human-beaver mating. If Jane and Hank had children, could their offspring fell trees in the backyard? Would their dam-building activities make them popular at school, or would this only be a hindrance to their attempts at social normalcy?

"How's post-high school existence treating you, Rowan?" Hank has donned an apron and is putting the finishing touches on their dinner for the evening. Pork chops and applesauce. Jane is attempting to rescue the steaming pan of now-burned peas.

"I can't complain. Just loafin' along."

"What about Danny? Are you two still hanging out?"

"Sure. Sometimes. He's working a lot."

"And you? You still putting in time at the old Sugar Shack?"

"Yup." Rowan swallows. It's like a cord has been pulled, draining her of juice. "Sherry's trying to score herself a franchise opportunity with Dairy Barn. The corporate suits came last week to check us out."

Hank's eyebrows pop into his forehead. "Dairy Barn, eh?"

"Mmm." Rowan shudders, tries to shake off the image of Mike in the parking lot, lecturing her on decency and the corporate code. She's considered quitting the Shack, so as not to hurt Sherry's chance for a franchise. Or coming clean to Sherry, so her boss can tell her what to do. There's no one else to tell, except for maybe Danny, but that doesn't seem like a good idea either. "I hate to say it," Hank's upper teeth latch onto his bottom lip, then let go, "but a franchise like that can't help but bring more business my way. And I do hate to say that." He holds up his palm, as though addressing an invisible jury of fellow dentists stationed in the corner of the kitchen. "They put sugar in every-thing at those fast-food places. Even the French fries. I learned it at my last conference in Cleveland."

Rowan nods, utterly uninterested. She tries hard to like Hank for Jane's sake, but talk of the intricacies of oral bacteria and the supreme value of flossing tend to leave her underwhelmed. At least it's a distraction from her Sugar Shack woes.

"It's reprehensible," Hank says. "Truly. Maybe I should talk to Sherry about handing out packs of toothbrushes and floss. Maybe that would—"

"Looks like we're ready to eat." Jane picks up a bowl of peas with a suspicious pale of black and heads toward the dining room. Rowan shrugs at Hank and follows with the rolls, relieved to be bypassing a focus on her, or anyone else's, oral needs. Time to stick food, the culprit, into their mouths instead.

Jane gathers Ben and Dr. Marks from the living room and Hank settles into head of the table status. Rowan captures her preferred spot, with her back to the picture of Jesus on the wall over the chest of drawers that belonged to their grandmother. Rowan understands that Jane and Jesus are extremely close, that they may even converse from time to time, and she can't get away from the perception of Jesus as watchdog in her sister's house. For all she knows, He reports back to Jane every thought that cruises through her naughty little sister's head. Rowan knows this is crazy, but it doesn't stop her from wondering just the same. And protecting herself as best she can.

"Here are the other people." Dr. Marks enters, Scotch in hand, and eases into the seat next to Rowan.

Ben follows in a wave of silence and what Rowan suspects is anger, plunking himself into the chair across from her. Ben and her father coexist in a bit of a rocky patch, always have. Leaving them alone together in the living room was probably not a good idea.

"Shall we say grace?" Jane sits opposite Hank and scans the family expectantly. Rowan, Ben, and Dr. Marks take this moment to look at their shoes, inspect their fingernails, and generally display their acute discomfort with all matters religious. Jane's conversion

26

to Christianity bloomed in her adolescence and the family continues to hope that it will fade into a background of other discarded teenage notions: bouffant hairdos, mohair sweaters, patent-leather shoes, and The Beach Boys. Except Mr. Christ seems to have stuck as far as Jane is concerned. Denial is all they have left.

Jane closes her eyes. "May God our Father bless this meal and everyone at this table with His abundant grace and mercy. We live and breathe in the shadow of your love, O God. In the name of our Lord Jesus Christ. Amen."

"Amen." Hank plants a napkin on his lap with his usual zest. "How's the painting job going for you, Benno?"

"It's going just wonderfully, Hankie. Couldn't be better." A splash of beer hits the table as Ben raises his glass in a toast. "Inhaling paint fumes, dragging my roller from wall to wall. It's inspiring. Truly."

Hank squints. "Glad to hear it. There's nothing like a little honest labor to get a man thinking about his future."

"Nothing," Ben says.

"That's great," says Hank. "Which reminds me. I've been meaning to talk with you about a new idea I had. I was talking to Cyrus Gordan—you know him? He's—"

"Actually, sweetie?" Jane breaks in. "I think there's something else we need to talk about."

Ben takes a gulp of beer. "Does this mean we don't get to talk about my plans for the future?" Mock disappointment frames his face.

"Maybe later." Jane's lips curve slightly.

Hank shuttles his dinner plate an inch to the left, attempting to reset his agenda for the evening. "I thought we were going to wait till the end of dinner." He looks to Dr. Marks for assistance and receives nothing but a friendly and indelibly remote smile.

"So did I," Jane says. "But I'm thinking this is better."

Rowan removes her feet from the floor, allowing them to hover in the segment of space under her chair. What could it be? She has an idea, but it's only a maybe. Nothing for sure.

She attempts to draw Ben's gaze to her own merely by willing it, but he's somewhere else. Not here. She wouldn't know what to do with her father's gaze even if she had it and turns back to her sister.

"Come on, Jane," she says. "What is it?"

Jane places her hands under the table, in her lap. Her eyes are grinning and her mouth catches up to them as she begins to speak. "Well, as you know, Hank and I have been discussing the idea of starting a family for quite some time. And it seems that now, we are. Starting, that is. A family." She smiles shyly.

"Jane, that's wonderful. Great news." Dr. Marks skips not a beat.

Rowan's feet touch ground lightly at first, then sink into the floor in a motion both certain and cautious. "That is so cool, Jane. That's amazing."

"Yes," Hank says. "We're incredibly pleased. We're hoping for a boy, but either one would be fine, really. We're not picky."

"Nor should you be." Dr. Marks's voice is at once scolding and kind.

Ben raises his glass in yet another toast. "Groovy news. About time we started propagating the species around here. When can we expect that Ben Jr. will be arriving?"

"He or *she* will be here sometime around Christmas," Jane says. "So there will be two births to celebrate, our Lord's and our new baby's."

Ben chortles. "Hey, I'm okay with you calling her Benny even if she's a girl. I have no problem with that."

"Thanks, Ben." Jane shudders.

"After all, we need a reason to look forward to the eighties at this point, after Three Mile Island. What with the state of this asinine country." Ben jerks on his chair, as if being ministered by an invisible string above his head. The No Nukes movement is a recent interest. He picked it up sometime during his senior year of college and carries it back to his politically apathetic family with all the enthusiasm of a new toy. "I just hope there'll be a world for baby Benny to grow up in."

"Ben." Rowan yanks the choke chain, but it's too late for that.

"I'm just saying. We have no idea what the fuck we're doing with all these factories of death scattered across this country. Three Mile Island is proof of our incompetence, that's all."

"Benjamin." Dr. Marks speaks slowly, as though not quite sure he has hit on the correct name.

"Yes?"

"Do you really think this is the time to be discussing the state of U.S. energy resources?" Dr. Marks's fingers ride gracefully around the perimeter of his placemat.

"Oh, I see. Phrase it as a question. Always the illusion of choice. Smooth one, Dad. The problems of the world never touch you, do they?"

"Ben." This time it is Hank who intervenes, his voice a pale shot at peace.

"Hank." Ben smiles. "Let me guess—the latest dental journal espouses the use of radioactive waste as the ultimate cavity killer. Plop it in your mouth and watch those nasty germs disappear. And for that matter, your teeth. Really, Hank, I'd love to hear you drone on and on about what a great dentist you are. How important it is that we: Floss. Every. Day. Because Mr. Hankie says so."

Hank takes a bite of pork. For the next few seconds, the only sound in the room is him chewing, then swallowing, this meat. Finally, finished with his task, he finds Ben with eyes both wounded and furious. "If you will excuse me, please." He rises from his seat and pounds open the door to the kitchen, vanishing from the dining room.

Jane stands and follows her husband, a quieter but just-as-angry variation on a theme.

"What was *that*?" Rowan knows better than to challenge her brother in front of her father, but she can't help herself. Her arms are tingling with the volume of the moment.

"What was what?"

"Did you hear what Jane said? Did you hear *anything*? What

29

were you thinking, picking on Hank after an announcement like that?"

"I wasn't even talking about that, Ro. I was talking about something else entirely."

"What, Ben? What were you talking about? Tell me, because I really don't understand." Rowan rubs her brow, as if this may help with her comprehension.

Ben opens his mouth to speak, looking first to his father, then Rowan. She spies a flash of rage in his pupils, in his jaw, that she has never seen before. Not in him, not in anyone.

"You don't get it. You have no fucking clue." He shoves his untouched plate of food into the middle of the table, patterns of pork and peas spilling over the rim. He is out of the room before either Rowan or her father has the chance to reply.

"Sorry, Dad." Rowan flattens her feet onto the floor once again, flooded with an experience she has yet to understand.

"It's not your fault." Dr. Marks appears almost untouched by the outburst. Only his eyes convey a reaction, and it looks more like assessment than anger. "We all know Ben is a bit high-strung these days. I suspect it's the ambiguity surrounding his future. No one likes uncertainty."

Rowan watches her father's lips move, the top and bottom one coming together, then apart. Nothing makes sense anymore. Ben has been angry before, but not like this. Not cruel like this. And her father is acting like nothing happened. Maybe nothing did.

"Right," she says. "Uncertainty. Bad." Her own restless life floats in front of her face, splashing toward another atmosphere.

"I'm going to go check on your sister." Dr. Marks unfolds himself from his chair and pushes it under the table. Rowan notices that, unlike any other plate on the table, her father's is free of food. He ate every bite.

The door shuts gently behind him and Rowan and Jesus are the only ones remaining in the room. She wants to turn, to gauge His reaction to the preceding events, but fears that this would only perpetuate a truly foolish game. She sighs instead, breathing

30

in the scent of cold pork and lemon cleaner. Outside, the sky is fading and the Midwestern crickets are warming up for an evening wall of sound.

"Happy times," says Rowan, eyeing her peas.

Strip

"I seriously do not understand why you watch this show. Wonder Woman's boobs are so pointy and bizarre. She looks like she's directing traffic." Rowan shoves Danny's leg with her bare foot, causing him to spill pop on his shirt. It's Friday night and the friends are sitting on Danny's bed, watching the closing minutes of what he won't admit to, but what certainly is, his favorite television program.

"Stop it, dumbass. It's almost over." Danny laughs and shoves her back, refusing to unglue his attention from the boobs in question. "They're not so bad. I bet she's quite effective at traffic control. I'd sure go wherever she took me."

Rowan rolls her eyes and takes another bite of her Rocket Bar. "I'm sure you would. She could drive you off a cliff with those things. Blind you with their enormity. 'Hey, boy! Over here. Just park it in between these two boulders.' I tell you, Danny, they're lethal. Big time."

"Shhh." Danny remains fixed on the tube, soaking in the beauty of the final battle scenes. Wonder Woman is dispensing her high-stepping brand of justice to the poor schmuck who dared cross her path. With kicks, twirls, punches, and close-up shots delineating the effect of all this action on her ample cleavage, the female superhero is surely having her way. Rowan manages to stay quiet in spite of herself, long enough to get sucked into rooting for Wonder Woman to win the battle and feeling a strange sense of satisfaction when she does.

The Incredible Hulk is on next, but Rowan knows they won't watch this one. Danny feels obligated because it's another show based on a comic, but this commitment does not include silence while the show is actually airing.

"Did I tell you I did some more work on the strip?" He hops off his bed and retrieves a stack of papers from the top of his desk, bringing it over to Rowan.

"You did just now." She polishes off the rest of her candy and lobs the wrapper toward the wastebasket on the other side of the room. "Damn." She misses by a mile. "What's my buddy Hector up to these days? Killed any corrupt evildoers lately?"

"Check this out." Danny tosses a page onto Rowan's lap. "I'm gonna put him in a major battle with Vince. A battle like they've never had before."

Danny developed his comic strip *Hector the Mighty* a few years back. He's a great artist, but Rowan finds that his story skills leave something to be desired. For starters, she tried to tell him Hector and Vince were stupid names for a comic book hero and villain. Danny will hear nothing of it. He insists there is no name more noble or fierce than Hector, none more imposing or vicious than Vince.

And then there's the issue of the characters themselves. Hector, despite his bountiful mane of flowing blond hair and a body buffed beyond perfection, looks suspiciously like his creator. Hector's love interest, Guinevere ("Danny, no—not Guinevere!"), despite her blue eyes and blood red hair, looks more than a little like the creator's best friend. Rowan has never had the guts to point this out to Danny, thinking it would only complicate an already complicated situation. She keeps the subject stashed away in a hard-to-reach compartment in the back stacks of her mind, labeled To Be Discussed Later.

"Wait a minute," Rowan says. She's examined the series of animated events and is not impressed. "You've done this battle before. You need to do something different this time."

Danny tucks a lock of thin brown hair behind his ear. "Different? What do you mean?"

"Like you should introduce a new character in this part. Mix it up."

"Why would I need a new character?"

"Because you do. Because it makes it *better.*" Rowan's fingers graze the figures on the page, absorbed by their potential. "Like here. Where's the suspense? Vince will attack Hector with his fire-wielding eyeballs and Hector will resist with his impenetrable skin. How many times have we seen that? *Way* too many."

Vince is Hector's brother. He started out as a superhero but ran into a snag with the constant do-gooding. Vince was born to be bad. Or, at the very least, naughty. The two brothers are now bound to perpetual battle due to their conflicting allegiances. Serious superhero strife. Rowan is responsible for the bulk of this background material, a fact she tries not to be proud of but secretly cannot help but be.

Another interesting twist with Hector and Vince, also courtesy of Rowan's imagination, is the relationship between their superpowers. Hector's impenetrable flesh is affected only by his brother's gaze of fire. And Vince's powers are weakened only by assaults on Hector. Rowan sold the concept to Danny by its paradoxical nature. More precisely, she told him it was deep and chicks would dig it.

"I can't change it," Danny says. He rolls his knuckles into his forehead. "It's classic. Good vs. evil. You can't wear that out."

"Whatever you say." Rowan stares into the distance—in this case a picture of Bruce Lee mid-kick in a poster over the television.

Danny wiggles backwards and props himself against the wall. "So what would you do?"

"Well," Rowan pries herself away from Bruce, "I would start it out like normal. Vince attacks, Hector resists. Hector body slams Vince, Vince crisps him. That's when you bring in the new guy." Rowan licks her lips and taps the edge of Hector's head. "Right here." She grabs Danny's gaze, drawing him in. "Say it's a long-lost brother. You could call him Coltar or something. And Hector and Vince are fighting in the woods and they can't see a damned thing. They're running around and they keep losing each other. But Coltar, he can leap."

"Leap?" Danny's face sours.

"Yeah, you know. Leap. Jump."

Danny wraps his arms around his T-shirt, refusing the members of The Eagles additional views of his room. "Leaping just makes him sound . . . you know."

"What?"

"You know."

"Like a fag?" Rowan grinds the word into her new creation, his dark armor turning pink before her eyes.

Danny crosses his legs, stares at his knees. "I guess."

"Then let's just say he 'jumps.' How's that?" Rowan can feel an upward pull, the breeze of Coltar's magnificence.

"Fine." Danny bumps his head into the wall behind him.

Rowan continues to feel the pulse of her skyward friend and attempts to shape him into language. "So, Hector and Vince can't see anything, but Coltar, he sees everything. He's got these super-powered legs that allow him to lea—to *jump* so he can help Hector. He can tell Hector where Vince is and facilitate the attack. See?"

Danny shrugs. "Yeah."

"It's radical. Coltar's true superpower isn't in the legs. It's in the perspective." Rowan joins Danny against the wall, the tall breezes swallowing her. She relaxes until she can feel herself fall solidly back into her body, rearranged by having flown. "See? That's some real power there. Per-spec-tive."

Danny sighs. "I'll take it under advisement, Marks."

"You know you love it." She grins, full of flight. "You know you can't wait for me to leave so you can draw it."

"Only thing I can't wait for is you to close your mouth, doofus. I can't hear the show." Danny hoists himself off the bed and flicks a knob on the TV to drive Hulk's roars back into the audible zone. He saunters back to the bed, eyes on the floor. He is trying not to smile.

"And you can have Guinevere watch the whole thing. She'll be simply *mad* with desire for Hector at the end of the battle. The whole teamwork approach really turns her on." Rowan thinks to slap a hand over her mouth after this last statement but settles for mouth closed and silence instead. She should know better than to bring Guinevere into this.

One of the arguably more tragic elements of the Hector/Guinevere pairing is the effect of the superhero's impenetrable skin on their relationship. Though he pines for the touch of the lovely Guinevere, Hector will never experience it. It is, alas, never to be. It is also, alas, a dilemma that reeks with familiarity.

Danny shakes his head. "Didn't I tell someone to shut up?"

"Bitter is an ugly color on you, boy." Rowan hands the papers back to Danny and scoots her body flat onto the bed, gliding under the radar of fault. "But you never did know how to dress. Let me watch the show here, will you?"

Hulk manages to get himself in an awful lot of trouble over the course of the remaining hour (the plot revolves around a nuclear reactor and the pesky villain who can't keep his hands off it), but somehow, miraculously, everything resolves itself just before the last commercial break.

"Someday that will be your guy on the small screen." The closing credits find Rowan leaning over the bed, searching for her shoes. "After *Hector the Mighty* hits the papers."

Danny groans. "Like that will ever happen." He takes a drag off a roach found during a slow moment in the show and offers her another hit.

"No, really. I'm serious." Rowan takes the roach and sucks out its residual value. "It will be fantastic. I can totally see it happening."

"You and yourself."

"Me and my killer vision. You have to trust me, man."

"Do I?" Danny stretches off the bed and wanders around the room, settling into a beat-up chair next to his desk. Though he's tall, nearly six feet, his collapsed posture and quiet energy give the illusion of a smaller person. Younger too. He's been out of high school a year and still looks like a sophomore: round face, expectant eyes, self-conscious gait. He grunts, pushes his legs out in front of him.

"I don't think Hector is ready for the big time," he says. "He'll be fighting his battles in Wakefield the rest of his life, I think."

36

His face rises to study not Rowan but a spot on the wall next to her. As if the dope has given him the ability to see the alternative edition of Rowan living just outside her physical form. "Better not to pump him up into thinking he'll be getting something he's never going to get."

Rowan stares at her friend and allows the current underneath his words to resonate inside her limbs. It's painful sometimes, hanging with Danny. "I told you about that girl at work, right?" she says. This is a stupid question. She knows she told him. She even tried spilling the whole story—Mike in the parking lot, the shoplifting—but she couldn't go through with it. For now, the Sugar Shack subject acts as a needed buffer, a way to steer clear of Danny's dilemma.

"You told me a bunch of times," Danny says. "She still driving you crazy?"

Rowan flushes. "Crazy, yeah. Did I tell you what she called my bookkeeping system?"

He nods again. "Old."

"No." Rowan jerks up on the bed, folding her legs underneath her. "She said it was *archaic*. What the hell is that about? 'Archaic.'" She clucks the phrase to herself, as if repetition will soothe away the insult. "Like she's so damn smart. If that's what college is going to do to me—insert a rod of knowledge up my butt and compel me to assault the world with the superiority of my rod— then I don't want it. Not at all."

Danny smirks and cups his hands behind his head. "What does she look like, anyway? You never told me."

"Ugly. She's ugly." Rowan watches the lie spill into the room and it catches her by surprise. She twists the truth even further as a way out. "She looks like the Incredible Hulk's long-lost sister. Really. Same facial structure. And skin tone."

"Sounds hot."

"You don't know the half of it." She shakes her head vigorously, an attempt to hold off her inner wanderings. Catherine the Hulk is already stomping through Rowan's brain, leaving a flurry of devastation in her path.

"I'm serious. I bet I'd think she's hot. I've always liked green skin on a girl." He rummages through the top drawer of his desk. "I could swear I had another one in here."

"You wouldn't like her, believe me. She's mean and prissy. And weird. She's *way* too in love with her own opinions."

"Sounds sexy to me." Danny has found it, mixed in with his drawing pens. He perches the joint between his lips and begins his search for a match.

Rowan can feel her legs grow heavy, Catherine's interior rampage leaving her spent, ornery. "I should leave." She places her feet on the carpet, a first step toward gone.

"But we were going to celebrate."

"Celebrate what?"

He holds her in a fuzzy gaze. "It's not every day you turn eighteen."

"Thank God for that." Rowan gathers sufficient defenses to say this with a smile. "Besides, it's not midnight yet. My birthday doesn't officially start for another hour. And I have to work tomorrow." She travels the distance to Danny's chair and jostles his floppy head. "Sleep well, spaz."

"Wait," he stretches out his hand. "Pull my finger."

"You wish."

S p e l l

"Rowan?" Sherry's voice filters in from the kitchen of the Sugar Shack.

"What?" Rowan barks back. She's in no mood for anything but silence. It's another hot day, and the Shack is packed with families attempting to beat the heat with strawberry, vanilla, and chocolate. The constant demands on her time and attention are beginning to drive her into a pit of short-tempered intolerance. "What do you want?"

Sherry chuckles. "How about we go out later and celebrate your big step into legitimacy? You're legal for 3.2 beer now. If that ain't worth a night on the town, I don't know what is." Her chuckle segues into a cough, followed by faint sputters.

"You okay back there, Sher?" Rowan pokes her head around the corner to find her boss composing herself over the grill with a freshly lit cigarette.

Sherry smiles lightly and nods toward the ceiling like she's in on a grand secret. "Never better."

"I can't go till later. My family's doing a thing at my house. The inevitable giving of gifts."

"That's cool. Little has a race at 7:40. We could meet at 9:00 over at Ollie's."

"Is this his first race? Tonight?"

"Yup. I gotta admit. I'm kinda proud. Bud says he's gonna make a real jockey out of him."

Little is Sherry's second son. The good son. A few months back he talked his Uncle Bud, Sherry's brother and manager of All Bets Off out in Loomis, into trying him as a horse jockey. Turns out he's got a real talent for it.

39

"Tell him good luck," Rowan says. "Nine sounds groovy. I'll meet you there." She can hear the chirping of little girls at the front counter but decides they can wait. She stares at Sherry and imagines there must be more to say, some other reason to stay here. But nothing comes. "I better get back."

"To work." Sherry simmers in her knowing smile. "When things slow down up there, you might go check on Miss Smarty Pants in the office. Make sure she's not rewriting the Bible or something. She was only supposed to be here an hour and it's already been more like two. Hey, maybe she's dead." Sherry pauses, trying on this last thought like a new dress: pressed fresh, form fitted, the perfect pick-me-up.

Rowan's knees wobble like a toddler's. "How come I have to do it? Why don't you?"

Sherry's slow-burning smile breaks into a complete grin. "Because I said so. That's how come."

"You suck."

"Yes, I do." Sherry lowers her voice and grows serious. "I'm actually quite good at it." She turns back to her burgers, whistling through a brush of smoke. "If you see Lee Majors, you tell him that. Tell him I got a set of skills worth *way* more than six million. The happiest man alive, that's what he'll be once I get ahold of him."

Mr. Majors' stint as *The Six Million Dollar Man* ended last year, despite Sherry's lettered protests to the contrary. Nowadays she stokes the fires with reruns of *The Big Valley* and the hopes that Farrah Fawcett-Majors will die of excessive beauty, leaving Sherry next in line for Lee's affections. Rowan realizes that Sherry has her tongue firmly planted in cheek regarding this subject, but worries sometimes that her boss might do something stupid anyway, like pack it up and book out to L.A. in her search for movie love. Rowan also finds Sherry's devotion difficult to comprehend, as Mr. Majors strikes her not so much as a man but a cardboard cutout resembling a man. Not to mention the fact that *The Bionic Woman* is clearly the superior show.

"I'll just tell him to follow the trail of smoke." Rowan wags her head at Sherry, drawing out her visit an inch longer.

"You do that, sugar," Sherry says, distracted.

Rowan understands that she's lost her boss to fantasy (Lee Majors's face is probably adorning the greasy burgers under Sherry's spatula at this very moment) and can no longer delay working. She slips back behind the counter to find that the bird-voiced girls are gone. Maybe they were never there in the first place. A passing examination of the dining area shows that the crowd is either finishing their orders or waiting for food from the grill. Rowan knows what she needs to do. Might as well get it over with.

She starts with a knock, hoping politeness will permit a quick and painless entrance.

"Yes?" The flare of annoyance in Catherine's tone projects easily through the flimsy wooden door. "What is it?"

"I, umm. I have to get something. In the file drawers." The concept twists round Rowan's tongue, sounding false and unnecessarily cheerful. It would have been better, she thinks, to have said nothing at all.

"Come on in."

Rowan enters carefully, so as not to activate any of the preset alarms Catherine seems to have installed in the atmosphere surrounding her borrowed body. In Miss Lowell's multiple visits to the Sugar Shack since her arrival at the store two weeks ago, Rowan has observed that penetrating a radius of closer than three feet around the young businesswoman seems to trigger warning devices in various forms. Such penetration, in Rowan's estimation, has manifested in phenomena anywhere from increased sharpness in Catherine's speech to critiques of Rowan's accounting abilities to direct requests to be left alone. ("Could you stop that, please? Can't you be your loud self somewhere else?")

Rowan often wonders if Catherine knows about her indiscretion, her criminal tendencies. Maybe Mike and Catherine had a little chat, and that's why Catherine's thermostat is permanently set to chill. Though she was like that the minute Rowan met her, so it could be she knows nothing. After all, Mike said he'd keep quiet, at least as far as Sherry's concerned. And it doesn't matter anyway, if Catherine knows. She's weird, and not a friend. Why should Rowan care?

As Rowan slides behind Catherine in a bogus quest to the file drawer, she feels the thrill of testing boundaries, gauging the effect of her presence on Catherine the Entitled, Catherine the Mysterious. It's like a roller coaster ride—climbs and falls in time and space, the resulting jumps and sparks inside her belly, her mind. Why is it so exciting, being around this girl? Indeed, as Rowan glides to the file cabinet and back, she feels stretched beyond herself, a momentum that wastes her, overwhelms her. She watches her energy shrink, reverse directions. And then she's curling inside herself, fusing into a thin line that snaps her into Invisible Girl. Another round of missing. Everything is gone except for a speck inside her that walks, that needs, that finds the door.

"Do you want to see what I've been working on?"

Catherine's question startles Rowan, bringing her back. She turns to face the junior accountant behind the desk. "Umm. Sure?"

Catherine pulls out a chair and motions for Rowan to sit beside her. "Come see. I think you'll be impressed."

"Yeah?"

"I should have showed you these earlier. But I got too absorbed in what I was doing. Look at this."

"Uh." Rowan secures a place on the chair, the plastic cool and serious against her bare legs. She pretends to pay attention to what Catherine is telling her—debit columns and profit margins and balance sheets—but she is not listening to a word. She is inside the secret fortress and is carefully assessing the terrain. Catherine shows all the signs of flesh and blood, a living being with a heart actively engaged inside her chest, but there's something extra about her, something numinous. Rowan observes the curls that land neatly on Catherine's shoulders, the voice that makes a direct line to its target, the freckled hand that circles the ballpoint pen that scratches numbers in the margins as she speaks. Rowan doesn't believe in aliens, in outer space phenomena, but it's impossible not to speculate on other dimensions at a moment like this one.

Catherine continues to speak, her lips and the sounds emerging from them formulating a language Rowan cannot hear. Until she notices the expression on Catherine's face, a mix of concern and amusement, and clicks back to sound. The college graduate has just constructed a sentence that may have ended with "opinion"—like "What is your opinion?" or "Do you have an opinion?"—but Rowan's not sure. She scoots her chair forward, trying to analyze how to respond to Catherine's inquiry. Any answer is bound to give away the fact that she hasn't heard a thing. She goes for a stall.

"Umm . . ." Rowan says. Her heart starts dancing against her ribs. It could be anything. Catherine could have asked her anything. Capital gains, world peace, petty theft. What's Rowan supposed to say? Panicked, she stares at the freckles on Catherine's face. Connect the dots. Catherine's freckles are like Connect the Dots: cheek to nose, nose to chin, chin to forehead. They make an airplane; Rowan can see an airplane in there.

"That's okay," Catherine says. "You don't have to tell me now."

Rowan nods, trying to focus. Catherine seems annoyed. Rowan finally made it inside the forbidden territory and she's blown it with her distractibility and tilted imagination. "Yeah," she says. "So. I'll get back to you on that."

"If you like." Catherine rotates her body so she's facing Rowan. "Since I have to wait for your answer on the invoices, maybe you can satisfy another curiosity."

"Curiosity?"

"There's something I've been meaning to ask you."

"There is something I've been meaning to answer."

Catherine laughs. An actual laugh. Her gums are a soft, clear pink. "It's your name," she says. "Rowan. I've never known anyone with that name before. Is it Irish?"

Rowan blinks, as if to will away this stranger in front of her. There must be a million ways to avoid this question. Too bad she can't think of any.

"I was just wondering." Catherine slides her hands down her lap, sweeping aside an unknown irritation.

"Yes," Rowan says.

"It's Irish?"

Rowan shudders. *Why this? Why do we have to talk about this? I can't. I can't do it. Don't make me.* The thoughts bang around Rowan's skull with such force she swears they must be audible. "Yes, it's Irish," she says.

"Are you Irish?"

Rowan coughs, stalling. She shakes out her remaining thoughts, searching for a change of subject, but comes up empty. "My mother was," she says finally. "I'm named after her. Rowan was her maiden name. Helen Rowan."

Catherine leans in ever so slightly, piercing a radius of another sort. "You said 'was.' Is your mom no longer here?"

"She's dead." Rowan tilts into the void behind her, maintaining the distance between them. "She died. In a car accident. When I was small."

"I'm sorry." Catherine appears to be genuine, but the words sound wrong. Like she mispronounced them. Stripped all the meaning out of them.

"Don't be," Rowan says. "It's none of your business anyway."

And then the room shines with empty, ripped free of content as the two girls sit on either side of the response. Catherine stares at Rowan for an instant, then fully registers the slap and turns away. Her mouth opens as if to speak to the page of numbers under her hands, but she swallows her reply.

Rowan remains frozen on her chair, unsure what to do next. She realizes this was the wrong thing to say, but it seems she owed it to Catherine somehow. For something.

"You can leave now." Catherine—tidy and composed—turns back to Rowan to complete the exchange.

The edict takes a minute to register, but when it does, Rowan lifts herself from the chair and allows her legs to guide her out of the office. The door closes with a bit more force than she would have liked, but she doesn't seem to know her own strength these days. Or anything else, for that matter.

"She's alive, then." Sherry scowls as Rowan emerges from the office and ambles over to the grill.

"Yes. Unfortunately."

"What's she doing back there? Calling her daddy to ask him what's two plus two?"

"No. She just—"

"I bet she's got a stack of college books with her. Probably sitting on them, right? Trying to figure out the formula for who hijacked her personality."

"There's no formula for that. Or for her nosiness. It's like she thinks she can—"

"What?" Sherry turns. She takes a breath, the sequined "Foxy Lady" across her chest expanding. "What's that little hussy being nosy about?"

"Nothing special," Rowan says. "She was just asking about me, my name. Trying to get all chummy."

"Chummy ain't in her." Sherry yanks on the belt loop of her squeeze-tight jeans. "You set her straight, right? Told her where to shove it?"

"I did."

"Good girl. That's my Ro." Sherry hands her a cheeseburger platter and pats her on the behind. "Don't ever say I didn't teach you nothing."

ℒ ℒ ℒ

The next half hour is spent in murky waters. What initially felt like justice—reciprocal nastiness, really—starts to acquire the stale taste of regret. Rowan digs at the ice cream with a small metal scoop, portioning out cool flavors to anxious customers, each one a person she's known since either her birth or theirs. She finds an undeniable sense of accomplishment in giving people what they want in moments like these. It stretches out her anxiety, broadening it into a place that resembles patience. Understanding. Chocolate chip. Rocky Road.

The part that won't go away, the part that lingers in her mind no matter how many times she tries to scoop it into nonexistence, is the thought that maybe she was a bit harsh. Sure, Catherine deserved it. Without a doubt. There's been nothing in Miss Lowell's behavior of the past few weeks to indicate that the young woman has any familiarity with the concept of manners, let alone the ability to use them. Yet the fact remains that Catherine asked her a regular, normal question, to which she—perhaps—could have given a regular, normal answer.

She tries out a few such responses to herself while dispensing cones and sundaes. They are, invariably, easy phrases, full of sweetness and gentility—"Why, how nice of you to ask," "I'd love to tell you all about it." Yet these stick to the end of her throat like an old piece of gum, a dry portion of insincerity. Rowan comes to realize that her response to Catherine's question was as close to appropriate as she could manage, as true as anything she could have offered. Unless she had gone deeper, ripping out the seams of decorum, expressing her resentment for the way Catherine's been frosting around the office for the last two weeks. But that would require a degree of sophistication Rowan suspects she does not possess. Probably never will. Not that Catherine deserves it anyway.

Rowan is lunging into a tub of French Vanilla, gathering a scoop for Tommy Jenkins, when her next challenge presents itself.

"I'm going now." Catherine's voice dives into the tub, grips Rowan's wrist. "I'll be back next week."

Rowan springs to attention, shakes out her wrist by releasing the scoop of vanilla to its cone. Catherine is hovering next to Tommy, a placement that appears to be making the high school freshman uneasy. Or is it aroused? Rowan hands him his cone.

"Far out," he says. He strolls off—loose-limbed, awkward—leaving Rowan alone at the counter.

"Next week," she says. "That's . . ."

"Seven days away?" Catherine snaps. She's holding her briefcase in one hand and nothing in the other. Her posture is tilted toward the briefcase, and the lack of balance makes her look vulnerable, though her face denotes otherwise. Chilly eyes, stiff mouth. "I assume the place will still be standing when I return," she says. Her voice is a plea, a sad song sung by a child. Rowan feels a wash of regret splash the back of her knees. "I'll be here," she says. "I'm not going anywhere."

Catherine's shoulders rise and fall as she glides toward the exit. The smoothness of this motion gives Rowan an idea. A crazy idea.

"Hey, Catherine, wait a minute."

Catherine stops but does not turn around. Rowan acknowledges her lack of commitment and honors its logic.

"It's my birthday today. I'm eighteen." The words roll out of Rowan's mouth with an ease that surprises her. She is coasting in warm, open waters. "We're having a little celebration tonight at Ollie's Inn, off the Interstate. Nine o'clock."

"Is that right?" Catherine inspects her feet beneath her as if daring them to move.

"Maybe you would like to come." Rowan had a feeling she would say this, but it is strange to hear it out loud.

"Why would I want to do that?" Catherine's hand massages the back of her neck.

"Because I asked you?"

"I don't think so."

Rowan assesses the folds of Catherine's shirt, checks the slight wavering in the golden yellow fabric that sticks to her shoulders. Ultimately, she supposes, it doesn't really matter whether Catherine comes or not. The idea was to right a wrong. That accomplished, they can both let it go. "Just thought I'd ask," she says.

Catherine stands, silent, between Rowan and the door. She hikes up her briefcase and lifts her head. Her posture is almost balanced. "Thanks for asking, though."

"You're welcome."

Catherine exits quickly and Rowan watches her go. She slips into her car—an old blue Thunderbird with a solid strip of rust around the rear fender. The gravel bucks under the tires as she speeds out of the parking lot.

Sherry appears from around the corner and pokes Rowan in the ribs. "What was that about?"

"What was what about?"

"I didn't hear you invite Miss Brainy to the bar tonight, did I?" Rowan has a sudden urge to clean the counter. "Not me." She grabs a rag and ducks her head. "Tommy Jenkins was chasing the caboose, though. Trying to get her number."

"Is that right?" Sherry waits. "I guess my ears were fucking with me. Like you'd want to invite that uptight harpy to your party. No way."

Rowan finds a spot of hot fudge and increases her efforts. "No way." In the fractured reflection of the cool, clean counter, it's almost true.

ॐ   ॐ   ॐ

Ollie's Inn is one of two bars in Wakefield. The other, JJ's, is run by the woman that Sherry's father left her mother for. Sherry makes a point not only never to go there but also to give Ollie's more than his fair share of her business.

She and Rowan are sitting in the back, in a booth by the jukebox. Sherry insists on oldies, songs from the fifties like "Great Balls of Fire" and "Short Fat Fannie." Rowan teases her about this, arguing that "doo-wop" is not an acceptable background vocal for a song and should be banned. Sherry reminds Rowan that rock and roll sprouted from the Fifties and the younger generation has its eyeballs on backwards if it can't recognize its own roots. Rowan agrees with this but reminds Sherry that roots are meant to be buried, a sentiment that only increases Sherry's efforts to educate her young charge. She's punched in "Leader of the Pack" five times tonight already.

"So, did you get lots of presents?" Sherry is nursing her second beer, a Budweiser from the tap. Her body is relaxed and her energy has started to inflate, a function of the alcohol. She's known more than one bar fight in her time.

"Dad and Ben gave me money, Jane gave me a sweater. No big deal." Rowan sips her 3.2 beer. Given the laws of the state, it's the only way you can get legally hammered until you turn twenty-one and graduate to hard liquor. (Rowan's favorite joke about the stuff comes from Sherry. "Hey, Ro, what do 3.2 beer and a couple making love on a rowboat have in common?" "I dunno, Sher. What?" "They're both fucking close to water.")

"Eighteen isn't all that important to me." Rowan swallows through foam, the cold spilling down the middle of her body.

"That's believable."

"It's true, though."

Sherry grunts and scoops up a few peanuts from the dish on the table. "When I was your age? Hooo boy. Age is freedom, girl. Don't know why you can't see that. Or pretend you don't." She pops a couple of nuts into her mouth and crunches loudly, grinning through her teeth.

"Whatever you say." Rowan plays with her napkin, twirling it in fidgety circles with her hands. "How did Little do? Did he race?"

"He sure did," Sherry says. "He did good. He lost, but he still did good. Jerry Jr. even showed up for it. He wants to join the Marines now, did I tell you?"

"No." Rowan leans over the table, the back of her T-shirt peeling free of the fake leather upholstery behind her.

Sherry's head wobbles forward. "You mean, I didn't tell you or I did?"

"Didn't. The Marines—what the hell? He's such a rebel. How's that going to work?"

"He's been telling his friends that his dad is in the service. That Jerry Sr. works for some special operations office in the East. Wherever that is."

"And he wants to join the service to be more like his dad?"

"Something like that." Sherry shrugs, finishing her beer. White bubbles slip slowly down the inside of her glass. "Except it's a total lie. Last I heard, Jerry Sr. was in Montana racing Harleys. I should have listened to my mother about that boy."

"You wouldn't have listened, Sher. Don't lie. And what is it you always say? About hindsight?"

Sherry chortles. "That it's a 20/20 tour of your own ass? So true." She points a finger in the air, signaling the beginning of round three. "Maybe the Marines will be good for little Jer. Smarten him up a bit. At least give him good posture."

"Nothing wrong with posture." Rowan drains her glass and slams her palms against the table. "And now it's time for some birthday music."

Sherry covers her ears. "No. Please. Not that crap you like."

"Get used to it, lady. It's the voice of a new generation." Rowan rises, her legs feeling the beer and a swift pull of nostalgia. For what, she's not sure. She makes it over to the jukebox, its soft light illuminating her reflection in the wide clear bubble display of songs from generations past and present. A quick hit of Invisibility takes over, blending her with the A7s and G5s of choice and inclination. She emerges, rejuvenated, and snaps in two songs— one by Fleetwood Mac and another by The Eagles. Tunes she knows Sherry will protest only a little.

Rowan yawns. There's a tape on top of the jukebox, and she leans in to get a look. *Fleetwood Mac, Rumors.* Weird, Rowan thinks. She just selected a song by them and here's the tape. Like a birthday present. Rowan slides the tape in her pocket, her fingers tingling with the motion. She wasn't going to do this again. And here she is, doing it. But it felt okay—or not okay, but necessary.

Rowan shakes her head, lifting her arms to circle her chest. This was the last time. She's eighteen now, so she needs to cut it out. And she will. Totally. She turns back to the booth, nursing a rise of resolution and regret. If she knew why she did this, maybe she could stop. Though it doesn't matter, because she's stopping anyway.

Rowan squints. Mary Jenkins, the owner of the bar, is hovering over the side of their table. Rowan can tell, even in the dim light, that Sherry is disturbed. Mary is probably entertaining Sherry with another one of her sordid sewage stories. Her husband Clancy, a plumber by trade, keeps her in steady supply. ("It's amazing," Mary likes to say, "what some people will flush down their toilet bowl.") As Rowan approaches the table, however, she sees that she is wrong.

Mary is not Mary but Catherine. Catherine who, apparently,

decided to come after all. She and Sherry are clearly having a difficult time of it.

"Catherine," Rowan says. "You're here."

Catherine nods firmly. "Yes. Yes I am."

"I didn't think you were coming."

"Neither did I." Catherine is noticeably disoriented, her cells constricting with the attention.

Sherry coughs and extracts a cigarette from her purse. "And I wasn't informed she was coming in the first place, so there you go. We're all up to date." Her lighter flares against the darkness and she inhales a deep drag. "The next question is, are you staying or leaving? Take your pick."

Catherine looks as though she might tip over. "Go. I should go. We had dinner in town and my father and I were in separate cars and I was just thinking I'd stop in and . . . I really don't know what I was thinking."

"You could stay for one beer." Rowan punts.

"One beer." Catherine repeats this like she's reading directions from a manual of How to Survive in a Wakefield Bar. "Sure." (Page 1 says, "Stay.")

Sherry hoists her elbow onto the table. "Well, this should be interesting." She flicks a batch of ashes into the tray in front of her and settles under a halo of smoke. "Make yourself comfortable."

It is clear that this comfort will have to occur somewhere else, however, as Sherry is making no attempt to create room for the unexpected guest on her side of the table. Rowan compensates for the error and crams herself into the corner of the booth, motioning for Catherine to plant herself on the expanse of sagging upholstery between them.

"Thanks." Catherine finds her seat but does so with difficulty. As though she has to fight with the molecules currently occupying the area in an effort to gain permission to land there. "Just the one," she says. "One beer will be plenty."

Sherry coughs. "We can hope."

The real Mary Jenkins appears, like the good fairy in an old story, and delivers the trio their beers. Their third, second, and first beers. Rowan, the middle bear, is feeling more of a buzz than she would expect so early in the evening and rolls her feet into the floor, hoping for ground.

The group begins the process of adapting to this odd alliance by paying extra attention to the sipping and swallowing of their respective liquids. Except for Sherry, who has the good fortune of adding cigarette usage to this equation. Rowan thinks of a few good things to say, but then decides they're actually pretty lame. For several minutes, their length stretched beyond recognition by the silence that saturates them, nothing manages to emerge from anyone's mouth except some forced and desperate throat clearings.

It is Sherry who finally casts the first line, with a broad, strained smile for added effect. "Hey, Catherine," she says. "You're an awful long way from Chicago. Where are you people staying, anyway?"

"At the Golden Lion Inn in Mason," Catherine says. She addresses Sherry directly, head bowed slightly, fielding the question like a pro. "It's right in the center of all the towns we're assessing. That way, we're never more than an hour away from anywhere we need to go. It seems to be working quite well so far."

"Mason. That's where you lived when you were a kid, isn't it, Sher?" Rowan wiggles her beer around the tiny puddle of water formed by the condensation off the sides of her glass. If she wanted to, she could expand this puddle to life size and dip in, a moment of clean, easy Invisibility, but there's far too much outside activity for such simple escape. "Isn't Mason where you had the farm and your dog Spider and all that? You should tell Catherine some of your stories. Like about the way your dad named you guys."

Sherry snorts. "You mean how I'm in between a Brandy and a Bud?"

Catherine tilts her head. "Between what?"

"Her dad named them all after alcoholic beverages. Right, Sher?"

Sherry addresses Catherine like she's forgotten whom she's talking to. Like she's forgotten she hates her. "Actually, my brother's name is Dwight. My mom insisted. My dad got away with Brandy for my older sister and then Sherry with me, but my mom put her foot down with my brother. Then the little guy gets born and my dad starts calling him Bud first thing. Drove my mom crazy." Her eyes swerve toward the spot above her head where the home movies are already rolling. Life on the corn farm. Barefoot in the mud and sun. "Mom loves the sauce, of course, but she didn't like the way my dad slapped it on each one of us. Dipped from birth like we got no choice. I don't mind. I'm not a big fan of sherry itself—don't like the taste, but you can't have everything." She shrugs.

Rowan's first song spills out of the jukebox. "Rhiannon," by Fleetwood Mac. The tape in her front pocket stretches against the fabric of her jeans. She peeks over at Catherine. Could Catherine have seen her take the tape? She was already here, after all. Maybe she saw. Rowan gulps her beer. No. She didn't. She's not acting weird, or any weirder than usual. Rowan can rest easy. Or try to.

"And how about Spider and the tractor?" she says. "Tell Catherine about that one." Rowan can practically see the stories in Sherry's mind and yanks at them like a single thread that unravels the reel. This is what they need—a tour of Sherry's wacky past to take their minds off their troubles. Sherry's got stories galore. Her crazy dog Spider and the day he drove the tractor. The ghost in the hayloft, whose howls they would hear after midnight when the moon was bright in the night sky. The old cow with farts so bad the family could smell them through the kitchen window when they were eating breakfast. Sherry hauls out one tale after another, slapping them on the table until the laughter is genuine and the night has pushed open another round of beer.

"Here's what I want to know." Sherry's face is pink, shining. She points at Catherine with a wavery finger. "Are there more like you?"

"What do you mean?" Catherine rouses from a silence that

53

has gradually made the transition from pained to peaceful. Other than the earlier location explanation, her contribution to the evening thus far consists of focused attention and the commitment to one more beer.

Sherry licks her lips. "I mean, is it just you? Or were your folks busier than that?" There are tiny lines sprouting from the corners of Sherry's mouth that Rowan's never noticed before. They look like a dry creek bed, before the water comes to fill it in.

"Ah, I see." Catherine smiles into her napkin. "Just me. My mom went back to school when I was little. She's an architect now. A successful one. She's amazing. And my dad was on the road a lot so, yes. Just me." She stops, tugging at opposite ends of her napkin with her fingertips. "I always wanted a sibling. A sister, preferably. But I did okay by myself, it wasn't so bad. I have a lot of cousins in Chicago—most of them older than me. My dad has a ton of brothers. The rhythm method fails again."

Rowan holds onto her glass like she's about to take another sip, but she's finding this impossible. She'd like to investigate the face that goes along with all this information, to catalog the interchange between content and expression, but she can't. It feels too risky, somehow. Rowan wedges herself into the booth until she can feel the corner meet her spine, flat wood against chicken-shit nerve.

"So, Catherine," Rowan says. "What did you major in? At college, I mean."

"Economics." The dim bar light and the beer seem to have brought out the curl in Catherine's hair. Loops of red-brown hang around her face like they, too, have something to say. "I minored in Women's Studies. Lots of interesting things going in that field. My mom turned me onto it, actually."

"*Women's* Studies." Sherry shakes her head at the dish of peanuts in front of her. "What the hell do you need to know about *Women's* Studies? What do they teach—the art of tampon management?"

Catherine, to Rowan's surprise, laughs at this. "No, not quite. We talk about the impact of feminism on current thought. The challenges women have faced in various disciplines throughout history. Looking at ways to overcome the current sexist structures—be it by changes in laws or overcoming outmoded patriarchal values. Stuff like that."

"I see." Sherry makes a face. "Patriarchal. Sounds like a disease."

Catherine nods. "Close."

"Hey, well, speaking of brainy things, you do know about our spelling champ here, don't you?"

"No, please." Rowan lifts her hands in a warning maneuver that is entirely too late.

"I did not know about that." Catherine grins like she's stolen one of Sherry's.

"Yeah, Rowan was a champion speller in—when was it?"

"Fourth grade." Rowan injects it with annoyance, though the pride can't help but leak out.

"State Champ. She can spell and define anything you throw at her. Fastest speller in the Midwest. Ain't that right, Ro?"

Rowan sees Catherine inspecting her and tries hard not to match the impulse. She wonders if Miss Lowell is impressed or merely amused. Either one makes her squirm and Rowan does just that, sliding against the shiny seat and studying the edge of the table. It's got a metal rim, peeling off at the end where it hits the wall.

"Try her." Sherry says, bombing through her purse for her lighter, a cigarette limp between her lips.

Catherine grins again, wider, sharper. "All right. Let's see. How about . . ." She searches the ceiling and returns with a word. "Picayune."

"You start off small, eh?" Rowan addresses the perspiration on Catherine's beer glass and quickly rattles off the correct letters. "Definition—of minor importance. Secondary definition—mean-spirited." She thinks to link these meanings to the past actions of her interrogator, but declines the internal invitation. At the very least, Catherine is exhibiting the behavior of an honorable guest.

"Umm. Mendacious." Catherine fires another.

"M-e-n-d-a-c-i-o-u-s. Prone to lying."

The ends of Catherine's mouth creep into her cheeks. "Ah, but you wouldn't know a thing about that, would you, Rowan?"

"No. I wouldn't." Rowan blinks. Her hand, she can't help it, drops to the front pocket of her jeans. What does Catherine know? How much?

Catherine continues as if nothing has gone wrong. "Here's a good one. Try this: xerophyte."

The game has slipped past the fun stage, yet Rowan can't help but keep playing. For one thing, Sherry is watching. "X-e-r-o-p-h-y-t-e. A plant adapted to growing in an environment providing limited moisture."

"And I *know* you know something about that." Catherine levels her target with a gaze at once challenging and absolutely clear.

Rowan sits stunned, unsure whether to duck or stay. Whatever Catherine knows, she doesn't appear to be offering condemnation. Just the opposite. Her eyes, her face—they're open, absorbent. It's like Rowan has never been seen before. Of course she has, but not really. Not like this. It's as if nothing else matters. The smell of alcohol in a room without windows, the laughter that circles the bar as one more joke gets told and one more drink gets poured, the jukebox haunting the background, sweet and low. These stand on the perimeter of Rowan's awareness, severed and distinct, Catherine's eyes solidifying their position. While Rowan sits dead center, undeniably seen.

If there's a proper response to such an investigation, Rowan doesn't know what it is. All she can do is stare back. It's like Catherine is prying apart the ions of Rowan's supposedly solid self, slipping effortlessly past what was, until now, thoroughly out of bounds. As she drifts around—inside Rowan? between them? inside both?—Catherine is on tour, at home, sated. Rowan stretches her senses to allow this as long as she can, which, in this case, is a buzzing on the outside lining of her flesh that intersects, ever so gently, with the soft wall of this other.

A blush that starts in her knees travels to Rowan's nose and spreads out across her face. She blinks a time or two, hoping to stop what must surely be the influence of the alcohol on her system. Causing her to drop all her defenses in front of a total stranger. Naked on a fake leather seat in a small-town bar surrounded by corn and roads that lead only to other towns and other bars. Naked in front of a person who is, from everything Rowan has seen so far, not a friend.

"Yeah, the girl has always been a bit plantlike. In my experience." Sherry taps a fistful of nails on the shiny dark table and chuckles to herself.

Rowan turns toward her boss, shifting from observed to observing, uncovering nothing in Sherry's demeanor to indicate she has even the slightest clue of what just happened. Sherry is calm, mellowed by the warm air and familiar surroundings. Rowan will find no clues here. She turns back to Catherine, hoping for at least a hint of explanation from those strange, roving eyes. Yet the instant she finds Catherine's face is the instant she is catapulted into a moment of closure—the sounds and sights and smells of the bar merging together as Rowan slides all the way inside herself. Hidden.

"Shall we keep going?" Catherine asks. She smiles.

Rowan tries once again to suss out the situation, to inspect Catherine in the same way Catherine has just inspected her, but comes up short. "I don't know."

Catherine's face is a blur. Empty of everything but the faintest traces of—though Rowan is not sure of this and understands she may be imagining the entire thing—the whir of connection between them.

"I don't think so," Rowan says. "I think I've had enough. I think I need to be heading home." There was another song, wasn't there? She punched in two songs—whatever happened to the second one?

The blank face speaks. "Do you want a ride? You've had a few more than me." Catherine says this like it's no big deal, but all Rowan can think of is a slow, silent ride that ends with Catherine's headlights on Rowan's front lawn and an awkward goodbye. She'd rather walk.

"No. I'm cool." She gives a quick nod to indicate that this is, indeed, true.

"I got one." Sherry is talking now. Her speech folds in on itself; everything out of her mouth sounds like one long vowel. "What's that word we were laughing about last week? The one that makes you sound like you're from New York?"

Rowan closes her eyes. Specks of green and yellow float across an acre of black. "Autistic," she says.

Ghost

The screen door to Thompson's Hardware opens easily, allowing Rowan a smooth entrance into Wakefield's unofficial town center. The center of town is supposed to be the statue of Colonel George Wakefield saluting the sky in a sixteenth-of-an-acre park, but no one in Wakefield pays much attention to statues. Thompson's has live bait and newspapers and cold beverages and an amazingly diverse array of small metal items designed to meet the hardware needs of each and every citizen in their modest town. That, plus the fact that Betty Thompson treats each customer like the long lost child she'd just about given up hope on until, lo and behold, the urchin marches through the screen door and back into her life.

"Well, look who's here. I haven't seen you since graduation." Betty's broad face lights up at the sight of another found soul. She usually adds a wave to the reunion, but she has her hands full with an order of night crawlers for Herb and Scott Vanasek, forty-ish twin brothers who still fish together in their lucky boat *Helga*. They greet Rowan in tandem, the "Hellos" bouncing between them like an echo.

"Is Danny around?" Rowan rolls onto the balls of her feet like a springboard diver.

"In the back." Betty adjusts her apron, mountain green and loose across her bust. "He's sorting through the new shipment of lawn supplies. You might take a look. Lord knows we could all do a little to spruce up that front yard."

"Will do. Thanks, Mrs. Thompson."

Rowan negotiates the wide aisles brimming with bins of this and racks of that. Like little gremlins, they are, begging for liberation. One item in particular—a wee roll of electrician's tape—catches her eye. *Pick me, pick me,* it yelps. Rowan shivers, swoops it off the shelf, and stores it in her pocket. Where it's safe. A crop of thoughts vie for her attention—*What the hell? What happened to stopping? You promised!*—but she shoves them away. She's busy. She's on her way to see Danny.

"About time you got here." Danny is sitting on a paint-splattered stool in the storage closet, knee-deep in boxes of chemical fertilizer and decorative lawn ornaments. "The fair started an hour ago."

"I know. Don't spaz out."

"Who says I'm spazzing?"

"Not me."

A white-faced servant with an arm attached to a lantern juts out from a box of identical servants. Rowan imagines that Danny is their master and just doesn't know it yet.

"Are we going or what?" she says.

"Keep your shorts on, Marks." Danny heaves himself up from his stool. "I have to tell Betty I'm done. Then we can go."

Rowan would have easily made it through this year's Corn Day festivities unscathed if Danny hadn't insisted, and she agreed, that they attend the town's Annual Corn Day Parade, Picnic, and Fair at the old town reservoir. Corn Day has always been a bit of a sore point as far as Rowan is concerned. She tries to tell herself it's stupid to have a whole day devoted to corn, especially because the crops are still barely out of the ground. She knows the whole point of the festival is to support the harvest, to give good vibes for the growth of the crops. And that's all well and good. But the really annoying thing about Corn Day is that it's always right near her birthday. Rowan should be used to having her birthday in the shadow of the festivities—a day worth pulling out the horses and the old folks and the high school marching band. The annual reminder that, although she may be turning another year older, there's always something bigger and better right nearby. But it never ceases to annoy her. Not that she would ever admit this to anyone—least of all Danny. It's far too petty.

They exit the store just in time for the tail end of the parade (a float of the Kennedy Middle School 4-H club, complete with live goats and bushels of tomatoes) and follow the bleats and hollers all the way to the reservoir. Once there, they're greeted by the spectacle of Ben's buddy Lyle and the Kirkpatrick brothers smashing up an old car for twenty-five cents a hit, courtesy of the local Ford dealership. This event, appropriately titled U-Whack-It, is always one of the most popular attractions at the fair.

Lyle swings the sledgehammer onto the grass next to his feet, his forehead sprinkled with sweat. He's got on a tank top that shows off the muscles in his arms—pumping through his flesh like trophies. "Rowan, where's your brother? I'm outta weed."

"You got me." Rowan shrugs. "I haven't seen him since yesterday. I'll tell him you were looking for him."

"You guys wanna do some damage?" Lyle points to the already battered car, sprayed with chips of glass, dents as big as potholes. "How about you, Dan the man? Take a pop."

"No thanks. I'm wasted from work. All I want right now is some food."

"Don't be a fag, dipshit. Just take a crack at it." Lyle barks it out. The Kirkpatricks chuckle.

"Shut up, Lyle." Rowan takes a step toward the car.

Lyle huffs. "Ahhh, I see. Got to send your lady to do the work for you, is that it? The fag's girlfriend to the rescue."

Danny kicks the grass. "Only fag I see here is you, Lylie. Trying to impress your boyfriends with your homo tank top and your disco jeans. Where'd you get those things, anyway? Fruits R Us?" He laughs, then turns and trucks away.

"Takes one to know one." Lyle bellows at Danny's back. He opens his mouth to speak to Rowan, but she bolts before he gets the chance.

"Nice shot." Rowan trots to catch up with her friend. "I never noticed before how faggy he looks." She swallows.

"How can you not notice? His pants are tighter than a girl's. It's no wonder he—*shit.*" Danny winces and Rowan looks. Sarah Scarpetti is strolling toward them.

"Maybe she didn't see us."

Danny clenches his jaw. "She saw us."

Sarah is clad in a red tube top, blue jean shorts, and white tennis shoes with tall white athletic socks. Her hair corkscrews around her face, Farrah-style, bobbing in and out when she walks.

"Danny. Rowan. What's going on?" She approaches them hopefully, as though a prize is involved.

"That's a nice candy apple you got there, Sarah," Rowan says. "Where are they selling those?"

"Over there." Sarah pokes a finger toward a smattering of booths comprising the food section of the fair. Sugar and meat products appear to be the major contenders for the town's dollars. "I heard you're going to New York. Is that right?"

"Sort of. Massachusetts, actually. Close."

"You're lucky," Sarah says. "I'm not allowed to go anywhere far. Only Erie County Community, and I have to pay for it myself."

Rowan can feel Danny's impatience pulling on her like the blanket off a bed. "Good luck with all that," she says. "I'm sure it'll be—"

"Danny, was that you I saw at church the other day?" Sarah's hopefulness reappears, obscured only partially by the candy apple in her mouth.

Danny nods and takes a step in the direction of away.

Sarah smiles. "Our youth group is working on making a costume for the football team. You know, for the eagle? I'm going to be a senior next year, but of course you know that. I can't wait to get out of there, but it's still cool to do something for the team. Go Baldies!"

The Wakefield High School mascot is the bald eagle, on account of the bird's unquestionable patriotism and the fact that it was Colonel Wakefield's favorite animal. It's a good mascot, except it tends to bring out the extremes in people—like the year the girls volleyball team shaved off all their hair in a misbegotten sweep of school pride. Though the team went on to take the North County championship that season, the Wakefield High girls athletic department has had a moratorium on head-shaving ever since.

Danny clears his throat, speaks. "It's not all it's cracked up to be, believe me. Enjoy your senior year. After that you're going to have to deal with responsibility and your life and shit like that. Don't rush it."

Rowan and Sarah stare at the boy like he's just announced he's radioactive. Danny hasn't spoken more than two words to Sarah in a single breath since they were both under four feet tall and sharing boxes of crayons to draw inside the lines of the Holy Bible Scenes coloring books at St. Joseph's Sunday school.

Sarah takes another bite of her apple and munches thoughtfully. "Yeah, you're probably right." The steep midday sun drops onto her face and Rowan notices for the first time that, even though Sarah's hair is a medium brown color, her eyebrows are light blond. Almost clear.

"See you, Sarah." Danny tilts his head back, squinting into the sun, and negotiates a quick exit to Food Land.

"What was that? Foreplay?" Rowan coughs up ten cents for a cotton candy and nudges Danny in the elbow.

"Like you would know *anything* about that."

"I'm just saying." She steers away from the obvious to the safer ground of shit-giving. "The girl has the names of all your unborn children tattooed inside her thighs. I think you ought to respect that."

"Shut up."

"Shut don't go up."

"Jeez." Danny covers his eyes in response to the sight of Rowan attacking the pink fluff-on-a-stick she's got planted in her fist. "Cut it out, will you? You're making me sick."

"Get used to it. I hear little babies get sick a lot too, you know." She opens her mouth and nods suggestively. "Little babies conceived in luuuv."

"Get over it, Marks. You're tripping on your own brain." He turns on his heel and saunters over to the Dunk-A-Dave booth. "I'm going to do something *productive* with my time. Unlike some other people I know."

"I'm productive." Rowan follows behind him. "Just like Sarah. 'How many babies should we have, Mr. Danny? Let's give them

63

all Farrah Fawcett haircuts. Even the boys. We can start a band. Danny and the Lame-os.'"

"Hey, kids. Bet you can't get me wet." Dave Rivers, owner of Rivers Autobody and chairman of the local Little League, hails them from the inside of his booth.

"Hey, Dave. Bet we can." Rowan waves at him with her gob of pink.

Every year, Dave Rivers subjects himself to this baptismal ritual, allowing himself to be dunked all day in a small pool of water to help raise funds for the new football field. Or the new gymnasium. Or whatever else new the town needs.

Danny pays a quarter and hurls a tennis ball at the target— a lever with a painted version of Dave's face. He nails it on the first try.

"Good shot." Dave's head bobbles over the waves of water sloshing against the sides of the tank.

Danny nods, rolls his eyes at Rowan. "Thanks."

Rowan stands beside her friend, occupying herself with the remains of her cotton candy. She should know better than to give Danny a hard time about Sarah but, on some level, she guesses she has her reasons. The ones circling round her escape.

"Your turn, Marks. Go for it." Dave plunks onto the platform, water dripping off his toes and returning to the tub. "Don't tell me you don't got an arm on you."

Dave was Rowan's coach back when she was the only girl on an all-boys team. Back before other boys on other teams from other towns started making fun of her developing breasts and she quit organized baseball for good.

She fingers her pocket for a quarter but catches something else—the roll of electrician's tape. The confidence she felt while taking it is gone. All that's left is sadness. And regret. She'd like to yank the tape from her pocket and chuck it on the ground, but what would that accomplish? Danny would see the price tag, he'd know where it came from. She could throw it at Dave, but that would be even weirder. He's staring at her now, Dave, with his wet toes and a hopeful look on his face. His hope hits Rowan the wrong way, an "Everything's all fucked up and I don't know how to fix it" sort of way. A way that slices through the facade of okay she stands on most of the time, leaving her open to all that's not. Moments like these always force her to wonder what's true: the most-of-the-time feeling, or this one.

"What are you waiting for?" Dave is grinning and Rowan looks away. His expression has so little to do with where she is right now.

She gathers up her voice from a place so deep it doesn't even feel like hers.

"Sorry," she says. "Not today. I don't want to start a tidal wave in that plastic pond of yours." She maneuvers her lips into a sort-of smile, a skill acquired from Jane. ("When you don't want to smile, just raise your upper lip. They'll never know the difference.")

The minute she turns away from the tub, Rowan realizes what needs to happen. It might not help, but it's worth a shot. What else is she going to do—stand here, fingering stolen goods? Danny takes her lame excuse in stride and, with a few waves and smiles, she extricates herself from the festivities with minimal effort. An easy out. Only one destination makes any sense now, and Rowan wastes no time in clearing a path to there.

෪   ෪   ෪

The pulse of Led Zeppelin pouring out of the garage tells her he's home. She figured this is where he'd be. What better place for an alienated, disgruntled college graduate than Ben's Dionysian Den—a space filled with music to slam the senses and enough drugs and booze to twist them into oblivion. Ben has surely found his niche this summer.

Rowan knocks, though she probably doesn't have to. There's no reply and she watches the mild roll of anxiety that starts at her toes and ends in her brain. The images kick around inside— Ben passed out on a sofa, dead in his own vomit; Ben hanging by a noose slung over the rafters of the old garage. Recently it's been hard to stay away from pictures such as these. Rowan reminds herself that their origin is her overactive imagination filtered through a deep love for her brother. Probably no need to worry, right? Sighing, she nudges into the room with a turn and push of the warped plywood door that separates Ben from the rest of the world.

"Sissie," he says. "What's shaking?"

He's alone, perched on the dark blue velour couch he picked up at the dump in an effort to "liven the place up." His primary accomplishment thus far has been the creation of a site much like the dump itself—a venue littered with crushed beer cans, old magazines, boys seeking treasure, the smell of decay.

"Where you been all my life?" He lowers the music an entire half-turn of the stereo dial, opening up the room for conversation.

"At the Fair. I brought you these." She throws a pack of half-empty cigarettes onto the couch, then collapses into the over-stuffed armchair on the other side of the room. She won't bother to mention that she lifted the cigarettes from a work shirt stupidly left on the ground while its owner was banging away on the U-Whack-It car. She won't bother to mention it because Ben won't ask, won't even wonder why the pack's not full.

"Lyle and the guys were there," she says. "They were asking where the hell you were." She squints to see her brother, the shades still pulled down even though it is almost two o'clock in the afternoon.

"I don't know. Where the hell was I?"

"You were here?"

"You got that right." In the dark, against the couch, Ben looks like a grinning ghost. An exact likeness of Ben, but not quite Ben.

"But what about—"

"I got all fucked up. I thought it was a regular workday until I remembered it was the day of the Corn. You got to respect the Corn." He flops a foot onto the cluttered table in front of him. "But I forgot. I got all dressed up for work and everything— see?" Ben sweeps a hand down the outside of his body, a show-case display of self. He's wearing his painter's outfit—white overalls and T-shirt spattered with a veritable palette of colors.

He looks like one of the Spin Art confections sold at the nearby mall in Loomis.

"Maroon. That's a new one." Rowan points to his knee. "Where'd you get that?"

It takes him a while to zero in on this body part, a possible function of the muted light. Or muted something else. Even when he finds it, his memory is slow in registering.

"The Franks," he says finally. "They're redoing their rec room. Puke yellow walls with burnt red trim. A dastardly color combo if ever there was one. But I say nothing. I'm just the paid help."

It occurs to Rowan she could slip a few questions onto the issue raised by Ben's last statement. Searching, probing, "What are you going to do with your life?" sorts of questions. But she doesn't have the nerve. She's caught her brother in a jolly mode. Might as well extend the levity.

"Hey, Benny," she says. "Do Psychic Jim."

His eyes fall from the ceiling and he addresses Rowan with glee. "Who?"

"You know."

"I do?"

"C'mon, Ben. Please?" She is eight years old to his twelve, skipping into a game they both love.

"Well," he says. "I'm a sucker for 'please.'" He folds his legs up on the couch, yogi-style, and flattens his palms together in front of his chest. His voice acquires a generic accent. "What do you desire to know?"

"Umm. It's ten years from now. Where am I and what am I doing?" She tries to resist, but even a silly question like this gives her the sensation of free fall: weightless, no boundaries. Gobbling warm, empty air.

Ben jerks in the illusion of Psychic Jim's unearthly entrance into Ben's earthly body. He breathes deeply as he "incorporates" Jim's spirit into his own.

"Let us see here," he says. "Hmmm. Yes. Very interesting."

"Ben." Rowan giggles. "I mean—Jim. What is it?" Her body twitches in response, a jittery mirror.

"By day, you are an investigative journalist, keeping the world free of roaming scumbags." His eyeballs roll back into his head, then forward again. "By night you are a badass superhero crime-fighter, continuing to keep the world free of the scumbag population." Ben as Jim stops to scroll the ethers. "That is it. That is all I see."

"Wow, Jim. Thanks for that." Rowan comforts herself with a landing on false ground. It is strangely reassuring.

Psychic Jim moans, and for a moment Rowan feels like she's really sitting with someone other than Ben.

"Jim?" she says.

Ben jabs an index finger into his forehead. "I sense you would like to ask me a question about our father. Is this not so?"

"Uh."

"Is this not so?"

Rowan nods slowly, improvising. "Yes. Yes, I would." She waits. "It's six o'clock," she says. "We're sitting at the dinner table. You and me and Dad and Jane. Dad is extra-quiet tonight. Psychic Jim: What. Is. He. Thinking?"

Psychic Jim wastes no time with this one. His hands grip his knees, his fingertips digging into Ben's spotted painter's pants—white and maroon, deep green and faded black. "He is plotting complete and total nuclear annihilation of Wakefield. The evil powers stored in his massive cranium will obliterate all living creatures in a manner of seconds." Ben's body wiggles, as if he is receiving an internal massage. He scans the space above his sister's head. "As he methodically chews his dinner, he considers whether or not to spare his children. How will he decide?"

"Ben. Cut it out." Rowan sits up in her chair. Something's poking her lower back—probably a beer can or a bong. "Dad's not . . . You don't have to—"

"He decides to spare his daughters. Only them." Ben's palms meet his belly and he emits a low hum. "All the rest will burn and crisp in a ring of indomitable terror. Especially Ben. That wicked, unworthy soul."

Rowan twists around, discovers that the beer can or bong is a plastic hand grenade. She tosses it out of the chair. "Dad's not a Nazi, Ben. He's just a guy. He's just a regular—"

"Ben? There is no Ben here." He's imitating Darth Vader now, an alternate attempt to remain anyone but himself.

"And he doesn't hate you, you know. He just doesn't understand you. There's a difference."

"Tell that to my lawyers." Ben is Ben again, but not without resistance.

"Why do you hate him so much all of a sudden? Dad's always been . . ." She trails off, knowing she doesn't need to explain to Ben how their dad has always been. "It's not like he's just turned distant and smart and unknowable. That's his steady state. What's the big deal?"

Ben is slumped over himself, a crumpled napkin of hair and clothes and color. "You wouldn't understand," he says.

Rowan pulls up an oldie from the stacks. Ben at twelve. It's winter and they're sledding at Devil's Hill. He convinces her to lie on top of him while they two-man a Flexible Flyer over the most dangerous part of the hill and they, of course, crash at the bottom, Rowan flying forward into a mound of snow and Ben jammed into a tree stump at the edge of the woods. He comes running over to check if she's okay, snow sticking to his eyelids and the rings of hair around his hat, and he stares at her with love and concern and another emotion. While she lies flat on the ground, afraid and happy and confused all at the same time. Rowan couldn't identify what Ben was holding inside himself that day and she still can't. She guesses that, if pressed, he wouldn't be able to tell her either.

"What don't I understand, Ben?"

He reaches behind him and draws up a blind. Sun smacks against the walls and table and curtains, adding to the sense of interrogation and loss.

"Okay," he says. "Like the other day. Dad was in the shed, putzing with all those old artifacts he's got in there. Grampa's bug collection and all that. And I'm out in the yard, right? I'm sitting there on my lawn chair, and what do I see? I see him with a *raccoon*. Not a real raccoon, Ro, but one of those fake ones. That taxidermy shit. Man." He pivots his head from side to side, as if trying to coax the memory out of his skull.

"Ben. Mrs. Collins gave that to him as a present. For all the stuff they've been through in the last year with Mr. Collins's cancer. It was a gift, a thank-you present. Nothing to get all psycho about."

"Psycho is just what I'm saying. He's flipped. He's gone from remote to zombie."

"No, he hasn't. You don't know what you're talking about. You haven't been here. You're not—"

"I know a hell of a lot more than you do. You have no idea." Ben is shaking. Every part of him. His arms, his feet, his head, his lips.

"What are you—"

"The man is seriously deranged. And you can't even see it. Can you?" Ben scowls, his eyes squinting, then releasing. "He's fucking with all of us. And there's nothing we can do about it."

"I could say the same for someone else." She doesn't mean to say it, it just slips out. Luckily for her, Ben doesn't register the cut, or at least doesn't show that he does, and a loud knock on the door marks the end of their private chat.

"Enter." Ben barks from his throne, having instantly become, once again, lord of his domain. He cranks the music up several notches.

Lyle stomps into the room. "Hey."

"Hey," Ben says.

"Hey." Rowan tries this as well, but it seems to have a different meaning coming out of her mouth.

"Lyle, check out this new record I just got." Ben bounds off the couch and Rowan notices a chunk of blueberry muffin sticking to the seat of his pants. "You got to hear this," he says.

She watches her brother move across the battered carpet, his body stiff with drugs and lack of activity and, just like that, Rowan is swamped with the Everything's All Fucked Up feeling. She doesn't have time to fight it, it comes over her so quickly.

"I'm going to head out," she says.

Lyle smirks. "See you, Rowan."

"See you, Rowie." Ben is coasting on the vibe of an entirely different brother-sister chat than the one they just had. "Nice knowing you."

"I guess," she says.

It's the hottest part of the day. A time when the only way to cool down is air conditioning or a dip in the reservoir—which, today, is otherwise occupied. Rowan takes off her sneakers and walks the long, wide stretch of grass that separates the main house from Ben's little one, losing herself in the sensation of feet to lawn. The green blades cushion her step—hard and soft at the same time. The Fucked Up feeling is still there, but so is a kernel of antidote. The lawn doesn't know confusion, doesn't know pushing away what's longed for more. Doesn't know wandering, or never being found. And, for a moment, neither does she.

Leak

"That's not how it works." Catherine taps her pencil against the desk and winds a piece of hair around her finger. "The percentage the corporation takes is the product of this formula, here." She draws a circle around the equation in question, adding an arrow for good measure.

"No, I understand. That's the problem. What I don't understand is how Sherry is going to pull any profit out of this place when she slams into numbers like that at the end of each month." Rowan slips one arm over another and drags them both toward her protesting stomach. She never did eat lunch today. Her hunger seems to be tempering her usual reaction to Catherine— the buzz, the thrill. There's still something there, but it's changed. Or maybe Rowan's just getting used to her.

"The added profits are from the draw of the franchise." Catherine speaks slowly, like she's peeling words off a page. "They'll more than make up the difference."

"I see." Rowan imitates the pace. "And you'll be creating new inhabitants of this town as well? AmeriBurger robots with huge wads of cash and a penchant for plastic food?"

Catherine's focus on the paper in her hands gets frosted over with something else. Rowan suspects it's anger, but she doesn't care. Sherry was supposed to be the one listening to this initial orientation to AmeriBurger fiscal procedures, but she didn't have the stomach for it and sent Rowan instead. Which, Rowan realizes, was probably a good thing. Sherry would have walked out four equations ago.

Catherine continues to stare at the beloved numbers, her face frozen in place. Rowan ponders the notion of Catherine-as-alien-life-form once again, as the bright eyes inside the older girl's perfect skin dart away briefly, then back to the page. Outer planetary involvement certainly would justify the look Catherine gave her at the bar last week. Rowan has yet to come up with an explanation for that one. Perhaps Catherine is here on a mission to pick out champion Earth spellers so she can shuttle them back to her home planet for amusement and hard labor. Rowan can see it already—her poor hands raw with blisters from a day at the pickax, her jaw sore from a night of entertaining the leader with obscure and off-color Earth words. She wonders what the food might be like on other planets. Is there chocolate available? She's not sure.

Rowan clears her throat. "No disrespect or anything," she says. "But these plans seem kinda unrealistic for this town. Why don't you let me run all this by Sherry and we can review it when you stop by next week?"

"Okay."

"Really?"

"Sure." Catherine's reply is punctuated by a drop of water falling on the corner of the desk.

Rowan checks the ceiling first, hoping it might be a leak in the roof. Until she remembers it's not raining. Then she tells herself it must be sweat. Catherine is nothing if not hard-working. This thought is crushed by the sound of a low sniffle emerging from deep inside Catherine's nasal cavities. A rich soppy noise that suggests an entirely different movie than the one still showing in the shadows of Rowan's mind. She clears out the chocolate and the pickaxes for a view of the current Ms. Lowell, suffering silently in front of her.

"Wait," Rowan says. "I'm sorry. I didn't mean we—that there isn't a way to . . ."

"It's okay," Catherine says. She bites her lip.

"Can I get you something? A drink? Or—or fries? Do you want some fries?" The minute she says this, Rowan is sure she has discovered the right course of action. She skittles out to the grill, snatches an order of steaming fries out of Sherry's hands

73

("Emergency," she says, by way of explanation), and rushes back to the office to deliver the prize to Catherine, now semicomposed and looking more than a little embarrassed.

Rowan flops onto her stool. She grabs one first, a starter fry, and grins as it eases down her throat. "Really. Try these. You'll feel much better." She chews heartily to demonstrate her point.

Catherine's face is round and open, a little moon. "I'm sorry about that. I guess I didn't realize how much pressure I've been under lately." She blinks. "This is my first real job out of college and I've been trying so hard to make a good impression. All I've been getting is a lot of suspicious looks and accusations of nepotism." She glances at Rowan. "No offense."

"None taken."

"And it's true, in a way. The nepotism part. My dad got slammed with extra work this summer and hired me to help him out." Catherine twirls one of the fries, fatter than the others, between her thumb and fingers. "I've wanted this for so long," she says. "To work in business. I want to run my own company some day. I've got a job with a management consulting firm in the fall, you know. Lewis and Wright, in Boston. I was hoping this summer would be my start, my auspicious debut. So far, it's mostly a lot of shit." She sniffles, then stares at the fry in her fingers. After what seems like an eternity, or at least the duration of an unbearably long commercial break, she lifts the fry to her mouth and begins to chew.

"Can I say something?" Rowan swallows, gathering shreds of nerve.

Catherine nods, still chewing.

"Well," Rowan taps the table with her fingertips for luck, "it might have something to do with the way you present yourself. I understand you want to make a good impression and all that, but maybe it would help if you tried to connect with people a little more. You know, laugh more often and stuff like that. To prove you're human." Rowan waits.

"I appear not human?"

"Kinda."

74

"Really?"

"Yeah." Rowan thinks to tell her about the foreign planet and the pickaxes but decides this would only distract. "Today, though. This," she waves a hand in the direction of the fries and the curls and the equations, "this is better."

Catherine's elbows hit the table, shoving aside her papers, and she studies the wall in front of her. Several photos, faded with age, have been fastened into the plaster with thumbtacks. Rowan and Sherry, arm in arm in matching blue bowling shirts, grinning viciously the night the Sugar Shack beat Bob's Piggly Wiggly in the finals of the 1977 Wakefield Bowl-a-rama. Sherry's son Little sitting tall on a huge black horse, serious as a soldier. Jerry and Little as young boys, lying on a beat-up couch in their pajamas, hands full of cookies.

"You know," Catherine turns and Rowan can tell—by the arch of emotion uniting her stomach with her throat—that Catherine is switching subjects of examination, "when I first met you, I thought you were a total snob."

"A snob?"

"Yes."

"Hmm." Rowan sits in the critique. This isn't the first time she's been told such a thing.

"With your looks, and the way you stared at my father, then at me. It was like we were beneath you."

"Beneath me?"

"Yes."

Rowan circles round herself, tries to cull a reply from the chasm of confusion in her mind. She finds herself in the bowling picture, sees the face that was hers peering from old eyes into this new room. What does she know now that this other self doesn't? Is there anything?

"My looks?" she says. "What do you mean by that? What looks?"

"You know."

"No, I don't." Rowan continues to stare at her old self, but the girl in the picture remains flat, mystified.

"I mean the way you look, combined with a sort of distance, a removal from others."

Tearing herself away from the photograph, Rowan attempts to fix her thoughts into some sort of order. How did the topic swing back to her side so quickly? And why does a potential compliment feel so unsettling? One thing's for sure—she is surrounded by an element utterly unknown to her. Like water, except not. Like air, except not. It sinks into her pores and engulfs everything she knows, pulling her farther and farther from the girl in the picture on the wall.

"I don't get what you mean, Catherine. About how I look."

"You're cool-looking. I don't know." Catherine sounds almost off-balance as she says this, then instantly rights herself. "Like no one I've seen before. Unique, or something."

"Unique or something."

Catherine laughs. "You have to stop doing that."

"What?"

"Repeating me."

"Repeating you." Rowan smiles shyly and Catherine returns the gesture.

"Or . . ." Catherine hesitates, her features organizing themselves to serious. "Or maybe it's none of my business anyway. Like you said to me last week. Maybe I shouldn't bother." This, like she's punching holes in a huge piece of cardboard—the one marked "Catherine and Rowan." The one covered with words.

Rowan's smile gets stuck in place, then evaporates altogether. It's like Catherine just wedged a brick between her eyebrows. Anything she could think to say is lost, sucked into the throbbing sensation between her ears.

Catherine reaches for another fry but thinks again and returns it to its red-and-white paper home. "I'm sorry. That came out wrong. It just threw me off, last week. When you shut me up about your mom. I was trying to be nice, and you—"

"What did you mean? When you said I was like a xerophyte? What did you mean by that?"

Catherine appears puzzled. "Hello?"

76

"What?"

"Hello?" Catherine repeats herself and Rowan observes that this is a pretty horrible answer to a genuinely serious question.

"Guarding the books again, eh?" Danny's voice grabs her from behind, like a claw.

She turns around and, sure enough, it's Danny. Danny, wearing sandals and jeans and a red T-shirt and saying something about going swimming, maybe later, and going to the movies after that. If she could listen to him maybe she could respond but she can't so, "Danny, this is Catherine. Catherine, Danny," is what emerges instead. And then she's basking in the glow of an interaction that should not be. Catherine and Danny should not be meeting. Like in those parallel universes she sees on the old sci-fi movies on Channel 58. One person's reality pokes into another's and the entire course of history is transformed forever. Wars break out. Mayhem ensues. But this is more than a little melodramatic and Rowan changes the channel, attempting to hunker down into the boring ordinariness of the moment.

"Are you okay?" Danny continues to stand in the spot where he landed when he entered the room.

Rowan turns to Catherine, thinking maybe he's addressing her. But he's not.

"What are you talking about?" Rowan says.

Danny scratches his nose. "You look weird. Different."

She focuses on the bottom of Danny's shirt, frayed with multiple washings. Behind her, there are sharp bursts followed by tapping, the sounds of Catherine rising from her seat. Probably leaving. Then speaking.

"I meant you don't belong here. That's all. Nice to meet you, Daniel."

"Danny." Rowan corrects her, though it's not what she wants to say.

"Nice to meet you too," he says.

Rowan catches Catherine's exit in the reflection of Danny's face—a body removing itself from a room, a door closed. No big deal.

Danny drops onto the chair vacated by Catherine. He picks up a fry and uses it to jab at the others remaining in the basket. "So that's the Hulk lady. She's a looker, Ro. You were holding out on me." He grins.

Somewhere between Danny arriving and Catherine leaving, Rowan managed to lift herself from her stool. She stands now, limbs buoyant and bulky at the same time. She guesses this is how the astronauts must feel. In space. There's the illusion of freedom, but you're really attached to a ship with a cord so thick you couldn't yank it away if you tried. "Yeah, I guess I was." She lifts one leg, then another, testing her suit.

"How about a swim? Sherry told me you were off an hour ago."

"I can't."

"Why not?" Danny's fry war has escalated. He's got one in each hand and they're smashing each other into an off-white pulp.

"Man. I was eating those." Rowan snatches the basket out from under him and pitches it into the trash. "Because I can't."

Danny, fryless, wraps his arms around his torso. "Because you're doing something with Catherine?"

"No. Jeez, give me a break. I just can't, okay?"

Like Catherine's exit before it, Rowan can see the effect of this remark on her friend's face. This time, though, it's an entirely different show. Danny's face is drained of everything but pseudo nonchalance, a careful placement of slack mouth under slippery eyes. *Look how much of a fuck I don't give. See that?* Like hell.

"I'm going home, then," he says. "The reservoir would have been too crowded today anyway. Later."

Rowan observes this second departure from the visor of her space helmet, the plastic bubble that insulates her from a noxious atmosphere. She is lucky, she supposes, to be protected in such a manner. Outside the store, cars rush and hum through the forty-five-mile-an-hour speed limit at more like sixty, and the birds, perched on trees and phone lines, chatter amongst themselves. Normally she might feel bad, or funny, about all that just happened, but the suit seems to be shielding her from emotions as well.

"What's going on back here?" Sherry merges into Rowan's

world, smelling of fresh onions and stale cigarettes. "You're pushing them away in droves."

Over at the desk, Rowan begins stacking Catherine's papers into a scattered pile. Catherine's handwriting is large and loopy—surprisingly sloppy. The papers fall together like old friends.

"Nothing's going on," she says. "Just the normal stuff."

Sherry leans in and tucks her finger under Rowan's chin, shattering the remains of the space suit. "You look weird. What's up?"

"I told you." Rowan pulls her head from Sherry's grip and continues her stacking task. "N-o-t-h-i-n-g."

"Hey, girl. I can spell too. B-u-l-l-s-h-i-t. How's that for a word?"

"I'm not lying," Rowan says. "I'm just—*fuck*." A piece of paper off the stack turns against her, slicing her pinky and drawing blood. "Stupid paper."

"Oh, honey. It's the little things that hurt the most, isn't it? I'll go get a Band-Aid."

Sherry's exit, the third in about as many minutes, finds Rowan alone, shaky, and profoundly off her game. She settles into the chair that was Catherine's, then Danny's, now hers. Still warm from the bodies before her. The heat feels claustrophobic and wrong—knocking her backwards instead of the right way. She inspects the thin line of red on the tip of her finger, a sliver of her insides exposed to the light and the air.

"The little things." She repeats Sherry's statement as an audible wrapping and studies her injured finger. Maybe it will clear up on its own.

Boil

"Why not?" Jane peers at her sister. "Why can't you just go out with him? What's the big deal?"

"You." Rowan snorts. "You're the one making it a big deal."

"Am not."

"Are too."

Rowan and Jane are sitting on the front porch of their family home, fanning themselves with their hands. It's almost dinner time and the part of a summer day where the inside of the house has absorbed all the heat the outside has to offer and is now hotter than its benefactor. Hank has shooed the females out of the kitchen, claiming he can't concentrate with them there, though they all know it's more on account of Jane's sketchy cooking abilities.

"He just got a promotion," Jane says. "Did I mention that?"

"You did, in fact. Four times. You—"

"His father says he'll be running the company before he's thirty. Quite impressive."

"Impressive. Yeah." Rowan pulls on the top of her T-shirt and wipes the sweat off her face. Today was a non-workday and she spent most of it lounging inside the house, immobilized by the heat and lack of structure. "Boy, oh boy," she says. "It's like bathwater, this air. Like we just need some soap and a rubber ducky and we're good to go."

"Rowan." Jane frowns. "Don't change the subject."

"Was there a subject? I don't remember any—"

"See, this is the problem. You. You're in the way of all the good things that could happen to you, if you'd just let them. I could—"

"Hi, Mrs. Schultz." Rowan waves at their neighbor, currently traversing their front sidewalk. Thank God for neighbors.

"Rowan, Jane." The older woman slows her pace. Back when she was still working, Mrs. Schultz was a schoolteacher. First grade. Rowan never had her, but Ben and Jane both did. The best part about Mrs. Schultz, other than her being a really nice teacher and all, was that every year, come Halloween time, she gave out special candy packets to all the kids in her class who came to her house for Trick or Treat. Rowan still considers herself gypped for not getting Mrs. Schultz in first grade.

"Jane, what's this I hear about you and a baby?" Mrs. Schultz smiles.

Jane nods. "Yes. A baby. I'm having one." Mrs. Schultz can't tell, but Rowan knows this is Jane's way of signaling that the brief conversation is now over.

"Well, glory be. Congratulations." Mrs. Schultz quickens her step. Perhaps she can read Jane after all.

"Thank you." Jane leans back into her rocking chair, a satisfied expression blooming across her face.

"Have a nice night, Mrs. Schultz." Rowan raises a hand and follows the neighbor with her eyes, hoping the added time will distract her sister from the pre-visitation topic. Which, of course, it doesn't.

"What's your problem, Rowan?"

"What do you mean?"

"I mean, you're not trying." Jane sighs and clutches the arms of her rocker. "You're not hanging out with anyone other than Danny. You don't seem to care about yourself, or your future. Don't you have plans, aspirations?"

"Plans?" Rowan hoists her legs off the porch floor and swings them onto her chair. This permits a view of her toes and the house next door instead of Jane and her worried eyes.

"Yes, plans." Jane huffs. "Like, ideas about how you want your life to be. What you're going to *do* with yourself."

Rowan smushes a foot into the wicker seat, feeling clunky and uncoordinated against the firm, woven surface. "I'm going to college. Isn't that enough?"

"I don't know. It doesn't seem like you want to go. Like you're not—"

"What do you want me to say? You want me to just randomly pick a career? Like, hey—how about I become a criminal? Make my own hours, score a ton of cash. How's that for a plan?"

"Are you serious?"

"What do you think? Do you think I'm serious?" Rowan glares at Jane, but only for a second.

It's gotten worse, since her birthday. It seems like every day finds Rowan stealing something, from somebody. The hardware store, Art's Gas 'N' Go, Ben Franklin's Five and Dime. She keeps telling herself she'll stop, but it only seems to amplify the compulsion. Like picking at a scab, aggravating a bruise. Maybe it's all she's cut out for, theft. Like, her true vocation. At least she's good at it. She hasn't gotten caught again since that one time with Mike. That one time that keeps plucking at her conscience, her nerves.

"You should come with me this Sunday," Jane says. "I think it could help."

"No way." Rowan plunks her feet back onto the warm ground of the porch, dragging a few fingers through her sweaty scalp. "No way, no way."

Jane clucks at her. "You've never been. Not once. How can you know—"

"Because I can."

"No, you can't."

"Yes, I can." Rowan tips her head into the damp wind creeping onto the porch from the yard below. "I'm a sinner. And sinners don't go to church."

"A sinner?" The low voice of their father cuts into the breeze. "Who's a sinner?" He takes a seat beside Jane, next to the door.

"No one," they reply.

Their father smoothes the khaki surrounding his long legs and stretches them out in front of him. "As long as it's not me," he says.

"No, Dad." Rowan says this to quell the surge of Invisibility approaching from deep inside, but it overtakes her just the same.

The surfaces of the outside—the texture of the breeze, her scalp, Jane's worry, her father's presence—they flip over on themselves, shrinking Rowan into a splinter, a speck of a thing. Barely there at all.

When she returns, Jane and her father are discussing Dr. Marks's work, a task only the two of them can perform with any aptitude or interest. Ben doesn't care enough to try and Rowan's attempts always leave her feeling like a hapless child, wearing Mommy's dress, trying to appropriate Jane's place in her father's affections. It was when Jane got married and finally moved out of the house last year that their father took to watching TV every evening.

"Rowan." Hank's voice seeps through the screen door. "Phone for you. I think it's Danny."

"Who?"

"Danny. Your friend, Danny."

Rowan gulps. She hasn't spoken to Danny since the other day, the day with Catherine and the space suit and the fries. She doesn't want to talk to him now, but what else can she do? It's as though the collective presence of Hank, Jane, and her father is a net, trapping her inside herself.

"Got it," she says.

She hauls herself off her chair, following Hank into the kitchen. He's frying fish and the whole house smells like a camping trip. She picks up the phone and holds it a half-inch away from her ear. Though it's nothing she ever witnessed, Rowan has been told that her mother used to do the same thing.

"Hello?" she says.

"Rowan?"

She is silent, hoping for a change of subject. Like this makes any sense at all.

"Are you there?" There's a crackle on the line and it makes Danny's voice sound wobbly.

"Where else would I be?"

"You tell me. You're the one who's being weird."

"Am not." Rowan sinks onto the talking-on-the-phone stool while Hank busies himself with a bowl of fresh string beans.

83

"Whatever you say." Danny sighs.

"I'm not being weird. I'm just—"

"*Superman* is at the Roxy. It finally got here. Didn't you see it on the marquee?"

Danny and Rowan have been talking about seeing this movie for months now. Ever since it came out last winter and got splashed all over the press as the best comic-turned-movie in ages. Like everything else in Wakefield, the movies at the local theater are always a step behind the curve.

"No," Rowan says. "I haven't been downtown lately." The urge toward Invisible presents itself again, but Rowan holds tight. The worst part is how little she cares—about Danny, about the movie.

"There's a nine o'clock show," he says. "We should go. Hank said you're about to eat dinner. We could go after that."

Rowan turns away from her brother-in-law, now whistling something vaguely jazzlike and snapping string beans. "Not tonight. I'm too tired." She flattens her torso over her thighs, proving her point.

"That's bogus. C'mon, Rowan. It's *Superman*." The crackle is gone and Danny's voice is clear, pleading. "You know you want to. What the hell is going on?"

Rowan understands that the pause following this remark will not change any subject but will merely buy her time. She definitely needs time. She sits up tall on the stool, then stands. The phone line permits her to travel to the back window of the kitchen, farther away from Hank. "It's not about anything, Dan. I'm just tired and I don't feel like going."

"Dan?"

"Huh?" She tugs on the cord, its plastic coils taut inside her palm.

"You never call me Dan."

Rowan inspects the tallest tree in their backyard. Wishes she could step outside but knows the cord isn't long enough. There's a scratching sound from Danny's end of the line. Maybe a match getting lit. Maybe his fingers on the receiver. She imagines he's probably on his bed, in his room, his father at the bar or downstairs passed out drunk, his mother watching TV. This is suddenly too much for her to hold in her hand, through a phone, a quarter-mile away.

"I have to go," she says. "We're about to eat."

"You're full of shit, Marks."

"I know." She decides this will have to suffice as a goodbye and hangs up the phone.

The Wakefield telephone directory lies on the shelf underneath the now-quiet receiver and Rowan examines its tattered yellow cover, wondering how many of the numbers she knows by heart. Stored inside herself with all the words and thoughts and memories. Eclipsing all the numbers she does not know, all the people she has yet to meet and would never call. The randomness of this collection—what has landed in her brain and what hasn't—strikes her as unfair. How much choice did she have in any of this?

"Could you do me a favor?" Hank is standing in front of her, a bowl of freshly snapped beans in his hands. "Could you start these for me? I'm going to give Jane a glass of cold milk. We're trying to watch her dairy intake."

Rowan nods and takes the beans from Hank. The bowl is heavy in her hands and it anchors her path to the stove. The water is already boiling and she drops in all the beans at once, the steam rising above the kettle and into her eyes. She blinks at first, shielding herself from the heat, then gives in, permitting her face to become brushed with a thin glow of vapor. The boiling water loops around, sucking the beans to the bottom of the pan, spitting them back for a brief stay on the surface. Rowan stands, guarding the scene. There is nothing to do but wait.

Splash

"You want more?" Sherry holds up the remainder of the chocolate milkshake she and Rowan have been sharing for the past ten minutes.

"Nah." Rowan shakes her head. "I get any fuller, I might barf cocoa soup all over my knees."

"Did I need to hear that?" Sherry's face ripples to sour and she places the shake back on the picnic table. "Tell me, Ro. Did I?"

Rowan chuckles, hands on stomach. "I'm sorry." Though she's not. Not totally. "I forgot to think."

They're out behind the restaurant, in the "Patio" section of the Sugar Shack. It was set up a few years ago to deal with customer overflow on hot days like today. No one ever eats back here, though, on account of the Jensens, the Shack's next-door neighbors, and their cesspool problem. George and Ann Marie Jensen keep saying they'll get it fixed, but this never does seem to happen. Rowan and Sherry have simply adapted to the smell—Sherry from her childhood on a farm, Rowan from her finely tuned powers of denial—and the Jensens' Garden of Delights, as they've taken to calling it, has become their preferred break spot.

"Mom?" Jerry Jr., dressed in the solid white of a short order cook, juts his head out the back door of the restaurant.

"Jer?"

"We're out of fries." He delivers this announcement with a level of urgency usually reserved for more dire matters. Like emergency tracheotomies or being held at gunpoint.

Sherry rolls her eyes. "In the freezer, dumbo."

"I looked." Jerry stomps the ground with a thick boot.

"Look again."

"Mom." He runs a hand through his greasy blonde hair. "They're not in there. I'm not—"

"Jer. Your hairnet. I told you we have to wear those now. Regulations."

"No way. I look like a total homo with that thing. And I'm working counter, not grill."

"Yeah?" Sherry scoffs. "Then why you asking for fries? Sounds like grill work to me."

"Bud told me to get them. And he ain't wearing no net. So I don't got to either."

"Bud's bald, Jer. There's nothing to net." Sherry shakes her head, her face etched with resignation. "You want to pay off your debt, you do the job. You want to do the job, you wear the net. Simple as that."

Rowan can see the not-so-quiet struggle in Jerry's eyes. He got busted a few weeks back for driving his motorcycle under the influence of a variety of substances. Usually Officer McElroy would rattle a young kid like him with a warning and escort him home. This time, though, Jerry and his state of inebriation took it upon themselves to inform McElroy that his daughter Peggy is a first-class slut who has slept with half the boys in Wakefield. While not complete fiction on Jerry's part—since age thirteen, Peggy McElroy has been blessed with the figure of a Las Vegas showgirl and the sense of adventure to go with it—Peggy's main crime is dumping Jerry for his best friend Steve two short weeks ago. And while Jerry would have been more than happy to outline, in vivid detail no less, Peggy's various faults and transgressions in the sexual arena, her father was not so keen on spending his Saturday evening in such a manner. He preferred to slap Jerry with a ticket and a night in Wakefield's only jail cell. Sherry came the next morning to post bail and Jerry now owes her a large sum of money. About two months' worth, in Shack time.

"I don't see why you can't help me find the damn fries," he says. "That's all I want. Why can't you—"

"I'm telling you, Jer. Just go look. Once more." Sherry's voice is quiet, almost peaceful. "If you still can't find them, I'll show you. You got to stop—"

"You always do this, you know? I'm trying to do good, and you fuck it up."

Jerry digs his fingers into the doorframe, his jaw tight. Rowan guesses he's debating whether or not to exit the situation. The expression on his face is familiar, though she can't place it at first. Then she does. It was a show she and Ben saw on TV once, about wild animals who chew off their own legs to get free of hunters' traps. That's the look on Jerry's face about now. When she was little, Rowan turned away while Ben stared at the set, fascinated. This time, she's the one who can't stop staring.

"I'll show you where the fries are, Jerry." Rowan rises from the picnic table, her legs sore from the heat and a day of standing. "I was about to leave anyway."

"That'd be alright," Jerry says.

"And put on your damn hairnet, bozo. I mean it." Sherry tugs on her shirt, a flash of pink in the mid-afternoon sun.

Jerry grunts.

Rowan leads him to the freezer and the large bags of fries in plain view on the middle shelf, below the maraschino cherries and the hot dog buns. She pats a bag with her hand, aware that she has nothing more to offer. "I hear you're thinking of joining the service," she says.

Jerry jerks a bag of fries off the shelf, holding it by the top corners, swinging over his boots. "Did Mom tell you that?"

Rowan has never really talked with Jerry, only hears about him from Sherry. She stares at his hands, wide and capable like a grown man's, and realizes she has no clue who this boy is. No clue at all. "Yeah, your mom told me," she says.

"Sherry don't know shit." Jerry hoists the frozen bag under one arm and props it above his hip.

"But she said you were—"

"She's got ideas. Ways she wants me to be. Got nothing to do with who I am. You dig that?"

Rowan nods. She feels like there's something she's supposed to say, but it's buried too deep. She's got no access.

"Thanks for helping me out," Jerry says. "I'll catch you later."

"Okay," Rowan says, still fumbling inside herself.

She follows Jerry into the kitchen, grabbing her jacket and car keys from the table next to the grill. Then lingers for a minute, momentarily distracted. Sherry's brother Bud is cooking onion rings and the smell, sweet and oily, stands beside her, soothing. She opens her lungs, breathing in the comfort until it circles her, pressing into each cell. The fumbling feeling is gone. Now there's just the calm.

"Someone was looking for you." Bud cocks his head. "I think she's still in front."

Rowan shoves the keys into the front pocket of her shorts and cinches the jacket round her waist. So much for calm. A clatter of fear, strained and wiry, starts at the point of contact between waist and jacket and flares upward, stopping just below her shoulders. "Did she say what she wanted?"

Bud shrugs. He's a big guy, beefy as a cut of steak. "Got me." He chuckles. "Send her on back here, I'll tell her what she wants."

Rowan tries to laugh along, but she can't. The only thing to do is walk away, past the grill, veering around Jerry and a batch of teenage girls at the counter, and present herself to the still, patient visitor by the front door.

"Catherine," she says.

Catherine smiles, a shy bloom. She is dressed for the weather, in shorts and a light T-shirt. Her brown leather business portfolio, the one that has accompanied her to the Shack for a month of visits, lies propped in front of her hips, underneath two straight, suntanned arms.

"There you are," she says. "I was beginning to wonder."

"Here." Rowan steadies her weight above her ankles. "I was here."

"Did you get a chance to talk to Sherry?" Catherine lifts a hand from the portfolio and runs it across the top of her forehead, pushing back the heat. Rowan remembers the alien girl who once inhabited this body, how strange she once seemed. Now she's just a human, on Earth. Almost boring.

"I did," Rowan says. "I've been meaning to call you, but—"

"What did she say?"

"What did she say?"

Catherine laughs again, louder, deeper. "I don't think this is going to work. Your usual Marco Polo routine. You're going to have to—"

"I know. Hold on." Rowan opens the front door and motions for Catherine to follow her outside. "I won't repeat you out here," she says.

It's a humid day and the heat falls on their bodies, wet and heavy. The door thuds shut.

"Sherry's not going for it, Catherine. The numbers don't add up. It's too big a risk. And she just got this new job—driving at the Demolition Derby on Tuesday nights. There's this guy, Roger, and he got her a spot. She's been wanting to drive those cars forever. She's thinking that between summers at the Shack, Driver's Ed during the school year, and now the Derby, she can crank out enough cash for a down payment on a house. That's all she really wants. Or the main thing she wants." Rowan squints into the bright sky, a bead of sweat forming above her upper lip. She licks it off with her tongue.

"Oh." Catherine curls round her portfolio. "Okay."

"We appreciate all you did. A lot of hard work and all that. It's not like she's not grateful, like *we're* not grateful, we just can't—"

"I should talk to Sherry. At least let me talk to Sherry. Then I can—"

"She said she's done." Rowan wipes her face with a damp wrist. "She said if you asked to talk to her that I was supposed to—"

"I get it," Catherine says. The disappointment in her voice is barely audible, swallowed by the softness in her tone. "You don't have to try to make it better. It is what it is."

Rowan tugs up her shorts, as if this might lift Catherine's spirits somehow. It doesn't work. "We could go swimming," she says.

At first it looks like Catherine is going to laugh. Then it looks like she might start yelling. Then she switches back to amusement once again. "Is this a habit of yours?" Her voice swoops up, pricks the air above their heads. "Trouble comes along and you feed it with beer, fries—now water?"

"No. I wasn't—"

"This is my first professional failure, you know." Just underneath the top level of Catherine's face, there is a rise of something urgent. A wave that threatens to, but does not, break. "You think dunking myself in some backwoods pond is going to fix this? Is that your plan? Wash off the smell of failure?"

"That's not what I—"

"Or maybe there's something about the water in this town I don't know about."

Rowan lifts her shorts once again, letting them settle back down on their own. "First of all, you don't smell that bad. Really. Second of all, it's not a failure. Not at all. You met me, didn't you? And now we're friends. Sort of." She adds this, just in case. She's still not certain what they are. "And third of all, the water in this town doesn't do anything—except cool you off. But that's enough for me. More than enough for you too, I bet." The sweat has reappeared on Rowan's upper lip, but this time she lets it stay.

"I can't," Catherine says.

"Why not?"

Catherine blinks. The wave crashes, rearranging her face. "I don't know," she says. "I can't think of a reason."

"How about that," Rowan says. She beams through the glare of sun. "Neither can I."

༄ ༄ ༄

They stop first at Art's Gas 'N' Go so Rowan can buy them a six-pack of pop and some potato chips. She insists on going into Art's alone—presumably to spare Catherine from paying, but really to spare Catherine from what Rowan may or may not do. As it turns out, Rowan happens to lift some Slim Jims from the shelf when Art's not looking. Luckily, Catherine doesn't have to know about it.

Instead of going to the reservoir, which will be swamped on a day like today with rowdy kids and short-tempered mothers, Rowan opts for the creek. There's a place just north of town that she and her brother discovered years ago. Ben and the boys put up a rope swing when she was in fifth grade, but the old thing finally broke after too much use and no one goes there anymore. Rowan knows this on account of being the better part of "no one." It helps her to think.

"Looks like all the backwoods idiots left. Now it's just us." She flops onto the ground, kicking off her sneakers and stretching her legs in front of her. "The creek is cool. You'll be surprised."

Catherine, still standing, inspects the wooded area sloping down to the wide pass of water below. "Is Danny your boyfriend?" she says.

"No." Rowan lifts her legs and massages her knees with sweaty palms. The sharp pull inside her stomach does not appear to be alleviated by the soothing of her knees. "Friends is all we are."

"I had a boyfriend in college. Larry. Friends is all we are now too." Catherine eases to the ground. She sits with her legs crossed and pats the earth around her, the dirt and the leaves and a small patch of flowers. "It's gorgeous here. Peaceful." She sighs. "I think I'm beginning to let go of my defeat."

"It's not a defeat, you know." Rowan wants to joggle Catherine's shoulder, wants to reconfigure all the pieces she doesn't understand and shape them into something she does, but restrains herself from this impossibility. "You did the best you could. Really."

"Easy for you to say. You're not the one who has to go back to your boss and father and tell him your sure thing just turned into nothing."

"But it wasn't. It wasn't a sure thing. Year-round ice cream never would have made it in Wakefield. We're too small and set in our ways. That's the town motto, you know. 'Change is bad. We fear change.'"

Catherine runs her hands down her legs. "And how about you, Rowan? What are you going to do when you get out of here?"

Rowan swallows. She feels the rise of an impulse, an urge to tell Catherine everything. Her dreams, her fears, her criminal tendencies. It's an impulse that's met with an equally powerful force, one that tells her to lay low, keep quiet.

"I don't know," Rowan says. She clears her throat. "I'm not sure about the whole future thing. There's always astronaut and firefighter. Those were my choices when I was seven."

"Good choices."

"Yeah. My career planning hasn't advanced much past that stage." Rowan clips a blade of grass from the earth and squeezes it between two fingers. Somewhere that seems far away but isn't, a bird sings into the hot afternoon sky. "Rollins is strong in English and Physics. I'm good at both of those. And then there's my spelling. That's sure to be worth big money some day."

Leaves scatter as Catherine turns on her side, propping her head up with one arm. "That's right," she says. "I'm keeping company with a champion speller. Very impressive. What'd you win anyway? A cup? A bowl? Or something more substantial?"

"Substantial. Good word." Rowan flattens against the grass, level with the bugs and the dirt. "I won a trip to Washington D.C. That's what happens. If you win the State, you go on to Nationals. My dad went with me—Big Fun in the Big City."

"What was it like?"

"It was okay." Rowan closes her eyes, pulling up the pictures she hasn't looked at in years. "It was weird, actually. Strange." She shudders as the memories barge into her awareness, crossing her legs in an attempt to mask the swell of discomfort. "I never talk about this," she says.

"What happened?"

Rowan waits. She feels the equal but opposing tugs—to tell or not to tell. She takes a breath, easing into speech.

"There were a ton of kids," she says. "From all over the country. All ages of kids. It was cool. We're all spelling our words and moving through the competition. There were seven rounds in all. But the fourth round was the weird one." She opens her eyes, scrapes the blade of grass against her cheek. The green is sharp against the tiny hairs that frame her skin, pushing them aside as the blade drags forward. "They gave me my word—legerdemain, it was—and I'm up on the stage, facing the audience."

"Were you scared?"

"Totally," Rowan says. She gulps. "My dad was there. He had a seat all the way in the back, but I could see him anyway. That helped. But it was still—like usually, in the more advanced stages of competition, you often have no idea what the word means or how to spell it. You can ask for origins and definitions and all that, but the spelling itself is mostly guesswork." Rowan stops, suspended between the rush of the creek below and the slip of leaves above. She's never gotten this far in the story before, always skips this part. She sits in silence for a minute, a final concession to the forces of caution, then tumbles past them.

"And so while I'm trying to figure out my word, looking at the speck of my father's face in the back row, I heard a voice. At first I thought it was someone on stage with me, another kid or a proctor. But I looked around me and no one was there. Just me and the voice that said it again—spelled the word inside my head. I didn't know what the hell to do. It was like cheating or insanity or something. I asked for the definition again, like that might kick me back into a place that made sense. They gave it to me, but all I could think about was the voice. I couldn't say anything—there was nothing to do but stand there. Finally, my time was up and I walked off the stage. That was it."

"Was it spelled right?" Catherine's gaze is uninterrupted, fixed on Rowan. "Was the voice in your head right?"

Rowan blanches. She shuts her eyes again, washing herself in a feeling of foolishness. So this is what it's like. This is what it's like to talk, to confess. She shivers. "It was," she says. "The voice was right. That was the weirdest part."

"Interesting." Catherine pronounces this with a mix of seriousness and play, and Rowan continues to stare into her eyelids, unsure how to close this subject.

"Rowan?" Catherine says softly.

"Yeah?"

"I don't think you're crazy, if that's what you're worried about."

"I wasn't worried." Rowan's eyes pop open, drinking in the field of blue and green above her.

"Who do you think it was? The voice?"

Rowan's leg itches and she scratches through her shorts. "I don't know," she says, hearing how that sounds. Wrong. It sounds wrong. "Sometimes I wonder if it was my mother. Back from the dead to help me win a spelling championship." She laughs, but not a real laugh. "Or not. I really don't know."

Catherine wriggles into to a sitting position. She links her hands together and inspects them for a long time. "I can't imagine what that must be like, to not have a mother around. Must be really hard. My mom is my idol. I want to be just like her. That might sound weird, but it's true."

"It doesn't sound weird."

"No?"

A mosquito whirs around her face and Rowan waves it away. "No."

"You know," Catherine reaches for the bag of food, "sometimes I find it hard to believe you're only eighteen."

"Why?" Rowan scratches her leg again, but only for lack of options. Itchy is not how she feels. Funny, maybe. On display, perhaps. But not itchy.

Catherine pulls out the potato chips and tears open the top. She jiggles the bag, then pops a chip into her mouth. "Lots of reasons. You remind me of my roommate freshman year. Molly," she says, through the chip. "She's twenty-one now, like me. Like you seem sometimes. She was a great girl—kind of rowdy too. Like you. We used to do some crazy shit." She chuckles, plops the bag of chips between them. "Sneaking into the Dean's Office after hours, bribing the security guard with booze and candy. We were bad."

Rowan flips on her belly, scraping her legs. "I can't see you bad," she says.

"We were. Though not always. We were mellow too. We'd light candles in our room and do tarot readings for each other. Stuff like that. Sometimes I think I was a little attracted to her. Or her to me." Catherine stops, letting the words coast into the open—spinning, scattered.

Rowan swallows. "Right," she says.

"We almost fooled around one night, but we chickened out. After that, we kind of drifted apart. I met Larry and everything changed."

"Hmm." There's a twig on the ground, next to Rowan's hand. She picks it up and starts twisting it into the dirt—a deep, easy motion. Until this strikes her as way too sexual and she drops the stick into a pile of leaves.

"So you two drifted apart," she says. Repeating Catherine seems the casual, sophisticated thing to do. The best way to demonstrate the many ways in which this is truly Not A Big Deal.

"Bolted in opposite directions is probably more like it," Catherine says. "I always wonder how that would have been. To be with her. They say your college years are supposed to be a time of experimentation. And now mine are over. Damn."

"Damn." Rowan senses she may be blushing and feigns interest in a large tree outside of Catherine's line of sight.

"How about you?" Catherine's voice sneaks over to Rowan, soaking her scalp, her blush.

"Me?"

"Have you ever . . ."

"No." Rowan jabs a toe into the soil, damp under the cover of leaves. "I've never really—I mean, I've never . . ." She shakes her head.

"I'm sorry, Rowan. I didn't mean to—"

"It's okay." Rowan rolls off her stomach, brushing dirt and leaves from her legs. "We should probably go swimming, though. I'm really hot."

Catherine giggles, and Rowan prays this is not in response to her last remark.

"Does anyone live around here?" Catherine stands, stretching out her legs.

"No. Not anymore."

Catherine chucks off her sandals and places her hands on her hips, elbows jutting out. She looks like an explorer newly arrived on conquered ground. "Do you think it would be okay if I took my clothes off?"

"Uh." Rowan nods. Her legs waver slightly, as if reevaluating their willingness to keep her standing upright. Inside her head, a mini-Rowan, dressed in a black judge's robe, snags her attention. *Knock, knock. Anybody home? Give me a fucking break. First the girl–girl thing, now this? What are you doing? And why are you smiling like an idiot?*

Rowan grabs her towel. "Excuse me," she says, and scurries down toward the water.

The creek is high for late June, and it pours over her toes, cool and clear. She strips off her shirt and shorts and glides into the wet, submerging her entire body in its rapid flow. Opening her eyes, like always, she lets the current carry her several yards from her point of entry, down the river. She pushes away water with flat palms, the surge thick against the pressure from her arms. The confusion of a moment ago fades into certainty. She is here, under water. She is swimming.

Finally, after a minute or so, she pops her head into the air, the stream at her neck. She's a good fifty feet from where she started. Catherine is at the bank—Rowan can see her hair and skin. Lots of skin. She thinks of staring but can't—that would be wrong. Like looking at other girls' bodies in the gym locker rooms or in the showers. Not a good idea. She treads water instead, limbs lifted and weaving, working against a current that has other ideas about where she should be.

"Just jump in," she says. "It's the only way." She yells into the approaching swell, yells against the tiny judge in her head still telling her to keep her mouth shut.

The skin and the hair dip a foot in, then out, sprinkling water onto the rocks. "It's cold."

"It's not *cold*. This isn't *cold*. This is bath water." Rowan dives under, then smashes to the surface. "I didn't bring you here for nothing, did I?"

The skin shivers, waits. "No."

"So. Jump on in." Rowan kicks a leg out in front of her, solid in the knowledge that she is no longer the same girl she was two minutes ago. "You're not going to wimp out, are you? Leave me in here all alone?"

Catherine takes a step forward. "Maybe," she says. The sun dives down against her body, illuminating her shape, her caution.

Rowan looks away.

Catherine pokes another toe in. "There's no leeches or crabs or anything like that in here, are there?"

"Leeches? Nah. Crabs?" Rowan waits a beat, long enough to get a rise out of the pale, naked figure on the other side of her vision.

"Rowan?"

"Yeah?"

"Crabs?"

"No crabs. Really. Just me."

The splash of Catherine's body against the stream is enough for Rowan to turn her head in the direction of the bank. The sound ruptures the air, then disappears into the rush of the creek and the low scrape of Rowan's breathing. Even when Catherine emerges moments later, several feet away, Rowan is still transfixed by the pressure of air against her lungs, edging back and forth, in and out of her surroundings.

"You were right." Catherine shouts.

"About the leeches?" Rowan's breath darts across the surface, toward Catherine.

"About the fucking freezing."

Rowan grins. "I told you."

☙   ☙   ☙

98

An hour later they're lying, sunning themselves, on the big rock that was once a jumping-off point for the rope swing. Much to Rowan's relief, Catherine's clothes have returned to her body. Her bra and underwear, however, have not. These items now lay huddled in a pile somewhere in the woods behind them and Rowan can only guess at their fate—what kinds of creatures might be inspecting them, laying claim to their shape, their color, their essence. Although, ultimately, it's none of her business.

There's little talking between the two of them, but this doesn't seem to be a problem. Language weaves in and out of long pauses filled with sleep or contemplation; laughing circles the silences that cushion lazy observations. After a gap much longer than the others, a good ten minutes or so, Rowan cuts into the silence with a fresh topic, at a right angle to all the others.

"What's your stand on Demolition Derbys?"

Catherine clears her throat. "As in cars crashing into each other at high speeds for the amusement of others?"

"Exactly."

"I'm against them."

Rowan swats a fly from her face. "I see."

"Why do you ask?"

"Sherry's first run is tomorrow night, out at the track in Loomis. I thought you might want to go."

"You did, did you?" Even with her eyes closed, Rowan can hear the smile in Catherine's reply.

"I did," Rowan says. All the riled, crazy feelings of an hour ago are still present, but in a muted way, lying stretched out flat against the rock, baking in the sun.

"I wonder what would make you think a thing like that."

Rowan shrugs, her shoulder blades lifting from the hard rock. "Ignorance, I suppose."

"That makes sense."

"It does, doesn't it?" Rowan's lips release the sounds and she sinks deeper into the steady surface beneath her. The pull toward missing introduces itself and she senses the beginnings of Invisibility—the padded quality of sound, the shifting of surrounding objects from

99

solid to liquid to vapor, her heart suddenly quiet inside of her. She is almost there, her transition into away, when she is stopped by a bead of sweat. A glint of motion between her breasts, inching slowly toward her stomach. It pulls her back, hooks her into this short stretch of time in which she finds herself.

Here.

Here on this huge rock that cradles her body, and Catherine's, like a giant hand holding two tiny pearls. Here in the rise and fall of her chest, and the infinite portion of skin holding the stubborn speck of water that will not accept her departure. Not this time. Beating herself at her own game.

"Yes." She says this because it is the only thing to say. Because she can.

Bash

"You did say we were going to *share* that popcorn, didn't you?" Catherine eyes the shiny, buttery clump being crammed into Rowan's open mouth.

"Did I say that?" Rowan grins. "Maybe your memory is better than mine. All that learning you done did in that college of yours."

They're sitting on the bleachers of the Lil' Indy Demolition Derby in Loomis. The preshow entertainment, trained dogs driving miniature mechanical cars ("Darling Dorothy and the Disco Dogs"), is wrapping up and the Derby is about to begin.

"Give me that." Catherine snatches the bag from Rowan's slick fingers.

"Oh, I see." Rowan licks her hand clean, one finger at a time. "When you want it, you just take it. No 'please', no 'may I'— just 'mine.'"

"It's called initiative. But maybe you aren't familiar with that word."

"Word? What's a word?"

"Oh dear." Catherine winces. "I take back everything I said about your maturity level. I was sorely misguided."

"You're Miss Guided?" Rowan smirks. "I thought your name was Catherine."

"You're a moron." Catherine shoves her in the arm. "And don't you forget it."

"Got it. You're a moron."

"Shut up."

"Will do." Rowan sits up and grabs a handful of popcorn, giddy with the interaction of the evening thus far. It's like the Derby has already started and only she and Catherine are driving.

She examines the field, the cars making their way onto the wide expanse of green patched with dirt and puddles of mud. Maybe these cars can bring her back into herself, into the person she used to be. If that's even what she wants.

She points toward the field with a fistful of popcorn. "Sherry should be coming on soon."

Catherine inspects the drivers, looking for blonde. "Does she know I'm here?"

"Now why on earth would I want to tell her a thing like that?"

"Because you're a—"

Rowan stops her with a flat hand. "Don't remind me. I'm a moron."

"Precisely." Catherine appears to grow tired of the cars on the field and switches her attention to the stands. "Awful lot of people for a Tuesday night. Doesn't anyone have anything better to do?"

Rowan smoothes her legs below her shorts. "Tuesday nights used to be real slow till they started offering two-for-one beers and all the popcorn you can eat. Now it's a madhouse. Sherry was lucky to get a Tuesday spot her first time out. They've even started putting some of the special drivers, the Saturday night hotshots, into the midweek line up. Tonight it's Killer Joe and his Mad Pinto. Sherry better watch out for him. He's got backing skills galore."

"I see." Catherine drifts to concerned. "I didn't know this was going to be so, so ..."

"Vicious?" Rowan checks the cars on the field. No Sherry. "She'll be here soon," she says softly.

Catherine studies Rowan for a second, then looks away. "How did you find yourself in the ice cream business, anyway? Your dad's a doctor. I assume you didn't need the money."

Sherry's face nudges into Rowan's mind—head tilted back laughing, cigarette in hand. Until the image gets blurry with smoke and distance and features that blend into someone else's—someone Rowan doesn't know.

"Just fell into it, I guess," she says. "Keeps me busy. And Sherry's a great boss."

"Sherry's something, all right." Catherine says quietly.

"And there she is." Rowan lifts herself up, then falls down on the bench. "Check her out."

Sherry is driving a bright yellow Nova. It belonged to her brother Bud—at least, it did until he crashed it into a tree behind their family house. Bud swears that tree wasn't there the night before. Regardless, two days later Sherry talked him into letting her convert the remains into a Derby car and, with a large amount of coaxing and a smaller amount of cash, here it is—decked out in a new paint job and looking spiffy, down to the details. "Road Kill," the name Sherry has dreamed of using on her Derby car for as long as she's dreamed of driving in the Derby, is spelled out on both sides of the vehicle in squashed red letters. The best part, and Rowan makes sure to point this out to Catherine, is that the bottoms of all the letters appear to be dripping blood.

"Huh," Catherine says. Though she's trying not to be, Rowan can tell that Catherine is impressed.

"How often do you see something like that?" Rowan says. "Really, how often?" It's only a bench in the middle of a stack of old bleachers, but Rowan settles in like she's the definition of luxury—like she owns the car, the arena, the entire experience.

"And there's Little," she says. "Little!" She calls out to Sherry's youngest boy, roaming the stadium with his hands jammed in his pockets. "Up here!"

The slender boy sees them, sliding through the crowd and into a place on the other side of Rowan. "Did you see the car?" he says. "Intense, man. I didn't think they were going to pull it off." He nods at Catherine. "Hey."

"I've been hearing rumors about you." Rowan clasps his neck, rocking him gently from side to side. "Something about a hot-shot young jockey, putting the old boys to shame."

"Maybe." He closes his eyes briefly, pleased. Except for the fact that he's a boy and has a face untouched by all-night partying and a lifetime of disappointments, Little looks exactly like his mother.

"Look at that. They're starting." Catherine leans in, no longer hiding her interest.

A horn blares from the top of the stands, signifying the beginning of the show. The crowd swells with volume, cheers for their favorite drivers, boos for the others. Rowan and Little join in, pouring hope on the yellow Nova at the far edge of the field.

"Go, Mom!" Little cries. "Kick some butt!"

"There she goes." Rowan jostles his knee. "Ready to do some damage."

Sherry charges into motion, maneuvering into the middle of the pack. From the bleachers, it's hard to see much of Sherry inside the Nova—the only sure sign is the bright blonde hair framing the bottom of her regulation helmet. The Nova, however, moves in a manner that is distinctly Sherry's. The car's first move is both shrewd and intrepid—easily dodging a Chrysler Colt at her left and an AMC Pacer at her right for a direct whomp into the rear bumper of Killer Joe's Pinto.

Little seizes Rowan's arm, screaming with glee. "That's my mom! Did you see that? That's my mom!" He turns to the neighboring bystanders, attempting to pull them into his vicarious achievement. "Road Kill," he says. "Check it out. The Chevy Nova's the one to beat."

And so it is. Before long, with slam after crash after fearless hit, the fan base for "Road Kill" spreads outward to include the entire south side of the stadium. Sherry, riding on the audible support, gives an inspired performance, disabling more than her share of vehicles on the field until only three remain—the Nova, Joe's Pinto, and a dark green Mercury Capri.

"Why is she smashing into the Pinto so often?" Catherine leans into Rowan's ear, the noise around them making normal conversation impossible.

"She has a crush on Killer Joe." Rowan yells back from a much safer distance than mouth-on-ear. "It's one way to articulate her affection."

As she turns back to the action, she senses Catherine's attention lingering on her, scanning the side of her face instead of the track, where everyone else is looking. Rowan pretends not to notice, but allows herself to absorb the range of her friend's interest—pocketing it silently, saving it for later.

The Capri is knocked out by an impressive assault on the part of the Pinto, as Joe nails the already frequently bashed vehicle with a mighty strike, ending its movement for the evening.

Little yelps with delight. "Far *out!*" He scrambles his slight frame into a standing position, straining for a better view.

"Here we go." Rowan follows Little to standing and tugs on Catherine's shirt, pulling her up as well. A reply, of sorts, to Catherine's previous inspection.

Joe starts backing toward Sherry in a particularly menacing fashion, weaving in and out of the clutter of disabled vehicles remaining on the field. The spectators boo and cheer in different pockets, according to allegiances. The Nova doesn't budge, standing its ground by the side wall of the arena while Joe closes the gap between them.

"Why isn't she moving?" Catherine is concerned, almost panicked.

"I don't know." Rowan stares at the yellow hood of the Nova, faded in the glare of nighttime stadium lighting. She tries to focus on the color, the form, the ongoing action, but Catherine's agitation is bigger than anything—bigger than Sherry or her car or anyone else in the stadium.

"I don't know." She says it again to knock herself into a steady state, away from the distraction, but it doesn't work.

Joe is close, almost to Sherry's front bumper, when the Nova comes alive, backing away from the Pinto in a slick fishtail turn and slamming it into the same wall Sherry was guarding only moments before. The Pinto coughs, sputters, dies. "Road Kill" roars into the main section of the stadium, battered and victorious.

Little jumps onto Rowan's back, spinning the two of them in a tight circle. "She did it! Mom did it!" He jumps down and wiggles toward the aisle. "Let's go find her. Come on."

Rowan thinks this would be nice, but is aware that she can

barely move. The noise and the lights and the inner commotion have left her about as battered as the Nova.

"We'll be along. You go ahead." Rowan collapses onto the bench and Catherine joins her. "I'm wiped out."

Little fades into the bodies of the crowd and Rowan fixes herself on the bleachers. Catherine, mere inches away, clutches the remains of the popcorn and breathes with effort, like she has run a mile to be here. Her pupils are shining and her mouth is open, as though in a pose of amazement, or wonder. Rowan catches herself staring and turns away. She's never seen anyone look like Catherine looks right now. She's not even sure how that is, other than ready, unguarded.

"How about that?" Rowan says, covering the shot of anxiety crowding her belly.

Catherine rubs her hands. "Should we go find Sherry?" she says.

"We should." Rowan watches Catherine's hands glide together, palm to palm, the pulse of self against self, unwavering. Her own hands clench into fists, then free themselves and flatten against the bleachers. Around them, people are stretching, milling, leaving their seats to go buy food. It's intermission—the tractor pull is next on the lineup.

"It might be better to wait," she says. "Just till the mob clears out around Sherry. If that's all right with you."

Catherine shifts on her seat, propping her feet against the recently vacated bleacher in front of them. "Why not?" she says. "It's not every day I have an experience like this."

"Me neither." Rowan positions her feet onto the bench next to Catherine's and immediately wonders if she's said too much.

Out in the center of the arena, crunched cars and weary drivers are removing themselves or being removed from the field. The mud has spread from a few small puddles to everywhere and on everything—grass, fenders, windshields, faces.

"That was fun," Catherine says, addressing her knees.

"Mmm." Rowan's stomach does a loop-dee-loop inside her body, like a tiny plane in the sky. She supposes it's Catherine's age—her experience, her self-assurance, her sense of entitlement—

that makes her so intimidating. So easy to tease one minute and so impossible to talk to the next. Rowan wonders if this is how college will feel—a jumble of nerves and shorted connections and fear and hope as a way of life, an everyday event. Maybe. And if so, in the face of this new life, she at least needs to try. Try to make this connection or whatever it is. Try to live in the experience, not merely nearby.

"There's a new movie coming to the Roxy on Friday," she says. "I thought maybe we could go."

Catherine shakes her head. "What's a movie?"

Rowan's shoulders sink into the rest of her body, relaxing for the first time this evening. "I guess I'll have to show you."

Guest

"Sweetheart. Bless your soul. How nice of you to stop by."
Danny's mother Audrey stands at the front door, motioning
Rowan to enter the house.

"I—uh. Thanks." Rowan steps into the house carefully, as
though avoiding shards of glass. "I was just—I was . . . walking.
Around. And I . . ."

Audrey nods, tucking her arms under her ample bosom.
Danny's mother has a timeless quality about her, like those moms
in Disney movies who traffic in profound truths and plates of
warm cookies. Rowan studies the flower print of Audrey's dress,
wondering if there could possibly be any cookies inside its
smooth folds.

"Rowan?" The folds sway back and forth.

Rowan's eyes climb into Audrey's, registering the concern
harbored there. "Thanks," she says. She backs toward the stairs.
"I appreciate your help. Thank you."

"He's in his room. He'll be happy to see you."

Rowan shrugs. Best not to argue. She turns and heads upstairs,
grateful for the predictable planks of wood under her feet. She
pounds out an even beat, massaging the queasiness out of her
ankles.

Danny's door is open, the light from his room puncturing an
otherwise dark hallway. Rowan approaches gingerly, respectfully.
An electric guitar solo slides off the walls and a thumping bass
rocks against her interior: Lynyrd Skynrd, a band Danny tends
to play when he's pissed off, melancholy, or a blend of the two.

"What?" Danny huffs. He's sitting at his desk, straddling his
chair. He looks out of place, like a visitor in his own bedroom.

"Just stopping by," Rowan says. "Seeing what's up." She stands near the door, next to the shelves housing Danny's comic book collection. His favorite, a vintage Superman comic published before he was born, hangs on the wall beside her, suspended in a plastic cover.

"What are you working on?" she says.

"Like you give a shit." He swerves in his chair, returning to his drawing. "Where the hell have you been?"

His anger hits her the wrong way. She imagines his fury bouncing off her chest and falling into an abandoned heap on the floor next to her. Not hers. This must be how Superman feels, with the kryptonite and all.

"Nowhere," she says. "I've been working a lot."

"Lyle said he saw you at the Roxy last night. With some girl he didn't recognize. The Hulk lady, I'm guessing. That Catherine." He pronounces her name like a weapon and Rowan feels it as such, little pings against her thighs.

"Since when do you talk to Lyle? What does that dickwad have to—"

"I would have talked to you if you'd been there. At the park. Remember baseball, Rowan? The game with the sticks and the mitts?"

"Yeah. Of course. But I—"

"And you still haven't said if it was her. Like I don't already know."

"It was her." Rowan thins out inside, portioning her energy until it's just one quiet line, up and down her body. Nothing to attack, nothing to blame.

"What's going on, Rowan?" Danny shoves his papers toward the far side of the desk, sending a pen skittering to the floor. "Skipping out before you even leave? Your old friends not up to your new standards?"

"Like I have standards. Right. That's what I'm—"

"Whatever you call it. You're still doing it. Was I never good enough for you? Was that it? You were just waiting till someone better came along?" His arms flex at his sides, coming to rest on the front edge of his desk. The thrashing guitar and bass relax into the next song on the record. A slow song.

"Danny." Rowan flows back into herself, holding his anger, her guilt. "We've been hanging out, is all. No big thing. She's . . . she's . . ."

"She's ugly as hell, for one. You were right about that." Danny turns and addresses Rowan directly, his eyes glued onto hers. "And she likes you, or you like her, or something. There's *something* weird going on there."

Rowan looks away. Superman continues to approach her through his cover of plastic. Never arriving.

"What are you talking about?" she says. "That's wrong. You're crazy."

"Crazy? You're the one who's crazy. We used to be buds, Ro. Then all of a sudden you ditch me like I'm some worthless sack of shit. I think Lyle's right. You're acting like you're in love with her. Your pervie new friend with her pervie new—"

"Lyle? What the *hell* does Lyle have to do with any of this? And why are you talking to him about me? None of this is anybody's fucking business." Rowan can feel a charge inside her chest, a spark that expands to fill her entire body. She holds it there, like a kettle, until it leaks through her feet and into the floor, shaping itself into something she can stand on.

"And talk about pervs," she says. "What about *you*? What about you waiting for someone you'll never get? What about you drawing some stupid comic book hero who looks just like you and his stupid girlfriend who looks just like me? Living out your fantasies in pen and ink. How pathetic is that? At least I . . ." She stops, breathless.

"At least you what?"

"Nothing."

Danny drops his head, his thin hair grazing his face. "You're full of it. You think you're so special, so much better than everyone else. Well, fuck you, then. Leave. I don't give a shit."

"And you think I do?" Rowan stands in place, near the door, willing her legs to leave. They won't. The anger underneath her feet turns to hurt and hesitation. Inside her head, thoughts whirl around aimlessly, unable to inject themselves into the conversation. How did everything get so fucked up so fast? Wasn't this supposed to be the good part? Where she and Danny got to enjoy this last summer together, free of everything but each other?

At his desk, all folded up with his drawings, Danny looks like a little kid—his T-shirt riding up his back and one leg sticking out to the side. In the window over his head, through the midday sun filtering into the room, Rowan squints and sees Hector: sword in hand, hair flowing, victorious after a long day of battle. There, in the atmosphere above his creator, Hector brings his sword to his chest, placing it diagonally across his heart. He finds Rowan and nods solemnly. She understands. He is precisely where he needs to be. Next to him stands Guinevere, with Rowan's hair and nose and long, thin body, cloaked in a ridiculous dress and looking anything but content. Her face, unlike Hector's, is desperate, panicked. She needs to leave. Now.

"Come on, Guinevere. We're getting you out of here." Rowan tugs at the tiny figure with her mind as Danny looks on in disbelief.

"What the hell are you doing, Marks? You're not taking any of my comics."

"I know," Rowan says. Guinevere loses the dress and slides into the corner of Rowan's brain. "We're leaving. We'll see you suckers later."

"Later." Danny slams his desk drawer, toppling his pencil holder. "Hope your big old ego can squeeze through the door there. Good luck with that."

"No bigger than yours, Superhero Boy. Have fun without me."

Down the narrow hallway that frames her escape, Rowan's footsteps echo against the cracked, plastered walls and against her heart, now beating rapidly once again. Deep in the background, Guinevere sits on a brand new throne, stunned, fanning herself and shaking with the weight of her host's exit.

"We'll be okay," Rowan says to her. "Who needs lame-o Danny anyway? Not me. Or anyone who looks like me."

Guinevere puts down her fan and shrugs, confused. She yawns, her dainty mouth opening wide inside her dainty head, and she closes her eyes, dropping quickly into a peaceful slumber. She hasn't slept in years.

F l i c k

Rowan and Catherine are sitting inside the Roxy, waiting for the show to begin. This is their second movie together. Tonight it's *Grease*, a film Rowan has absolutely no interest in seeing. Not that Catherine would ever know this. Catherine, having missed the movie in its first go-round last summer, got a souped-up summary of the plot and a shining endorsement of the choreography in a phone call from Rowan last night. Rowan imagines she'll have to answer to this amplification of the truth later in the evening, but suspects Catherine won't care all that much. For whatever reason, Catherine seems to find her smart, funny, and—though Rowan is still not sure about this one—charming.

They're sitting up in the front. First row in the front. Rowan contends that this makes for a more intense viewing experience. Fleetwood Mac slips into the theatre sound system, a crackly version of "You Make Loving Fun." Rowan sings along, quietly and off-key.

Catherine groans. "I hate this band."

"Hate?" Rowan slides her sneakers against the sticky concrete floor. "Hate is such a strong word. Besides, Stevie Nicks is a-mazing."

"I'll say she's amazing. As in she's amazingly vapid and has an amazingly large drug habit."

"You know nothing about it, my friend. Have you ever listened to any of her songs? I mean, really listened? Stevie's got it all—light, dark, birth, death. She's talking to the *people*, man. To the masses."

"Like you—"

"'Rhiannon.' Have you heard that one? Do you know what it's about?"

"Not really, young one. But I'll bet you're going to tell me." Catherine's tone is soft, like a quilt. It's almost enough to knock Rowan into an inability to continue, but not quite.

"She's a witch. Or something. And she's got these powers. But they're, like, out of our reach. Except they're not. Because really, it's what we all are. We're all witches, in this weird way."

A couple of things are true. One is that Rowan has no idea what she's saying. The other is that she is unable to stop herself from saying it.

Catherine chuckles and pats her on the leg, her fingers light against the top of Rowan's thigh. "You're the only witch I know. Really. Your secret is safe with me."

Rowan swallows a Milk Dud. "Mmm," she says. Her thigh is throbbing, rendering her mute.

Stevie Nicks is interrupted by the cheesy movie theater music that precedes every show at the Roxy. The lights dim and Rowan shoves herself deeper into her chair. Thank God for previews. The screen is washed in color and the audience is instructed not to talk or litter or allow their babies to cry.

Rowan sighs heavily, feeling the coarse fabric of the old theatre chair seep through her shirt. She reminds herself to take advantage of this time in the dark, next to Catherine, to try and neatly discern and arrange all of her emotions in relation to her peculiar friend. It might be easier if her thigh didn't continue to buzz with flecks of an invisible pulse. A phenomenon that makes tidy organizing just a tad more difficult.

It's nothing she's ever encountered before, the package of hyperactive joy, dread, and insecurity that seem to accompany any outing with Catherine. And ever since Catherine's mention of Molly, ever since the introduction of a subject absolutely unacknowledged in Rowan's life up to this point, it's only gotten worse. It doesn't help that the subject matter, and its accompanying cluster of impossible emotions (at least for Rowan), have been completely off limits ever since. She wonders sometimes if they could just talk about it, explore the myths and misinformation and lack of substance of the whole thing, then maybe the awkwardness between them would disappear. Or maybe not. She's not sure. They'd have to try to know.

As it stands, it's like they're circling a giant statue, a joint effort, a creation about which neither one of them will speak. At least, not directly. Yet they continue to chisel away with a jibe here, an insult there, constructing what appears to be—when Rowan can slow down long enough to sneak a glance—a large, imposing female figure. Extremely large. And extremely naked, Rowan suspects, though she's afraid to investigate too carefully. Everything between them is fueled by this dance, these twin drives of creation and censorship. Pretending the figure is not there is as vital to her existence as the continual efforts to coax her to life. Though Rowan and Catherine are cautious, avoiding direct words, direct invocation, they are branded by Her shadow, Her shape, Her form. They cannot leave and they cannot stop this.

Other times Rowan wonders if it's just hers, this stuff in her head. The drive, the enormity, the discomfort—maybe it's all just what she's imagining between them. Maybe Catherine threw out the information about Molly to indicate what's *not* important to her, who she's *not*. Maybe Rowan is taking this to a level that Catherine had no intention or inclination to explore, not even verbally, and Rowan's imagination is having a laugh of its own—taking her to a place that, quite simply, does not exist. The huge, shimmering figure lives only in her mind, exhausting all her energy and will, disallowing her ability to have a normal, regular friendship without turning it into something crazy, something unreal.

As the previews end and the movie begins, Rowan dives into her cinematic experience. Catherine's head is propped against the seat and her breathing is barely audible, allowing Rowan an unobstructed view of the screen and her own reactions to it. *Grease*, she decides with authority, is the perfect movie for this occasion. Even though John Travolta and Olivia Newton-John look old enough to be the parents of the high school students they are supposed to portray, the movie is nevertheless a wholesome, uncluttered jolt into a teen romance simple in scope. Boy meets Girl. Boy loses Girl. (Though it's more like Girl loses Boy because he's too embarrassed to admit he likes her in front of his friends.) And finally, most satisfactorily, Boy gets Girl back.

Rowan gets snared at this last part, though. It starts when, underneath the image of John and Olivia, as Danny and Sandy, reconciling with a passionate lip lock, she spies the flicker of another image entirely. Rowan kissing Catherine. Except she can't imagine this clearly and the picture smears into a mound of colors and confusion, firing yet another round of debate on the insanity of this whole thing vs. its lack of existence altogether.

The insanity side scores some major points when Rowan realizes that, for as long as she can remember, she has always checked out the female portion of a make-out scene. In the past, she told this barely conscious part of herself that her interest in the woman, or girl, was a matter of identification. Technique, perhaps. Moving into the feminine person she would someday become, kissing the manly man on the other side of her face. Now, with the introduction of Catherine and the ensuing nonexistent vs. crazy debate, Rowan's interest in All Things Female is more than a little suspect. Treacherous, even. Or perhaps, most simply, insane.

At last, the credits roll and light enters the theater once again. Rowan sits slumped in her chair, exhausted. It's as if she just emptied and deconstructed the entire contents of her cortex, while everyone around her sat quietly, unaware of the mess and the smell of delusion. And now she has to act like everything is fine. That nothing, nothing at all, is happening in her particular under-stuffed chair in the front row of the Roxy this evening.

Catherine leans forward, yawning and stretching her limbs. Her hair is in her face and she looks at once tired and rejuvenated, relaxing into a rhythm Rowan has yet to understand.

"So," she says. "Why did you think I should see this movie?"

Rowan waits a few seconds before replying. She wants to speak from a calm place, somewhere unaffected by all things Catherine.

"No reason," she says. "Good. Corny, but good."

Speaking is surprisingly easy. Score one for the Nothing Strange Is Going On side. She reminds herself not to spend so much time alone with her own thoughts. Trouble is invariably the outcome.

While Catherine searches under her seat for her belongings, Rowan pauses to remember the extraordinarily high number of times similar misunderstandings have occurred—though perhaps not to this degree—as the result of her wildly unmanageable brain activity. Statements gone unheard due to extracurricular apparitions appearing beyond the speaker in question. Facial gestures not seen but imagined underneath the stretch of skin masking the "true" expression. Pockets of emotion, whim, and theory that migrate from fiction to fact to absolute conviction in as little as minutes, as long as months. Or years. She bravely exposes herself to the facts before her, this history of fantasy gone horribly wrong, and vows to abolish this destructive pattern once and for all. Starting right here, right now.

A vow she keeps for all of four seconds.

Catherine rubs an eye with her fist. "I mean, ultimately the whole thing was full of shit. The way everyone's embracing the fifties all of a sudden. We've come a long way since then. Or at least I hope we have. Maybe we haven't. It's confusing, you know?"

"Yeah," says Rowan, not knowing.

"There was something else in there, though." Catherine rubs her eye again and falls back against her chair. "The whole romance bit. It got me thinking about things."

Rowan freezes. *Things.* The way Catherine said it, like the term was a lid on a vast collection of items. Buried treasure, maybe. Or thorny, sticky sewage that would take months to clean up. Hard to say which. Rowan promises the vowing side of herself that she will banish the imaginings and speculation soon, real soon. But this. This *things.* What did that mean?

"Rowan? I thought that was you." Jane and Hank, seemingly out of nowhere, are standing in front of Rowan and Catherine in the front row of this theater.

"It's me," Rowan says.

"And this is . . . ?" Jane draws the line, waiting for her sister to fill it in.

Which she does. Automatically. Jerking up in her chair, triggered by the concern in Jane's expression. "This is Catherine. My friend, Catherine. Catherine, this is my sister Jane and her husband Hank. They're married." Everyone laughs except Rowan, who is a few beats behind. By the time she catches up, with a brief fake smile and a knowing look, hands have been shaken and a light patter of conversation has been established among the laughing three. Rowan manages to stay on the sidelines, throwing in the occasional agreement here and there—yes, college blah blah, Wakefield yes, blah blah business school, blah blah blah—until it's over.

Almost.

"I'm surprised Rowan isn't here with Danny. They always come to the movies together. It's nice to see her branching out." Jane addresses Rowan when she says this, as if her sister is behind a clear, soundproof barrier that makes for easy viewing while being discussed.

"Yup." Rowan stands, dismantling the observation booth. "That's me. Branching." She inches toward the door off to the side of the screen—followed, luckily, by Catherine.

"And speaking of branching . . ." Rowan says. She grabs the door and twists it open. Outside, the air is thick and black. Warmer than the theater.

Jane watches them leave, holding onto Hank's hand like a tether.

"Bye," says Catherine, slipping through the closing door, speaking for them both.

❧ ❧ ❧

The headlights of Catherine's car snake across Rowan's front lawn and up onto the porch. In the dark, under the glare of the automobile, the Marks house looks deserted—like no one has lived there in years.

Catherine shuts off the car. At the end of the pavement ahead of them, off to the right, Rowan can see a low glow emanating from Ben's garage apartment. Her brother must be indulging in his latest hobby: Carlos Castaneda and psychedelic mushrooms. A potent combination, according to him.

"When you said the movie made you think about 'things,' what did you mean by that?" Rowan has been struggling to ask this question ever since they got free of Jane and Hank, but it isn't till now, under the protective cover of Catherine's car with the beacon of Ben beyond, that she has the nerve to give it voice.

"I don't remember."

Rowan knows, in an instant, that this is not true. She also understands, in the same instant, that Catherine will not tell her what is. She closes her mouth, waits.

"What happened with Danny?" Catherine's index finger traces the rim of the steering wheel, bumpy with notches for where the fingers go.

"What do you mean?"

Catherine grasps the wheel, her fingers closing and unclosing around the bottom of the curve. "Why don't you see him anymore?"

Rowan remains silent, replaying the fight with Danny in her head. If only she could transmit this picture by sheer force of will—from her mind to Catherine's, an immediate transfer.

"Rowan?" Catherine squints.

"We had a fight. It was about you, actually. About me spending so much time with you. He said I was stuck up and I think I'm better than him and he told me to get lost, basically. So I did." Rowan catches her breath. It feels so big, out in the open. Especially the part that didn't get said.

"Why does he care so much about you spending time with me? I mean, what's wrong with that?"

Perhaps Catherine is saying this because she already knows the answer. Perhaps not. Either way, Rowan figures—what's the harm in saying? It's Danny's opinion, after all. Not hers.

"He thinks there's something going on between us," she says. "That there's something beyond friendship here. Like that."

"Is there?"

Rowan blinks. The large sculpture they have danced around for weeks, the one so long in a blur, rises between them and Rowan sees for the first time that, yes indeed, this woman is naked. As naked as they come. *Of course. Of course there's something between us.* But how can she say that? She is silent for as long as she can be, for as long as anyone could be, until there is nothing left to do.

"Yeah," she says.

The sound reverberates off the dashboard, causing the naked lady to dip, sway.

"Hmmm." Catherine's hand lifts from the steering wheel and slides into Rowan's. "I thought there might be, but then I thought maybe it was just me."

"Just you." Rowan's fingers explore the simple flesh of Catherine's hand—this small, confident, unexplained hand. Is she imagining this as well? Her fingers squeeze harder, testing for illusion.

"Ouch." Catherine laughs. She pulls her hand away. "You're not into doing damage or anything, are you?"

"No, of course not. Sorry." Rowan imagines bringing Catherine's palm to her lips, wonders how this might feel, what it might do to both of them. She stares at her lap, caught in a field of pictures.

"It's not like I do this every day," Catherine says. "I still can't explain any of it. I've tried, believe me. We should probably leave this whole thing alone. It's crazy. Isn't it?"

"It is," Rowan says. "It's pretty weird." Though that's not what she's thinking. She's thinking this is all she wants.

"We could just stop now." Catherine slips her hand back into Rowan's. "I mean, nothing's really happened yet."

"Nothing," Rowan says. "Nothing's happened." If only she could remember to breathe. In, then out. In, then out. Easy, really.

"Or we could see where this goes. Where it takes us. That's another option."

"It is?" Rowan swallows. She remembers a double Ferris wheel she went on with Danny a few years ago. It stopped once when they were at the very top—taller than any building she'd ever been in—and they rocked back and forth in the middle of the sky. The lift, the risk, the lack of gravity—all those things were with her then, just like now. Practicality is the least of her concerns.

"I need to go," Catherine says.

"You do?"

"Yeah. Long day tomorrow."

"Long day today." Rowan lifts her sneaker into the empty space under Catherine's glove compartment. The gentle, rocking movement of the Ferris wheel reconciles her foot to the black.

Catherine tightens her hand around Rowan's. Her touch is fluid, calm. "I'll call you," she says.

Rowan thinks of all the bad movies she's seen where this is it, the last line of a relationship settling into the sour pit of over. But that's not this.

"Thanks for the ride," she says. She turns and fumbles for the door latch through the wrap of dark.

"Sleep well, girl." Catherine grabs her keys and cranks up the ignition. The engine roars to full and she taps the gas, giving it even more.

Rowan removes herself from the car without a sound and stands alone in the driveway as the old T-bird pulls away. She sinks to sitting on the gravel surface, scattered rocks digging into her ankles. She wonders if she'll ever be able to move again.

Uncle

"You got any Sevens?" Sherry grips her cards with the intensity of a prizefighter. The Shack closed an hour ago and she and Rowan are in the front of the diner, indulging in a favorite nighttime routine. The screen door is open along with all the windows, letting in a muggy breeze and a stray mosquito or two. In times past, they've been known to play this game till three in the morning.

Rowan pauses an instant, then delivers the bad news. "Go fish."

"Damn you, Rowan." Sherry smacks her hand on the table, creating a wave in her bottle of beer. "You never have anything I ask for. If I didn't know better, I'd say you were cheating."

"Me? Come on now. You know that's not necessary."

"What? You don't need to cheat, because I'm going to slam your ass no matter what?" Sherry hiccups, licks her glossy pink lips. "Or you don't want me to call you on it?"

"Only one whose ass is getting slammed here is yours. You got any threes?"

Sherry studies her cards a little too carefully. "No."

"You are *such* a liar. Don't even try it. You asked me for threes four turns ago. And I *know* I don't see any Threes on your side of the table. You going to start calling me blind now?"

"Damn." Sherry surrenders a thhree of spades and a three of hearts. They're playing the book version of the game: double deck, four-of-a-kind to match. Sherry's favorite.

"How about some fives?" Rowan lays a hand on the table, palm up. "Give 'em here."

Sherry takes a swig of beer. Her face is thick with flush and swagger. "Shit. You're on fire tonight, girl. Maybe I should quit while I'm behind."

"No need to quit now. Things are just getting good." Rowan plunks the four fives in front of her. "How about some eights?"

"Ha." Sherry shimmies in her chair, cleavage heaving. "No eights. Go fish."

Rowan draws the queen of diamonds and nestles it between the rest of the cards in her hand—an assortment of clubs and spades. Catherine's eyes peer out through the flat face of the queen, and Rowan folds her cards together, blocking everything but the nine of spades from view. The last half hour was the first break in a week of Catherine-only thoughts. A week of "Catherine hasn't called since that night in the car and I don't know what the hell is going on." She needs the respite.

"Hey, Sher. What's up with you and Killer Joe? You never did finish telling me what happened after your first date."

"That's because it's too racy to be told. Let's just say the Derby ain't the only place he uses them backing skills." Sherry drains the remains of her beer, foam and all. "How about a queen? You got any of those?"

"What about Roger?" Rowan prods the card from her hand and releases it to Sherry. "I thought you were crazy about him."

Sherry stacks the four queens in a tidy pile. "I am. I'm crazy about both of them. Why stop at one stud when you can have two? Speaking of which, you got any? Twos?"

"Go fish." Rowan sighs, an imitation of the sound she hears in movies when the best friend is giving the leading lady advice in matters of the heart. "Nothing wrong with a little caution. That's all."

"Caution? Who needs caution when you got raw animal magnetivity on your side? I don't need no stupid caution. That's for fools." Sherry clucks. "Like Farrah Fawcett. Did you hear what she did?"

Rowan shrugs, not caring. "No."

"She went and left Mr. Lee Majors all for me, that's what. I knew it was only a matter of time before he was mine. Now

123

I've got *three* hunks of beef at my disposal. One of them bionic."

"That's nice. Now gimme your tens." Rowan drops a hand in her pocket, clutching the small porcelain deer she stole from the Five and Dime this morning. She was doing much better until this past week, when Catherine stopped calling. She'd started to tell herself she was maturing, but it's a hard sell now. What with the porcelain deer, and the Rocket Bar the day before, and the box of staples the day before that. Rowan slips her hand from her pocket, exhaling to steady her focus. "Tens," she says. "I need all your tens."

"No tens. Fish your heart out." Sherry pops open another bottle of beer. "And speaking of ideal men, whatever happened to Danny? How come I never see him anymore?"

"I don't know. No reason." Rowan shivers. The motion, inexplicably, prompts an image of Lindsey Wagner, as The Bionic Woman, to bound across the vast plain of Rowan's mind, her speed enhanced by computer-generated legs. Rowan wonders what she's running from.

"Bullcrap," Sherry says. "There's always a reason. Everything's got a reason."

"No, it doesn't."

"Like hell. You know as well as I do that—"

"It was nothing," Rowan says. The Bionic Woman increases her speed, whipping past wheat fields, towns, supermarkets. "We just kinda grew apart."

"Apart my ass. You're holding out on that boy, aren't you? I don't know if I should congratulate you or take you across my knee and slap you. I'll take some jacks if you have 'em, though."

"No jacks. And it's not like that with Danny." Rowan pauses in what it's like. The Bionic Woman is gone, leaving a light coating of dust behind. It's empty, it's confusing, it's not possible to explain— that's what it's like. "You got any kings?" she says.

Sherry smiles slyly. "Maybe."

"C'mon." Rowan grabs onto the edge of the table and gives it a yank. "Give them to me."

"Only if you tell me what happened with Danny."

Rowan groans. "We're over. Whatever it is we were is over. That's it. That's all there is to know."

"Hmm." Sherry inspects Rowan like she's scanning a list of ingredients for the one she hates. She finds it. "It's that Catherine, isn't it? You only want to tag around her now. Leaves no time for your old boy Danny. That's it."

"That's not it. There's nothing like that going on. Not at all. And you owe me some kings. I told you about Danny, so fork over the kings."

Sherry frees the king of clubs from her fan of cards and presents him to Rowan. "You don't deserve this, you know. You didn't tell me *shit*. And, for the record, I never said it was 'like that' with you and Catherine. You're the only one who said that."

Rowan gulps audibly, then curses herself for doing so. "You got any aces?"

"No, but I bet she does." Sherry places her cards on the table, face down. "I bet she has a whole stack of cards stashed away where no one can see 'em."

"I don't play, actually. Don't have the time."

The voice confuses Rowan at first. Then doesn't. She turns in her chair to find the long-lost Miss Lowell under the Exit sign, one hand resting on the doorframe. Punctuation on the longest week of Rowan's life. She squints, shaping Catherine into an exclamation point. Then a period. Then a question mark. How long has she been standing there, anyway?

"Don't worry, I got nothing to do but get the hell out of here." Sherry shoves her chair from the table and stands tall, smirking at both girls. "Besides, I think the oven's on fire."

Rowan unglues herself from Catherine and watches as Sherry slings a white leather purse over her shoulder, slides her palms down the sides of her faded jeans.

"But, Sher," Rowan says. "The oven's not on."

"My point exactly." Sherry's boots clack against the linoleum as she saunters toward the back of the Shack. "Ain't no trouble to turn off something that's not on in the first place. You'll lock up for me, won't you?"

125

"Uh, sure," Rowan says.

Sherry cackles. "See ya. Don't do nothing I wouldn't do."

The back door whams shut and Rowan swears she can hear Sherry muttering on the other side. She tucks a hand in her pocket, checking for the porcelain deer. Still there. Smooth, small, stolen.

"Sherry hates my guts, doesn't she?" Catherine glides over to the table and plops into the chair opposite Rowan. Sherry's chair.

Rowan pulls her hand from her pocket. "Yes," she says. "Yes, she does."

Speaking of hate . . . Rowan scrolls the options in her mind. She could lead with anger, à la Sherry. Though hers would be of a more direct sort. *Where the hell have you been all week?* for starters. That would certainly get the conversation rolling in a lively direction. And possibly chase Catherine away. She definitely does not want Catherine away.

Then there's the concern angle. *Where have you been all week? I've been concerned about you.* Like Catherine would buy that. Given the assessment skills Miss Lowell has exhibited thus far, Rowan suspects that bullshitting is probably not the best approach.

She reaches for the cards scattered on the table—face up, face down, red backs, blue backs, kings and queens and aces—and starts to separate the two decks. She wants Catherine to stay. If only she could think of a strategy more effective than keeping her mouth shut and sorting cards.

"I'm sorry I've been out of touch." Catherine picks up a card and studies it, then places it on the table. "We've been . . . busy. Finishing up contracts with all the folks who are signing on for franchises. It's almost more work than my dad and I can handle." Her face is a fixed piece, obscuring any information except the words out of her mouth.

"So, you've been busy?" Rowan continues with her sorting project, the red deck from the blue, insuring that each family of cards is in its proper place among the two piles of scattered rectangles. It's like each card is a part of her body, a part of the vast array of sensations traveling through her that she cannot

126

even begin to name, and she is finding each one a home—a refuge—here on this table on this muggy summer night.

Fuck you, Catherine. Fuck you and your week of silence and your hard face and your idiotic excuses and the meek, pathetic loser I've become in your presence. That would work. That's what's real here.

"Yeah, I figured you were probably just that," Rowan says. "Busy." She finishes placing the last few cards in their proper piles and starts the process of drawing the first deck together.

"It's been hard," Catherine says. "Too much to do and not enough time to do it in. You know?"

"Mmm," says Rowan.

"Though I've learned a lot. I really have. I had no idea how much was involved in the process. All the paperwork. And the personnel issues. It's . . ." Catherine folds her arms and rubs her palms up and down against the sides of her T-shirt. She's acting like she's cold, but she can't be cold. It's way too hot outside to be cold. "You look weird," she says. "Are you all right?"

Rowan keeps her eyes on the cards. "Who, me?"

"That's who I'm talking to, dummy." Catherine's blank expression cruises to amused.

"Catherine." Rowan's tongue scrapes the roof of her mouth. "Are you trying to piss me off? Is that the plan here? 'Hmm. What to do tonight? How about I go over to the Sugar Shack and yank the chain of that Rowan girl? It's been a while since I've had the opportunity to aggravate the *hell* out of her.' Is that what you're going for?"

Her mouth clamps shut and she bites her lip. She is in a cauldron, heavy and black, with steam sifting up and around its bulky body. Catherine is still in the room but no longer visible, lost as the moisture from the huge pot saturates her hair and arms and attitude and renders her gone, untouchable by Rowan's anger or concern or anything else. Fat bubbles of vapor hover around Rowan as well, coating her with righteousness. She is protected. She is sheltered. She is immune from the effect of Catherine and her strange, stupid ways.

"No. That was not my intention. I wasn't trying to upset you."

127

Catherine's assurance, and the rest of her with it, travel from their place across the table to a spot about six inches from Rowan. The cauldron breaks apart and Rowan is left with Catherine beside her. Right there. Catherine's sandals have escaped her feet somewhere in the journey and her toes are delicate and white, like abandoned gems, luminous against the dark linoleum. Rowan spies on them, willing them to move—a wiggle, maybe, or a step. But this is entirely unsuccessful. Wanting is not enough. She'll need to do a lot more than want.

"I missed you," she says. "I didn't know what happened to you." *Fucker,* she thinks to add, but stops before she allows this. She stares at the toes again but they're quiet, still.

"Rowan?" Catherine's voice is as quiet as her toes.

"What?" Rowan won't look up.

"Come on." Catherine tugs on Rowan's hand.

She shouldn't allow it, but she can't help it. Rowan lets Catherine pull her from her chair and lead her to the back office. Rowan still won't look up, though. She's still staring at Catherine's feet, the way they lift and fall with such ease. Like that first day, when she imagined Catherine on the float. Entitled and victorious. Has anything changed since then?

"Are you sure Sherry's gone?" Catherine asks.

Rowan looks up at last. Catherine is sitting on the desk, on top of the papers and the ledger and the pencils and pens. "Yeah. I heard her car. But you—"

"Don't make it so hard."

"Me?" Rowan sputters. "Yeah, right. Like I'm the one who—"

And then Rowan is unsure what is hers and what is someone else's. Catherine pulls her close, slips past the imaginary line Rowan has placed between them. She kisses Rowan's cheek and then her mouth. Just like that. Soft meets firm, cool meets warm, a mix of lips and arms and motion. Catherine's tongue tastes like mint, like relief, like challenge. Rowan meets every movement with confusion at first, then awareness. She understands now what's hers and what isn't. Surrender and initiative, one and the same, her body shifting beyond itself, blending with another's.

"Jeez." She pulls away, her mouth unhooking from Catherine's. "You okay?"

Rowan tries to gather together the threads of need that have fallen from their interior hiding place, fallen all over Catherine, all over the room. "That depends," she says.

Catherine drags her thumb across Rowan's cheekbone. "Depends on what?"

"On your definition of 'okay.'" Rowan's belly twists into her ribs. The clatter between her legs that started when her lips found Catherine's grows stronger. She scoots closer, navigates the small of Catherine's back with a flat, warm hand. "Or maybe it's just me," she says. "I'm the definition." Her other hand cups the slope of Catherine's head and draws her in. This time she is more sure, more certain of what she wants. And how to get it. Finally, it is Catherine who pulls away. "You're a feisty thing." Her breathing is shallow, her eyes muted.

"And you're not?" Rowan tugs on a strand of Catherine's hair, watches it unravel, then wrap back together. "You never told me where you were all week."

"I was hiding." Catherine's voice is a solid line. "Weren't you hiding?"

Rowan assesses the shape of Catherine's shirt, how it swells under the breast section of the fabric. "No," she says. She swallows and her throat pounds against her neck. This must be what they mean in songs, when they use the word "want." She never knew. "I was wondering . . ." she says.

"What?" Catherine squints.

"I was wondering what you were thinking. About me."

"About you?" Catherine's eyes leave Rowan's face and inch down her body. "What gave you that idea? That I was thinking about you? Was it something I did?"

Rowan can't play. She inches toward Catherine. "I feel like I'm going to explode. Really. I'm all over the place. I don't know what to do."

Catherine grows serious. "I can fix that."

She rises as if managed by hidden levers, grabbing Rowan's

waist and pulling her onto the desk. Ledger, papers, pens—Catherine pushes them all aside, her motions swift and sure. Her cheek scrapes Rowan's as she climbs on top of her, her pace increasing to charged, sure. She grabs the top of Rowan's jeans and loops off the top button. The zipper splits open as her hand pushes away the material and finds the center of Rowan's concern.

Rowan gasps. She is shocked at first, then simply desperate. As Catherine slips inside her, fingers quick, driven, Rowan jams her thighs up, then down, matching Catherine's rhythm. She tries to be cool, tries to maintain the package she has presented thus far—smart girl, funny, restrained, orderly—but is utterly unable to do so. She discovers that if she pulls her hips away, then shoves them back into the stroke of Catherine's hand, she can intensify the sensation that threatens to break her.

Until it does. It's the moment Catherine's fingers find her nipple, tweaking it through the stiff cotton of her shirt, that the rise shifts to a fall, Rowan's entire body releasing itself to Catherine's hand. It's nothing she's ever felt before, the jerks and shakes delivering her body, stretching her farther than she thought she could go. It's almost frightening—the tension, the out-of-bounds need, the fulfillment. Invisible Girl was nothing, nothing at all, compared to this.

When her body stops, finally, it does so on its own. Her mouth is dry and a thin buzz of release runs underneath her limbs. She keeps her eyes squeezed shut until she can no longer bear either the suspense or the potential embarrassment. She needn't have feared either. Catherine, light and speckled, traces a finger along the top of Rowan's forehead and brings her lips to rest where her finger leaves off. She is radiant, Catherine is, glowing with ownership.

Rowan's mouth opens and she speaks inside a smile. "Was that sex?" she says. The syllables strain against the dry skin of her mouth. She's only half-kidding.

"Yes." Catherine chuckles. "Yes, it was."

"Ah," Rowan says. "What do you say we do some more of that sex stuff?"

"Sure." Catherine frees her hand from inside Rowan's pants and cups it, warm and wet, against the back of her neck. "This time, you get to drive."

Bacon

"Dad?" Rowan pokes her head into the battered shed at the end of their backyard. "Are you in here?"

Dr. Marks sits at a workbench, hunched over, his face drooped forward. For a second, she thinks he must be asleep. Until he speaks.

"Rowan," he says. "You got my note."

When Rowan arrived at the house late this afternoon, there was a note taped to the fridge. Her father's handwriting, unusually neat for a doctor's, instructed her to "Come find me" when she got home.

She found this odd on two counts. First of all, her father is not a note man, prefers to deliver his news, what little there is of it, in person. Second of all, Dr. Marks has never made a habit of telling others what to do. His patients, perhaps; Rowan knows they must, inevitably, be instructed to take this and swallow that. But even then, she suspects this information is presented in such a manner that the patient feels, at root, that Dr. Marks is telling them only what they absolutely need to know. What, on some level, given enough time, they could have told themselves.

With his children, even less was offered. Rowan grew up watching other kids of other fathers getting earfuls of orders—sharp, harsh, strewn across the lawns and bedrooms of her peers. Never so with the Marks clan. Indeed, Rowan and Ben made many a game, including Psychic Jim, out of guessing what coursed through their father's brain.

But now there is this. This "Come find me." Rowan pushes the shed door and enters the cramped quarters currently occupied by her father. As with everything else she's encountered in the week since she and Catherine started up, the shed and its contents, every one, remind her of her friend. The sun invading the dark room is the same sun that revealed Catherine's sweet naked body at the banks of the creek. Her father's work desk, cluttered and calm, evokes the desk in the back office of the Shack. The desk where Rowan lay down flat, a week ago now, with Catherine on top of her. The desk where Rowan discovered how to make Catherine moan, then holler. A dented yellow clock, perched on top of an old walnut cabinet full of screws and nails and various items of unknown origin, tells her two things—that it's 5:05 p.m., over ten minutes since she last saw Catherine, and that time makes about as much sense as anything else these days. Everything—everything—is up for reevaluation.

Including her father. Here in the late afternoon light, in this shed Rowan's grandfather built ages ago, Dr. Marks appears tired and worn, like an old wallet. The recent changes in Rowan's life allow her to examine her father and see two entirely different men: the first, a fellow human—an adult, a being who has participated in the full spectrum of activity, as she now has; the second, someone she still understands not at all. Even an event as life-changing as love doesn't alter her vision enough to peer inside this man more than an inch. And that, too, may be imagined.

"I just got in," she says. "I saw the note and came right out."

"I appreciate it," he says.

"What did you need?" Rowan takes a step forward, inhaling the scent of turpentine and rotting wood. She hasn't set foot here in ages. When she and Ben were younger, they played a lot of nighttime Hide 'N' Go Seek in this yard. The shed was always the best place to hide on account of it being so scary, no one would look for you in here. Ben won many a game that way.

Rowan's feet crunch against the planks of the floor. "Is everything okay?" she says.

"Everything's fine. Just fine. It's probably nothing."

"Nothing. What's nothing?"

Her father's palms stroke the sides of a large glass case in the middle of the workbench—her grandfather's old butterfly collection, the latest in a long line of Dr. Marks's fix-me-up projects.

133

"I don't know what to do," he says. "Perhaps you can—I was thinking you might be the one to . . ." He taps the glass at the top of the case, brushing away a smudge of dirt.

"I'm not—what do you want me to—"

"I tried to talk with him, but he won't open up about anything. He's always been a bit of an enigma, but lately . . ." He squints at the glass.

"Ben?" Rowan stammers. "You mean Ben?"

"Talk to him for me." Dr. Marks moves his hands to the bottom corners of the case and prods the collection forward. The wood moans against the table, resistant in its size and weight. "Maybe you can find out what's troubling him. Or perhaps you already know."

"I don't know anything." Rowan hears her voice and feels the bare truth of this pronouncement. Then, in response, what she does know comes to mind. Catherine, and everything this entails, invades her reality once again. Rowan scratches her nose, a shot at bringing herself deeper into the room that succeeds only in drawing her deeper into Catherine. Her scent is still on Rowan's fingers.

"I can try talking to him, if you want," she says. "I'd be happy to do that." She buries her hand in her armpit.

"Thank you. I do appreciate that." Her father's eyes find hers and tap out their gratitude. Like Morse code, her father's affection.

Rowan leaves the door ajar as she slips out of the shed. A cover of clouds has blown in, the light in the backyard milky and ominous. Why is it, she wonders, that sunlight is seen as good and lack of it is seen as bad? Why can't it all be okay, everything about life? Why do people have to make judgments about things they don't understand?

Ben's apartment is quiet today—no music, no chatter. Only Ben and, to Rowan's dismay, Lyle. The boys are sitting on Ben's ridiculous blue couch in what looks to be a bong-inspired haze. Lyle, eyelids at half-mast and lips puckered in a derisive grin, appears to be the less absent of the two. Ben, as usual, is the amplification of absent.

"Dig it," Ben says. "That's what I'm talking about. You never know where the inspiration's going to come from. Like my sis, here. Like Rowan."

"Ro-wan." Lyle grunts. "Yeah."

"Look at that face," Ben says. "Like blank. Or not blank, but new. Like nothing's fucked with it yet. Like that."

"Right," Rowan says. "That's me. All perfect and jolly. No problems. Right."

She traces the circumference of the apartment and props herself against the sink of her brother's makeshift kitchen. The kitchen is classic Ben, with a half-sized fridge and an antique hotplate ("Why cook on a real stove when you can use fake electric wood instead?"). The sink, an old industrial-strength number pilfered from one of his painting jobs, is by far the grandest item in the ensemble. Ben calls it The Throne and lavishes it with the kind of attention most people reserve for their children, or a beloved pet. Rowan can only pray he doesn't use it as a urinal.

"Haven't seen you at Wednesday Night Baseball for a while now, little Ro. But then, I hear you got your hands full these days." Lyle's voice scrapes against the hairs on Rowan's arms. She takes a breath to ease away the annoyance.

"I'm surprised you noticed, Lyle. What with your head jammed all the way up your—"

"I guess you got better things to do with your time." Lyle sneers. "Or so I hear."

A frying pan sits on the counter next to her, a single slice of bacon lounging in a puddle of grease. Rowan gets to thinking. If she jammed the pan on top of Lyle's skull, would it send the bacon flying? Would the sliver of pork stick to the ceiling, or would it stay in the pan?

"Shut up, Lyle. Only thing you know about is the territory of your own ass." Bam. Pan on head. Bacon flying.

"Better than the freaky territory you've been exploring lately. Danny told me about you."

"Danny told you about nothing."

"Girls, girls." Ben hoists himself off the couch and slides into

135

the zone between his friend and sister. "No fighting. It's bad juju. Can't be having that in here. So shut the fuck up, will you?" He coughs and spills into his big stuffed chair, his energy drained by the plea.

"Like I need this shit." Lyle stands, staggers. "I'll be back later. When she's gone." He pauses over Ben's chair and the two have a brief, wordless conversation before he leaves altogether, slamming the door behind him.

Rowan takes the strip of bacon and pitches it into the trash—a crumpled brown Piggly Wiggly shopping bag on the floor of the kitchen. She glances over at Ben, his arms and legs flopping out of the big stuffed chair, his lips twitching almost imperceptibly. What, she wonders, is going on in her brother's head right now? Does he know about her and Catherine? Did Lyle say something? Not that Lyle really knows anything anyway. But still.

Her feet get itchy from worrying and she wedges off her shoes, one by one. She needs to feel the floor on her skin, even if it is only Ben's kitchen floor—dirty and sticky and untended. At least it's real.

"Benny," she says. "What's . . . what are you . . . how's everything?"

"Huh?" He picks at a patch of black paint on the knee of his painter's pants. Then watches it fall to the floor.

"It's been a while." Rowan swallows. "Like that. I just wanted to see how you were."

"Don't be a dumb ass, Ro. You know how I am."

"Sure I do. But I'm also—"

"So you don't got to ask. If you start asking, then it's like . . . like you don't know." Ben picks up a magazine smashed into the corner of his chair and slowly turns its wrinkled pages. She can't tell if he's actually looking at anything or just pretending to. He stops at one page in particular and squints, his mouth softening and falling open. It's as if a tightly woven curtain lies between him and everything around him and he's always trying to assess what lies right in front of his face.

"Have you ever wondered why Dad never got remarried?" he says.

136

"No. Not really." Rowan's toes roll off Ben's floor, hang there, release. "Why?"

He closes the magazine and drops it into the chair. "I think it has to do with the fact that he's socially inept. He can't deal with real people in the real world. Either that or he's a fag or something."

"That's ridiculous." Rowan falls against the counter. The unfinished edge pokes at her spine. "What are you talking about? He's not—he dated Miss Collins from the hospital. That nurse. Remember her? They went out, on and off, for over a year."

"Till he dumped her because he couldn't handle it. That's not normal. Everything about him is not normal. You're growing up here and you think everything is okay because it's all you've ever known, but then you leave this town," Ben's eyes get bigger, his speech faster, "you leave this town and you find out there's a whole other world out there. All kinds of things you'd never even imagine. This life here is just a small speck, a tiny hair on the beast of the Universe. And you can't even see it. You think this is all there is. What a joke."

"No. It's not a joke." Rowan's fingers stretch around the lip of the counter. "Dad never remarried because he never stopped loving Mom. It's not complicated. And Dad's not fucked up because of it."

"Bullshit." He turns away from her, shaking his head with effort. He fixes on a point in front of him and his jaw grows slack once again, his lower lip loosening from the top one.

"Ben?" Rowan slips on her sneakers and travels into the space her brother is studying so intently. If she had a hose and some water, she could spray him a few times. Anything to bring him back onto the planet.

"Talk to me here, buddy," she says. "What's going on? Where'd you go?"

It seems to make no difference that Rowan is occupying Ben's studied space. Every ounce of his energy is going into communication with, and maintenance of, something she cannot see. She waves her hands above his head, stomps her feet against the old shag carpet, but Ben is immune to all of it.

"I came here to see how you were doing," she says. "Because I'm worried about you. Dad is too. We were just trying to figure out how to help."

"Dad?" Ben wails. "What the hell does *he* have to do with this?" He finds her face. He's furious. "You came here because *Dad* sent you?"

"So what if he did? He cares about you, Ben. So do I. We're trying to—"

"He doesn't care about me. He doesn't care about you, either. And now he's got you doing his bidding. Like a trained monkey. Snap his fingers and you—"

"I came here because I wanted to." Though the minute she says this, "here" seems to slip out from under her. She hardly recognizes her brother anymore, hardly recognizes herself. An image of Catherine, or someone like her, skims the area behind Rowan, tickling the angle of her elbows. Then it's Danny. Then her mother. Reinforcements. She takes a deep breath.

"Dad belongs to both of us," she says. "Whether you like it or not. Maybe you want to cram your head into a pile of drugs, ignore the world while it flies on by, but I'm not going with you. I don't even want to watch."

As the words empty her mouth, Rowan feels lighter and lighter. Almost sheer. She checks behind her for support, but whoever was there is gone. Now it's just her.

Ben winces. "You don't understand anything. Not a damn thing."

"So you keep saying, Mr. *Mysterious*. Like you have some big secret that will explain why you're acting like such a prick."

"As if you—"

"Spill it, Benny. Tell me what's so special. Tell me what you got going on, or what you found out. What do you know about Dad that's so damn bad?"

"It's not that simple." He hesitates and, for a moment, she thinks maybe he's going to keep talking—explain himself, even. But when he wiggles his finger inside the bottom pocket of his painter's pants and emerges with a fresh bag of weed, tapping the rest of his pockets immediately after in a search for matches, Rowan realizes that any explanation from her brother is fantasy at best.

"That's right," she says. "That's the answer. Toke up. That'll fix it." She shoves aside an old beer can with the toe of her sneaker. It rolls a few inches, then stops.

When Rowan was about seven years old, she and Ben discovered a huge pine tree on the periphery of the woods surrounding the reservoir. It had two branches near the top that were flattened like chairs, and they would scramble up the tall tree and slip onto those branches like birds. They could see so many things from that height—acres of woods and the perfect circle of the reservoir and even, when it was winter and the leaves were gone from the trees, the roof of their own house. Sometimes they would sing songs up there. Because they could. Because they had been lifted into the sky, far away from where others might laugh at them or remind them not to make such sounds.

Standing here, in the middle of Ben's room, Rowan is this young girl all over again, climbing up the tree that still lives inside her body. If only Ben were with her. She can't even tell him how scared she is, how lonely to be climbing this tree all by herself. It's not something she knew till just now.

"There's a reason." His voice reaches her at the top of the tree. "There's a reason I can't tell you."

She shivers. "Not good enough," she says. "I want to know."

His eyes find hers and for a second, just one second, she prays he'll join her on the other branch. Brother and sister cradled by wood and sky. But he doesn't. He's gone.

"I can't," he says. "It wouldn't make sense to you anyway."

"Don't you get it?" Rowan's pulse quickens, thinning her patience. "You're fucking with me. You say you're protecting me, or whatever the hell it is, but all that's happening is I'm losing my brother. Is it worth it? Keeping your special holy whatever-it-is to yourself?"

"Maybe." He locates his matches and yanks one from the pack, striking it against the thin dark strip on the other side. "It's hard to say."

The flame finds the fingerful of marijuana pinched into the cup of his bong. Ben waits until the tall glass cylinder is filled with smoke, then takes a hit, swallowing everything. He offers it to Rowan, but she refuses. His anger is gone, she can tell. What's left is quiet and enormous. Like sorrow.

"You know what's happening, don't you?" she says.

He takes another shot off the bong, holds it inside himself, lets go. "What?" he says.

"You're acting like Dad. There's no difference. Everything you're accusing him of, that's you."

"Fuck you. Would Dad say that? I don't think so."

"Like that proves it? Jeez, Ben. If only you could—"

"It does. It does prove it."

Rowan checks his face, tries to locate her brother behind the dope and the smoke and the bluster. "I give up," she says. "Seriously. If you're not going to—"

"I don't care. It doesn't matter. We're all fucked anyway."

Ben dumps his bong on the table and marches over to the tiny bathroom behind his kitchen. He tumbles inside and latches the door behind him. Rowan thinks he may have said "goodbye" under his breath before the door closed, but this is probably a story she's telling herself. He probably said "shithead" or "asshole" or something like that. He probably said nothing at all.

Toy

Rowan sits in her room on the edge of her unmade bed, Magic 8 Ball in hand. She purchased this marvel of divination several years back, when she was about twelve years old. The purchase was preceded by two years of wanting to buy, but being too shy to ask for a device as foolish and trivial as a Magic 8 Ball: a black plastic orb housing a finite number of answers to the infinite number of questions the lucky holder of the magic item might be inclined to ask.

In Rowan's case, the first question was the most important. It was, indeed, the reason she purchased the 8 Ball to begin with.

"Was that my mother's voice in the spelling contest?" That question. The one that never left, no matter how she tried to escape its insistence and concern.

And the reply: "All signs point to yes."

Never mind that she asked the same question later, and later again, and got different answers each time. The first response fastened itself to her memory, to the vision of a mother built solely on imagination and hope, and it guided every inquiry brought to the black ball from that time forward. The possibility that once, just once, the heavens might speak. And they might say: Yes. Without any doubt.

A white octagonal decal frames the black "8" at the top of the ball, faded from years of use. Years of earnest questions and arbitrary answers. Rowan chides herself for holding the shiny toy at this hour of night (past midnight), at this age (officially an adult), and at this point in her life. It's Catherine. That's the only explanation for the pull to foolishness here. There's something about Catherine that drives Rowan forward into a sense of both grown and small, an existence at once fully realized, intricate in articulation and form, and absolutely clueless. Rowan likes to fool herself, likes to pretend her affair with Catherine is mostly the former, mostly a full-on shove into adulthood, glorious and rich with substance and meaning. But she knows the truth is more like this. More like the spectacle of her, on a messy bed, in the middle of the night, addressing profound questions to a parlor toy. She suspects that this activity sums up her life in more ways than she could count on the fingers of both hands. Fingers otherwise occupied with the query of the moment, one ripe from weeks of storage.

"Does Catherine love me?"

Rowan scrunches her eyes shut in the asking, steadying the ball with a tired grip. She waits a minute or two, letting the ball absorb the weight and urgency of the inquiry, then flips it over for the answer.

"It is decidedly so."

Thrill, in the form of an ache that surges down her legs, supplies the second response to the question.

Rowan places the ball in her lap, feeling immediately embarrassed for having asked. In the fifteen days since she and Catherine slipped into sex (sixteen days really, considering it's past midnight and officially a new day today), there have been several moments of clarification for Rowan. Where she stands, who she is to Catherine, stuff like that. The best one came a week ago. That's the one she's planning to hang onto. Planning to try, at least. If the trivial over-questioning of a ball of plastic doesn't get in her way.

She brings it up now, a private show. The two of them at the creek, feet in water, pre-swim. Catherine had already removed her clothes, her usual routine. Rowan, clinging to a minor sense of modesty, had stripped off her shirt but not her shorts. As if this would give her an edge, being the modest one.

They were just getting settled at the bank of the creek when Rowan went for a question. Straight out of the gate. Like the run-hungry horses in one of Little's races. The ones he tends to win.

"Remember that first night, when you came to my birthday at Ollie's Inn?"

"Mmmm," Catherine said. She waved her feet up and down in the stream. She seemed to be not listening, yet also seemed to know exactly what Rowan was going to say.

"Do you remember how you looked at me? Near the end of the night? Stared at me when we were talking about xerophytes?" Rowan let the question sit. Then, "Do you remember what you were thinking about? What you were seeing?"

"Mmm." Catherine continued to pull on her store of spacy omniscience. "I do."

"You do? Seriously?" Rowan couldn't help but be alarmed. She didn't, she realized once the question was asked, really expect an answer. "What was it?" she said.

Catherine dipped a hand in the creek, bringing a few drops of water to Rowan's knee. "I totally remember what happened that night. I'll probably never forget."

Rowan couldn't decide: Did she want Catherine to hurry up and answer the question, or did she not want any of this, whatever it was, to stop?

"You really remember?" she said.

"Really." Catherine watched as the drips hit Rowan's leg, then splashed onto her own. "I was looking at you, when you were spelling those words, and I was thinking about how much you reminded me of Molly. And then I realized it wasn't so much that you were *like* her, as I was feeling like I used to feel around her." Catherine's voice grew hushed. "Excited. On edge. Like that."

"Ah," Rowan said. Her toes twitched once, twice.

"I realized I was attracted to you," Catherine said. "Like, really attracted. And I knew something was going to happen. Don't ask me how, but I did." She reached behind Rowan's head, tracing the line of skull to neck. "And I wanted to tell you, but I couldn't. Sherry was there, and even if she wasn't, I couldn't just blurt it out. Not like that. So I waited."

"Huh. I didn't—"

"But I was right. Totally right. Wasn't I?"

Rowan shivered. "You were."

"It's all that wisdom I got stored inside of me." Catherine's hand slipped between Rowan's thighs. "On account of my extreme old age."

"Yeah, you and your geriatric perspective."

Rowan could have taken her then, flattened her body against the leaves, teasing out a response entirely unlike the one just given. But she wasn't that desperate. Not yet. She would be later. Three hours later, in fact, in the hotel room Catherine swore her father wouldn't enter until after 6 p.m., a promise she kept. There on the soft wide bed with a painting of a wheat field behind it, there on a mattress and sheets that went on forever, Rowan would revel in her newest skill, her best to date. Making Catherine come.

The shudders that roam through her lover's body, through both their bodies, are the only thing Rowan can permit herself to rely upon these days. Trust in the sense of eyes-closed, arms-engaged, open-air faith, stretching off her studied reserve and leaving only want. That's where the desperation comes in. Rowan is so sure of this desire, and what she will do to feed it—her hand plunged into Catherine's body, a swollen mouth traveling across damp flesh, tiny moans flaring into the sound of her name—that any doubt, any notion that this is wrong or strange or unnatural cannot lodge in her mind for longer than a second. The pull, the urgency of Catherine's skin and smell and need—these are what coat Rowan's awareness, her life.

The 8 Ball remains motionless in her lap, her fingertips barely touching the shiny black surface. She thinks to ask about Ben, about his troubles, his anger, but her wise plastic friend traffics only in answers of Yes, No, and Maybe. Not long treatises on the plight of the middle child, only boy, sensitive-beyond-belief, drug-ingesting, mess of a man her brother has become. No toy in Rowan's possession can tackle that one.

And then there's her thieving. Maybe the 8 Ball can solve the dilemma of why. Why is she so compelled to take things from stores, from people? Sure, the compulsion has died down a little since she and Catherine were reunited, but it hasn't stopped. That would take—what? Rowan sighs. It would take more than the 8 Ball, she knows that much. Her little black buddy may be magical, but its capacities to change behavior are, as far as she knows, limited. Better to allow the ball to stick to what it does best.

Like the other question on Rowan's mind. One more in line with the 8 Ball's short, concise response style. This question, like the first one, has been brewing in Rowan's head for weeks. Given that the two inquiries are inextricably linked, it's only natural that she should pose both questions on the same night. Right? Rowan sits in a feeling of foolishness for a minute, a rapid reevaluation of this entire process coupled with forceful reassurances of her complete and utter insanity, that is overcome, finally, by a wash of wanting to know.

"Will Catherine and I stay together?"

Rowan does not wait this time, leaves no room for deliberation or cosmic processing. She lets the ball speak.

"It is decidedly so."

Her mouth drops open, then snaps shut so quickly she bites her tongue. What are the odds of this? Both Catherine questions, both replies "decidedly so." This is surely a sign. An oracle from the gods, in whatever form they might exist, that Rowan and Catherine are an item, a unit in time and space, glued together by the stuff of love, sex, fate, passion. Meant to be.

Rowan hobbles off her bed and drops the 8 Ball back into the top drawer of her dresser. There's been enough truth-telling for one night. Outside her window, somewhere in the backyard, two cats are howling at each other. Rowan wonders if they're fighting or having sex. Or both. The sounds—low, sustained yelps shifting rapidly into shrieks of extreme alarm—remind her of Catherine. Perhaps it's the sensual undertone of the cries. Or the intensity of interchange between the two beasts. Or the fact that the sounds are smashing into the dark—the portion of time that is unknown, unclaimed, unexplained. Or perhaps it's simply that everything reminds her of Catherine. It's probably that.

Rowan falls back onto her bed, exhausted by the pictures

roaming around her. Earlier, today, that's another scene she can't avoid. She's tried to. Most of the day has been a resistance to this one.

They were in the T-bird, parked, holding hands. It was the middle of the day, Rowan on her way to her shift at the Shack, Catherine on a run between Loomis and Elyria, stopping by Wakefield to say hello, no big deal, except for the lift in her eyes and the rush in Rowan's stomach when she saw her.

It started with a question, but this one wasn't planned. It rushed out of Rowan's mouth like a cough, and she had no choice but to speak the words.

"What about you and Larry?" Rowan said. It was so easy, once it was out of her mouth.

"Larry?" Catherine pulled her legs from Rowan's and placed them back under the steering wheel. "What about him?"

"How did you two get together and all that? What happened?"

"It's a funny story, actually. I thought I told you."

"You didn't, though." A few seconds ticked by while Rowan studied the can of pop lying on the floor underneath her. Her legs, without Catherine's against them, felt prickly, raw. "A funny story, eh? Do tell."

Catherine cleared her throat. "We were in traffic. Off campus. I had this shit-box of a car at the time. An old Pontiac of my dad's. And Larry was driving the car in front of me. He saw me in the rearview mirror and fell in love with me on the spot. So he said. He slammed on his brakes in the middle of the intersection and I bashed right into him. He figured it was the only way he'd get a chance to meet me. He didn't realize we both went to Freemont."

"That's dumb." Rowan chuckled.

"Yes, it was pretty dumb. It worked, though. Dumb but effective."

"Hmm," Rowan said. What was she thinking, bringing Larry into this? What a stupid idea. The thought of Catherine with anyone else made Rowan's brain hurt. Like a paradox—a bird without wings, a car without wheels, a foot without—

"Anyway," Catherine yawned, twisting in her seat, "that's how Larry and I met. It was a lot easier with Molly. Random college lottery threw us together. And there was no excessive damage of automobiles in that one."

"I see." Rowan dipped her fingers into the crevice between her seat and the door, plucking at the fuzzy material covering the floor of the car. "But I thought you said you and Molly were never together. I mean, *together* together."

Catherine pulled open the ashtray, saw it was free of ashes, flipped it shut. "We weren't. But now, since you, I see that we were, in a way. It's just . . . we were both too scared to . . . you know."

"I know."

"Rowan," Catherine's hand wandered over to Rowan's belly, peeked inside her shirt, soothed the surface underneath, "you're not, like, jealous, are you?"

"No," Rowan spit it out. "I'm not, like, anything." The floor beneath her sneakers was sticky with pop spilled from the empty can between her feet. Her feet made a ripping noise as she lifted them from the car mat.

"I'd say you're like this." Catherine pulls her hand from Rowan's and uses her fingers to trace the inside of Rowan's arm. "And this."

"Quit bugging me." Rowan squirmed away as if she wanted to rid herself of Catherine's touch, though neither one of them believed it. Before long, Catherine had torn Rowan's upset to shreds, and all that was left was the sensation of fingers on skin, the friction of Catherine's exploration against Rowan's willingness to allow it.

When this went as far as it could, given they were in a parked car in the middle of a sun-drenched street, Rowan pulled Catherine's hand from her arm and chauffeured it back to the driver's side.

"Tomorrow?" she said, the syllables threading in and out of tight, shallow breaths. Rowan, broken, pasted herself back together. "I'll see you tomorrow, okay?"

"Tomorrow." Catherine blinked. "Yeah, that could work." She

skimmed her hands around the rim of the car seat and lifted them to grasp the steering wheel. "I have to work all day tomorrow. Maybe tomorrow night."

"You could come over." The murmur inside Rowan's shorts was growing stronger. Just being with Catherine was enough to turn her inside out.

"I could." Catherine glanced at her, rising into a smile, and Rowan understood that there was never anything in her life as easy as this, as smiling back at this girl in this car on this day.

Except maybe thinking about it later.

Rowan turns her head to read the clock. Almost one a.m. She scoots up to the head of her bed, kicks her legs under the sheets, and drags the covers up to her armpits. She'll brush her teeth in a minute. Wash her face and shut off the lights, those things too. Those are all things people do. For now, though, the layer of cotton around her body and the pictures of Catherine infusing her brain will not allow movement of any kind. She finds it ironic that her head and the 8 Ball, both round objects full of mush, are capable of such completely different responses to the subject at hand.

Out in the backyard, the cats continue to have at it, weaving their way into domestic bliss. Rowan instructs a hand to travel under the sheets and slip inside her shorts, beginning a nighttime routine of a different sort. The howling cats circle and fuel her movements, lapping her into clarity.

Dive

Four plates of spaghetti frame the Marks' dining-room table, steam spiraling above each one. The recipients of this food—Jane, Hank, Dr. Marks, and Rowan—are all seated and munching salad, the cooler alternative to the still-too-hot-to-eat spaghetti. Salad has become a nightly staple on this table, ever since Dr. Marks emerged from a recent nutritional seminar a convert to the cause of vitamins, vegetables, and no red meat.

By some strange turn of events—Rowan is not quite sure how this happened—a conversation about gardening has taken a sharp left and veered unexpectedly into a lively discussion on the topic of her future. She is doing her best to dodge the cannonballs as they are fired, one by one.

"And then there's writing." Jane speaks through bits of lettuce and diced carrots. "You've always been good at that."

Hank nods in eager agreement. "You were in that journalism class, weren't you?"

Rowan doesn't respond. She put too much dressing on her salad and is tracking the progress of one of her tomatoes as it makes a break for the outer regions of her plate, chugging through a pool of oil.

"That's right." Jane stabs her fork into a slice of cucumber. "She did all those music and movie reviews for the high school paper. Even though I didn't understand most of what she was saying, it was well written, I know that much."

"Rowan's always liked to write." Dr. Marks slides several pieces of lettuce into his mouth and chews carefully. "I remember once, when she was four years old, she was sitting at an old typewriter we had set up in the living room. She typed a pageful of letters and called me over to see if there were any words on the page."

Rowan lifts her eyes from the tomato. "Really? I've never heard this before."

"You always were inquisitive," Dr. Marks says.

"Hmm." Rowan returns to the intrepid vegetable that, with much effort and the generous aid of her thumb, has now made it clear across her plate.

"So," she says. "Were there any words on the page?"

"There were a few."

"Really? Like what?"

"'Bean' was one of them, if I remember correctly. You were thrilled about that. You always did love beans."

Rowan checks her father's eyes, the light deep inside them. Will he stay here? On her early words and the attention he gave them? Or will he turn the page?

"Jane," he says. He swallows another bite of salad. "Most delicious. Indeed."

The Jane page. The next page is always the Jane page. Rowan lets her thumb sink into her plate, into the oil.

"Thanks." Jane says. "It was easy enough to make. I got the tomatoes from Mrs. Roth, at church."

"There's always doctoring." Hank rounds up some stray chickpeas with the aid of his knife. "It is the family business, after all. Ben let it go, but you could still be generation number three."

Instead of responding to Hank's remark, a reply that has a high probability of leaking into the realm of the smart-ass, Rowan commits herself to a couple of croutons and a tomato. Not *the* tomato. She'll let that one go.

"A doctor. Yes." Jane places a hand on her belly, sighs a sigh of the blissfully pregnant. "Rowan would make a wonderful doctor. She's smart. She's kind. I wonder why we never thought of this before."

Hank beams. "Takes one to know one, as they say. Sometimes the obvious is right there, staring you in the face."

There are several directions in which to take this irreparably flawed topic and Rowan considers just a few. Jane's pregnancy. Always a good bet. Hank's practice. Boring, but chock-full o' minutes. Her dad's work. Indecipherable and potentially short-lived. Ben's troubles. Last resort only. Rowan pulls a question for Jane out of the tangle of options and is about to commit it to language when, lo and behold, the high rattle of the kitchen phone interrupts her calculations.

"I'll get it." Rowan bolts out of her chair so quickly she startles herself. Her brave tomato dives off the plate and onto the table. Free at last. She skittles into the kitchen, closing the door behind her.

"Hello?" She already knows who it is. Or hopes it is.

"Rowan?"

It's Catherine. Of course it's Catherine.

"That's me," Rowan says.

"What are you wearing?"

"Shut up." Rowan sinks to the floor. She's never ready for this.

"No, really. I'm serious. What do you have on?"

Rowan looks down. "Jeans and a T-shirt."

"Which T-shirt?"

Rowan drives a hand to the top of her knee, then down the other side, holding on. "The yellow one. With the pocket."

Catherine is silent a minute. When she speaks again she sounds funny, like she's underwater or on drugs. "I love that one."

All the things Rowan can think to say are flattened by her emotional response, which is akin to being slammed with great tenderness. If she knew how Catherine managed to do this, maybe she could fend herself against it. Or, at the very least, retain her powers of speech when faced with such remarks.

"We got a new account today," Catherine says. "Over in Elyria. We probably won't be able to finish it this summer, but I'll be able to do most of the preliminary work."

"Cool," says Rowan.

"It is. I like the beginning part. It's fun."

Rowan nods, then remembers Catherine can't see.

"What are you doing later?"

151

"Nothing." Rowan straightens her legs against the floor. She finds it best to feign casual when hit with direct inquiries such as this one. She tells herself this gives her an edge in the *Who's More Into This?* game. Though she suspects she's the only one playing, which, by definition, makes her the loser.

"How about I come over when we're done here? Later." Catherine's voice has shifted yet again. This time it's loud and clear. She sounds like she's in the other room.

Rowan looks over her shoulder. "Later's good."

"Good."

The line clicks and it dawns on Rowan slowly, like a new day itself, that the conversation is over.

She hustles back to the dining room and finds her seat. The vegetables on her plate seem to have reorganized themselves in her absence. But this is, of course, absurd. She is surely imagining this. Why would Jane, Hank, or her father take such an interest in the contents of her plate? She sighs heavily. Sometimes, like now, this whole thing with Catherine—as much as she loves it, loves her—is a bit much to bear.

"Who was that?" Jane is pouring an impressive layer of Parmesan cheese on top of her spaghetti.

"No one," Rowan says.

Jane clucks. "No one? How is that possible? You were talking to yourself?" A forkful of spaghetti, coated with cheese, disappears into Jane's mouth.

"Kinda."

"Was it your friend? Your new friend?"

"No." Rowan squints, hiding the lie. "It was Danny. We're hanging out later."

"That's too bad." Jane adjusts her weight from both hips to just one, groaning ever so slightly. "I thought you'd widened your horizons."

"Nope," Rowan says. "My horizons are still the regular size."

"Honey?" Hank purses his lips and twirls his fork into a pile of noodles. "Why don't you finish your story? About Billy Regis and the cult."

152

Jane brightens. "Oh yes. That's right. So anyway . . ."

While Jane embarks on a lengthy and detailed description of the plight of poor Billy, strung out on his guru and free love and "God knows what else" in the wilds of California, Rowan slides a chunk of carrot across her plate. Her carrot can't escape, but she can. Maybe. She stops the carrot mid-slide, flexes her toes, and bears down for the grace of Invisible Girl, but there's no one there to play. Her toes release and grind into her shoes. Ever since that first day at the river with Catherine, the day that leaving was not an option, Rowan has been unable to resuscitate her old game. A few times, maybe, she's been close, but full escape is, apparently, no longer possible. All she gets is what's right in front of her face, a phenomenon that fluctuates in acceptability depending on the venue. Catherine, she'll stay for that. Anything else is a hard sell.

Like this. Misbehavior from somewhere across the country breaking into a random Wakefield living room. The low hum and pause of her father's attention and concern. The percussion of fork on knife, knife on plate, fork in mouth. Ice cubes vying for position in glasses of pop and bourbon.

"Rowan?" Hank's question slips inside her mind, just under the clinking ice.

She looks up quickly, peers into Hank's open mouth, and answers with what's in her own.

"I have to go," she says.

"Go where?" Hank is curious and attentive, eyes bright.

"Nowhere. I'm not hungry."

"Not hungry?" Jane leans over her plate. "But you didn't even touch your spaghetti."

"I touched it. I just didn't eat it." Rowan stands. "I need some air."

Dr. Marks nods with solemn understanding, like Rowan is the x-ray technician confirming his diagnosis. A spiral fracture to the family tolerance zone. Prognosis—full recovery.

Jane and Hank are not so trusting. "But . . ." they spurt, sharing a voice.

"I'm fine." Rowan flaps a hand in their direction, clearing the air of the worry puttering toward her. "I'll be on the porch."

The light as it hits the front yard is stretched and worn, as though tired from three months of warmth and illumination. A sign that even though it's only the beginning of August, autumn is already curling back the edges of what still looks like summer. Rowan ignores this in favor of the obvious—a yard sodden with heat and the smells of an evening in full bloom: wandering cars, low-flying birds, kids out on the street for an after-dinner bike ride. These sights and sounds approach her gently, without expectation. She begins to relax.

She settles first on the rocker, but finds the movement disconcerting and switches to the padded wicker chair she always seems to end up on. Another inevitability. Waiting for Catherine may be on the list as well, but Rowan doesn't attempt to categorize anything as vague and untamed as waiting. Though when at least a half hour goes by, judging by the shadows that crawl across the sidewalk from medium-long to longer, she starts to ponder the meaning of the term later. That was all Catherine gave her, in terms of arrival time. "Later." A concept that holds true, even now.

Circumstances inside the house have certainly changed, she knows this much. Dessert was served, followed by the arrival of Ben. The first had the chirps and sighs of a welcome addition; the second was clearly circumspect. And now there's the beginnings of a brawl. Ben and her father. This won't be a physical confrontation, Rowan's sure of that—neither man has the guts or desire for fists and blows. But it sure sounds heated.

Just how heated becomes evident a minute later, when the bodies of Jane and Hank filter onto the front porch, apparent casualties of the battle.

"Party's over, eh?" Rowan peers up at her sister, bordered by the initial tracings of a deep pink sunset.

"It certainly is." Hank says. "All this upset isn't good for the baby. We're going home."

Jane extends a wordless farewell, her shoulders hunching

and falling in what looks to be a cross between apathy and frustration.

"Sorry." Rowan says to the backs of her sister and brother-in-law, disappearing into Hank's car. Not that it's her fault. But still. After a short interval—ten minutes tops in shadow-lengthening time—the inside of the house settles down. While this respite affords Rowan a slim share of relief, it mostly gives her a chance to gather up the forces necessary to see Catherine. Catherine who will, surely, be coming any minute.

Rowan closes her eyes, the first step in her construction project. She's tried this before and it always falls apart, but perhaps this time she'll get lucky. Besides, there's nothing else to do out here this time of day.

It's an inner column she needs, one of strength, patience, and reserve. It's the only thing she can imagine that could help her get through time with Catherine, time that always seems to leave her tilted in the direction of Wacked. As if every one of her internal organs has been turned inside out, branded with Catherine's likeness, and then set back in place like nothing happened. Except it did. And every cell sings "Catherine."

But what can she use to build her inner fortress? What will protect her against Catherine? Rowan pauses, evaluating. The Three Little Pigs, what was it they used? Straw first, then wood? Then . . . bricks! She squeezes her eyes tight, straining to find the ground of her interior. One brick—it all starts with one. Rowan takes a deep breath and pretends to be brave. She heard once that this is what courage is: taking action in spite of fear. She places the first brick down firmly, wedging it between the root of her spine and the circling chaos. And that's that. The rest comes easily, brick by brick, building and building until they form an impenetrable pillar that spans from the bottom of her spine to the top of her skull. A castle of fortitude promising freedom. Immunity from the Wacked.

"Come here often?"

Rowan's eyes pop open and show her Catherine, leaning against the far post at the top of the stairs. Catherine smiles, or

155

maybe it's a smirk, and the bricks collapse like a child's tower made of blocks and overzealous ambition. Like it was constructed to fall. Rowan looks down, embarrassed. There, between her feet, is a pile of pink dust, steaming and defeated.

Catherine lifts herself up hips first, stands waiting. "Are you ready?"

Rowan takes one last look at the remains of her project, then rises above it.

"Ready," she says.

෯   ෯   ෯

No one is at the reservoir this time of night. And after an evening at the movies (*Oliver's Story*, a sorry choice) and a stop at Art's for gas and pop (and Rowan's obligatory free-of-charge item), the reservoir seems like the only place to go.

They're sitting at the top of the hill, part of a bank that surrounds the entire area. In the winter, little kids come here to tumble down the gentle slope on sleds and flying saucers. Devil's Hill, for the big kids, is behind them, tucked away in the woods behind a layer of trees.

"I'll race you to the bottom," Rowan says, struggling to decipher Catherine in the muggy dark. Though they're sitting side by side, clouds are blocking the stars and the moon and it's hard to see much of anything.

"What do you mean?" Catherine says.

"I mean, we roll down the hill. See who gets there first." Rowan is already horizontal, ready to play.

Catherine's shape pushes aside pieces of black and drops flat against the ground. "You're on."

Rowan stays quiet for as long as she can manage, building up the suspense. She inhales the scent of dirt and clouds and half-finished pop. Now. Now is the time.

"On your marks, get set. Go!" She shouts louder than she needs to, amping up the fun. The bank beats against her hips and shoulder blades, tossing her down its expanse like a friend who means well but plays too rough. She forgot what this is like.

"Ouch." She crashes at the bottom to find Catherine already there, chuckling between breaths.

"What did you do, cheat?" Rowan says. It's even darker down here than at the top of the hill.

"Just because I beat you, I must be cheating?"

"That's not what I meant." Rowan relaxes into the ground. In the center of her awareness, right above her belly, the hill game continues. The swirl of initiative and motion, rumbling thrill—she's still barreling down some hill, somewhere.

"Hey," she says. "Did I tell you about Sherry's latest conquest?"

The inky blob that is Catherine is absorbed by the bank. "You didn't," she says. "But I'm not surprised there is one. Do you think she has a drinking problem?"

"No way." The words fly off Rowan's tongue, like they do when someone calls her a liar, or tells her there's something she can't do. "She likes her beers, but she's not an alcoholic or anything." *What the hell, Catherine? What the hell is this?*

"It just seems like she's always drinking, is always loaded. Looks like an alcoholic to me."

Inside, Rowan is still falling, the hill is still letting her. "Well, she's not. Sherry's whole family drinks. That's just the way they are. It's not a problem or anything."

"I don't know. My dad drinks. A lot. Sherry sort of reminds me of him."

Rowan blinks, though there's no reason to. It's already dark.

"It wasn't so bad when I was in elementary school," Catherine says. "When he was home more. Then he started going on the road, and the drinking took off. He and mom would fight about it like crazy when he came home. Now he stays away most of the time. Mom doesn't seem to mind. She's got her own life. And it's not like he's a mean drunk. He's just a drunk."

"I see." Rowan lands at last, quiet inside and out. "I'm sorry." *Isn't that what you say at a time like this?*

"Thanks," says Catherine. "It's hard sometimes. But he and I

157

are cool. And my mom and I are cool too, so," she laughs, "I guess that makes me cool as well."

Rowan lifts her legs into the air and her feet play with the black. "You're a lot more than that."

"It's just I worry sometimes about what I've been given—from my parents, from my culture, from this world so far. How do you even *start* to go about building something good with all that gets thrown at you from birth, you know?"

"Sure." Rowan looks away.

"Take this, for example. You and me. Sometimes I think this doesn't even exist anywhere but here. This new way of being together, of connecting with someone else. It's like we're on the moon or something. Everything is lighter, allows more. You know?"

"Sure," Rowan says again. She rolls onto her side, props up her head with one arm, and squints to see Catherine's face in the dark. It's too hard, though, and she closes her eyes instead, pulling it up from memory. An easy task. Catherine's face pretty much lives on the other side of her eyeballs anyway.

"I should write a book." Catherine's voice is drifting up from the ground. She must be lying down. "About reconditioning. About breaking out of what you've been given and fashioning it into something better—a clearer way of being in the world. No obstacles. No rocks to trip you up."

"Mmmm," says Rowan.

"Like recently, for example. I've started taking a shower at night. Since it's been so hot lately. And last night when I was lying in the hotel, all warm inside the sheets, I realized it's like my day starts at night now. Like the sleep and the dreams are where it begins, and when I get up in the morning, it's a continuation of that. You know what I mean?"

"Yup." Rowan opens her eyes. She has no idea what Catherine is talking about. "I know exactly what you mean."

There's a bunch of different things orbiting her mind, options for a moment such as this one, but she doesn't wait to sort it out. She picks the easiest one. The pounce. She huffs her body onto

Catherine's, the breath escaping both their lungs and slipping onto their faces.

"Uff." Catherine runs a finger against Rowan's eyebrow and follows this with her lips. "You smell like chocolate," she says.

"I had some before. At the store." Rowan could say she purchased it but that would be a lie. She shifts to silence.

"I don't remember you buying chocolate."

Rowan waits. She's imagined telling Catherine about this from Day One. *I'm a thief. I steal. What do you think of that?* Is this the time?

Catherine pulls her leg from under Rowan's and pins her with it. "Where's mine?" she says.

"Your what?"

"My chocolate." Catherine adjusts her leg on top of Rowan's. For a semi-small sort of person, Catherine's legs are surprisingly heavy. "Didn't you buy me some?"

Rowan swallows. "I can't answer that."

"Why not?"

"Because I can't."

"Oooooh." Catherine arches her hips, slides her lower leg between Rowan's. "Not talking, are we?" Her hand searches for the back pocket of Rowan's jeans and positions itself inside. Gently at first, then with more authority, she encourages Rowan to ride against her. "You going to make me force it out of you?"

"Maybe." Rowan's hips pursue Catherine's leg automatically, without thought.

"You're fucked, you know." Catherine chuckles. She works her leg in deeper, so the slightest movement on Rowan's part is met by friction. "Totally fucked."

"So you say." Rowan pushes into Catherine, into her leg, her confidence. "I'm not the only one," she says, "who's fucked. I'm—"

"Shhhhh." Catherine's hand presses harder, pulling Rowan into speed, into getting what she needs through her.

Rowan finds Catherine's neck with the edge of her cheek, anchors there while she falls in and out, again and again. "I can't . . ." she says. "You can't . . ."

"But I can," Catherine whispers.

Rowan grunts, pushes faster. "Uh," she manages. It's too much. When she can feel herself coming, just about to, Rowan tries to hold back. But it's too late. Catherine, who knows exactly what's going on and loves it, rolls her fingers into a fist inside the back pocket of Rowan's jeans, shoving faster.

Rowan groans, her hips breaking open. This is it. This is all she can stand. She slams into a giant come, surging into Catherine's leg and the shore of her neck. Rowan's hips, her belly, the drive of unbroken need, falling into Catherine and out against the dark, digging and releasing and wanting more. Again.

When she's done, Rowan lies quietly. Somewhere out beyond where they are, a mile or so away, the brakes of a car squeal, then disappear.

"Whoah," she says. "That was . . . whoah." She speaks softly, almost hoping Catherine won't hear.

"I told you." Catherine's hand wriggles free from Rowan's pocket and thumps to the ground. "I told you I'd force it out of you."

"I guess so." Rowan coughs this out, burying her head in the grass. The earth smells sour, like vinegar.

Catherine's lungs expand to press both bodies up, then down. "So," she says. "About that chocolate . . ."

"Rowan?" In a way that should surprise her, but doesn't, given it's so familiar, Jane's voice glides down the hill and into Rowan's ear. The glare of a flashlight follows. "Is that you down there?"

"*Shit.*" Rowan loosens herself from Catherine and plops onto the ground. "What the hell is she doing here?"

The voice grows louder, the flashlight brighter. "Rowan?"

"I'm here." Rowan yells, straight into the air. She waits, half expecting the words to drop from the sky and into her mouth. They don't.

"Something's happened to Ben. You need to come with me." The voice at the top of the hill cracks and a column of light lands at Jane's feet. Jane, for some reason, is wearing rain boots.

Rowan sits, trying to line up everything in her brain. Chocolate. Stealing.

Sex. Jane. "What's happened to Ben?" she says.

Jane's boots flicker. Rowan wonders what her sister might have seen, why the light is staying at the top of the hill.

"I don't know," Jane says. "You need to come with me. We need to go."

Catherine finds Rowan's knee and gives it a push. "Go with your sister," she whispers. "You need to go. I'll be fine."

"Did she see anything?" Rowan ducks when she says this, as if truth is a body that lives under the normal range of perception.

"I doubt it. We were just lying here. There was nothing to see. Don't worry." Catherine's fingers tighten around Rowan's. "You should go."

"I'm coming." Rowan sends her reply up the hill and rises to leave.

Catherine chuckles beneath her. "But you already did."

"Shut *up*, will you. She's right there." A slap of air beneath her shirt reminds Rowan her pants are unzipped and she quickly seals them shut. Catherine is a muddy blur against the grass, and all Rowan can think is how much she wants her, needs her.

"I'll call you," she says.

"Don't worry about it." The blur folds into a sitting position. "Just go."

ॐ ॐ ॐ

The passenger seat of Jane's car is stiff and cold. Rowan cranks open the window to let in air, not caring that this adds to her discomfort.

"Where are we going?" she says.

Jane is driving, glowering at the windshield. She hasn't looked at Rowan since they got in the car. "To the hospital," she says. "Dad called me to say that Ben was in an accident and to come find you. He said your car was still at home but that you left. He told me to look for a blue Thunderbird. Said he saw you take off with that girl."

"Catherine."

"Catherine." Jane's foot tilts against the gas pedal and houses fly on by. "You said Danny. Before, at the house. You said you were hanging with Danny."

"What happened to Ben? What kind of accident?" Rowan locks her palms together and jams them between her legs. Sex is still running through her limbs, pouring out of her hands and feet.

"I don't know. That's what we're going to find out." Jane shakes her head as the traffic light trades yellow for red. "Shit."

"Jane." Rowan turns to see her sister's impatience bathed in a faint red glow. "I thought you didn't swear."

"There's a lot I don't do." Jane blinks. Red drops to green and her accelerator foot pounds the floor. "All kinds of things."

The next eleven minutes, the time it takes to get to Erie County General Hospital, are spent not talking. All except for one minute, the final one.

"Back there, at the reservoir, it looked like you were lying on top of that Catherine girl." Telephone poles, bleached white with streetlights, mark the seconds. One. Two. "Were you lying on top of her?"

Rowan cranks the window open another notch. More air, that's what she needs.

"No," she says. "Why would you ask that?" She says this like it's a stupid question, like it's the stupidest question she's ever been asked. Then lapses into silence. All subjects are off limits if there are no subjects at all.

         ❧   ❧   ❧

They step on the square rubber entry ramp and the huge glass door breaks into two, welcoming them to the Emergency room. Erie County General has been around longer than either visitor, longer than both of them put together and multiplied by three. That's the feel of the place, too. Older than bones, and big and calm and hungry enough to take those bones back, if you're not careful.

"Look," Jane says. "There's Carol."

Carol Browne was a classmate of Jane's. Slept with more boys than anyone. Now she's a nurse at County.

"Let's find out what's going on." Jane tugs on the sleeve of Rowan's jacket and leads her across the lobby.

As they approach Carol, as they near the wide, empty reception desk, Rowan feels as though her heart has been portioned into two chunks, chopped in half like the entry door, and that each chunk has fallen straight through her system and down to her ankles. She is here, wandering through this white, sterile place, and she is dragging the remains of her heart around her ankles like two small, bloody bodies. It's messy, frighteningly red, and not at all sterile. Rowan wonders if Carol can see this, if her training included detecting such things.

"Jane. Rowan. I've been waiting for you." Carol pulls a sheet of paper from a stack of charts and scans the page. Her face is fuller than it used to be, puffed cheeks under tired eyes. She is an adult now. Grown.

"Where are they?" Jane says.

"Your dad's in with the doctor. He'll be out soon. Have a seat over there. I'm sorry about this, Jane."

"About what?" Rowan stamps a foot against the floor, disregarding the possible mess. "What happened to Ben?"

Carol assesses her with immense patience. Perhaps she can see the chunks after all. "I only know there was an accident. Your dad should be able to tell you the rest. I really am sorry."

"We know," Jane says. "You're doing your best. Thank you."

An orderly colony of chairs guards a pair of vending machines off to the left. The waiting room. As they turn toward it, Rowan scrapes her sneakers against the floor, anticipating the drag of her heart below. But there's nothing. She doesn't even bother to look. If she's lucky, she may have lost it completely, leaving her without the responsibility of that sloppy organ, be it in one part or two. More likely, though, the chunks have weaseled their way back inside, stuffed themselves into a body overwhelmed by too much in one day, by this white glare of a space, this emergency room. Rowan feels a thumping at her throat and concedes to the latter.

The vending machines are consoling company, in their way—large, peaceful, humming. They take the place of the conversation no longer happening between Jane and Rowan, filling and surrounding it with the ever-present reality of fresh hot chocolate, triangles of white bread and bologna, chips in a bag. Rowan examines the long row of choices from her chair, the buttons she can press to make her purchases, but decides food is not the answer here. There is no combination of selected numbers and letters that will supply her with an open line of communication with Jane. And there's certainly no code for getting Catherine off her skin. Even here, waiting for news about Ben—what is he, dead? who knows?—there is Catherine. Skirting in and out of her pores, commanding her focus and attention, breezing just below everything that exists. Rowan could pretend herself a victim, dragged round and beyond the bounds of normal, out of the life she knew before, but it's not like that. It's like this.

Jane squirms in her chair, fretful, and people walk by, serious or laughing or in a hurry, but finally it is their father who is walking toward them. He looks funny, though. Off-kilter. Like he's put his shoes on backwards, or maybe it's his whole body that's on wrong. He comes to a halt, standing slumped and jittery in front of his daughters, leaving more distance than most people might allow.

"What?" Jane speaks first. "What happened?"

"It was the car," he says. "We had a fight."

"About the car?" Rowan stammers.

"No. It was the—he took my car. After the fight. He was drunk."

"After we left," Jane says.

Dr. Marks nods. He's a wreck. Stuck and stilted, with a face Rowan has never seen before. Sorrow, thick with it.

"Is he okay?" Jane says.

"He's alive. The car, it crashed—he crashed it into a tree." The words come slowly, as if each one is being massaged and inspected before being permitted to leave. "Cracked ribs and abrasions. It could have been worse. Much worse. The alcohol

164

may have softened the blow," Dr. Marks fades away, eyes climbing into the floor, "may have saved him."

"Can we see him?" Rowan tries to catch her father's line of sight but can't. She addresses his feet instead. "Can we go talk to him?"

Dr. Marks shakes his head and his lips curl inward. "Not tonight. He's sedated. He needs to rest. Tomorrow, though. Tomorrow morning." He finds his daughters, gives them a glance each. "You girls should go home. Rest. Come back tomorrow."

"Are you okay, Dad?" Jane peers up at him. "You look awful."

"Fine," he says. "I'm fine." He's shuddering almost imperceptibly, like he's plugged into a low voltage socket or is reevaluating, moment by moment, where, exactly where, to place his body in the field of space around him. "The best thing to do is to go home, get a good night's sleep, and come back in the morning. He should be conscious by then."

Jane takes a sip of air. "Can we drive you home? Anything? Is there anything we can do?"

Rowan would like to speak as well, tries to, but only emptiness emerges. She grabs a bite of air instead, a sign of solidarity with her sister.

"No." Dr. Marks takes a step back. His long legs look thinner than usual, less stable. "I'm going to stay a while to make sure he's okay. I'll get a ride home with one of the other doctors or sleep in the staff room. Don't worry about me."

"I will." Jane stands and smoothes the front of her blue cotton jacket. "I'll worry about you and Ben both. Promise me you'll sleep soon? At least that."

Their father's head edges up and down and some of the sadness slides off his face.

"At least that," he says. "I'll do that."

Rowan pries her body off the chair and up into the lounge. Her legs are rickety, as though walking is something she rarely does. She remembers the pieces of her heart from earlier and chides herself for such a melodramatic image. Everything's fine. Ben's fine. She's fine. Inside her chest lives a happy heart with two eyes and stick-figure legs, dancing. Both parts whole.

"You take care, Dad," she says. "We'll see you in the morning." She nods at him, willing him to agree, which he does.

As they leave him, gliding through the glass exit door that splits in half once again, Rowan realizes she feels worse for her dad than for Ben. Ben is at least sedated. Her father, roaming free, untethered, seems so much more delicate. The best thing would be for sleep to wipe the worry off his features, off everyone's, and then let tomorrow be more like most days and less like today.

Jane and Rowan manage to avoid any real talking, spending the car ride home mumbling brief bits about Ben and keeping their eyes on the road. This is a relief for Rowan who, though still worried about Ben, finds herself, now that she is alone with Jane once again, continually charging back to the light on her sister's boots at the reservoir. Rain boots in dry weather. A beam that scooted down the hill and then quickly back to base. The boots.

Rowan stands in front of her house, hand on the top rim of the car door. "I guess I'll see you tomorrow," she says. The inside of her palm against the door feels raw, as though the metal is contacting nerves and not just their casing.

"You're not going to tell Dad, are you?" Jane says. "About you and that girl?"

Damn. Rowan blinks. She was so close.

"No," she says. "What do you mean?" She delivers a cough into a clenched fist, substituting sound for the thoughts, like worms, sprouting inside her brain. *What the hell is this? An inquisition?* She grips the top of the door with her other hand, still raw, and steadies herself against the asphalt. This is almost over. Except, before she can stop it, one of the worms breaks loose.

"What, Jane? Jesus would disapprove? Is that it? Because I know that's what you're thinking."

Rowan can't see Jane's face, can only see her hand patting the seat Rowan just left. "No," Jane says. "It's not that simple. I don't know what Jesus would say. I just don't think we should tell Dad."

"Right. Thanks for the advice." The door-hand contact evolves beyond irritation into flat-out pain, radiating from palm to arm to breast to belly. Rowan grips harder, a counterintuitive reflex, before waking to sense and prying her hand, fingers first, off the door.

Fine

The first thing Rowan notices, after the artificial light blows open her pupils, is that the hospital in the morning looks exactly the same as the hospital at night. Even Carol looks the same, though as Rowan gets a little closer, she discovers it's not Carol at all but another nurse in the same uniform. Wanda, the morning nurse. Wanda who, as it turns out, is an extremely helpful young woman, informing Rowan that Dr. Marks was visiting Ben earlier today and may still be, and that Jane already came by, left, and will be back soon. Room 232, on the second floor, Wanda says that as well. That's where Ben is.

After saying her goodbyes to her new friend, which are surprisingly sentimental for such a short acquaintanceship, Rowan commences a slow march down the hall. Though she was in bed all night, a large portion of that time involved not sleeping. Now she's tugging her body around like a yawn, a mouth that needs to close. She remembers the beds in the staff room and wonders if they're free. A slab of even semisoft would feel so good about now. She stops for a second to soak this in, allowing the tiny Rowan between her ears to take a tiny nap on a tiny bed when, off to the right, a flash of red and the smell of coffee catch her attention.

It's the hospital gift and coffee shop, and the red belongs to the girl behind the counter. Rowan steps to one side, committing only to a view from the hallway, and peruses her options. Coffee, that's one, but she knows to pass on this. Coffee always gets her skittery, anxious—a full tank of the wrong kind of fuel. What else? She gives in and sidles over to the store, understanding that she's supposed to be in a hurry to see Ben. Not stopping to shop at a silly store that exists only to shine away, with food and trinkets, the pain and anxiety that brings people into this building in the first place.

"Rowan? Is that you?" The red shirt speaks.

"Yup. It's me." Rowan knows this much is true, though it takes her a little longer to figure out whom she's saying it to. Finally she realizes. Trish. Trish Reynolds.

"I thought so," Trish says. "I couldn't tell at first. You usually walk faster than that."

"Do I?"

"From what I remember." Trish smiles sweetly, wraps a dusting towel around a small glass globe with a miniature cat inside. When they were younger, Trish was an outcast of sorts—a poor kid from the south side of town, an aura of neglect hanging around her like dirt. Now she's all filled out, shiny, her red shirt barely containing everything she's become.

"You wanna buy something?" she says. She sets the cat globe on the counter in front of her.

"No thanks." Rowan positions one arm around her torso, attempting to protect herself from any further inspection, any more comments from Trish's mouth about how she usually is or isn't. "I mean, I could," she says. "Maybe I will."

Trish smiles again, and Rowan can see the two front teeth crossing over each other, a sign of membership in a family that couldn't afford braces. It's still a beautiful smile, though. The crossed teeth add character, a resilience Rowan envies.

"I didn't realize you were working here," Rowan says.

"Just started. I was over at the feed store before. But those boys—too rowdy. Too much pinching me where I didn't want it. My sister got me this job here."

"Nice." Rowan blushes.

"Maybe. It's been boring so far. But it's good to see you."

"Yeah." Rowan reaches into the display case, on the outskirts of Trish's vision, and fiddles with a package of fireball candies. All Trish has to do is turn around—for something, anything— and these babies are Rowan's. "Last I heard, you were headed for the service."

169

"That was the plan. Didn't work out."

"Why not?"

"Changed my mind. It wasn't for me." Trish lifts some scraps of paper off the counter, drops them in the cash register, and punches the door shut. Her movements are precise, deliberate. Rowan remembers how Trish used to be, how she used to move. This is all so different.

A bunch of summers ago, when Rowan was twelve and Trish thirteen, they both went to the YMCA camp out in Mason—Trish on a church scholarship, Rowan on her dad's money. They were in the same cabin and, even though Rowan never would have hung out with her in school, they became friends. Trish was the first person who told Rowan she came across like a snob, a notion that shocked her at the time. Trish talked rough and told stories about her family that Rowan thought she must be making up. She was fascinating, an amalgamation of fire and mystery and generous verve. It was a relief to be around someone so open, so unguarded.

Rowan stands stiffly in front of the counter, looking at the gifts. Maybe she should get a present for Ben.

"I'm sorry the service didn't work out," she says. "Though if it wasn't right for you, I guess it's good you figured that out."

One night during that summer, Trish had a bug in her bed—a spider or a cricket or something—and she got scared. She snuck over to Rowan's bunk and slipped under the covers, but backwards, head to toe. As if anything else would be too bold, too hazardous. Rowan lay there all night, motionless like a stick on the ground in the woods—gentle, fallen. When she woke up the next morning, Trish was gone, safely back in her own bed, but Rowan carried that night with her whenever she looked at or thought about Trish after that. For the rest of the summer, it always made her feel guilty, like a bad thing had occurred, even though she hadn't moved a muscle. Or maybe that was what felt so funny—the not moving, the feeling of frozen.

She ignored Trish when they returned to school in the fall, first by polite but distant exchanges, eventually pretending not to see her even when she was right there in front of her. It's not like she didn't feel awful doing it, she did. She simply couldn't fit Trish and who she was and what had happened between them into life at home and school and Wakefield.

"And how about you?" Trish rubs her cleaning rag against the glass counter, buffing it to clear. "What are you up to now?"

"Not much. Working at the Sugar Shack. You know, with Sherry Howard."

"I know Sherry."

"Yeah, so. And I'm ... I'm going to college soon. In September. Rollins University. In Massachusetts."

Rowan finds herself becoming transfixed by Trish's red shirt. There are white letters on it, talking about a company or a school or something, but that's not what's got Rowan on edge. It's the red, and the way it fills out in front and then lies on the cool flat of skin, like the upper arm where the surface of Trish's flesh is quiet and tan and covered with delicate sun-bleached hairs. The arm won't stop moving, either—pushing the rag against the counter, portioning time into pieces of up, down, side to side.

"I'm thinking of doing some school myself," Trish says. "I want to work with people more. I'm thinking maybe a nurse. Or an ambulance attendant." Her face expands with the thought. "That's what I'd really like to do."

Rowan nods and, to get herself out of the red, imagines Trish working in an ambulance. Trish, in uniform, leaning over a sick or injured patient. Look—it's a female patient. Look—Trish is propping her head up. Look—she's giving her mouth-to-mouth. Oh dear. Rowan glides back into the red.

"I have to get going," she says.

Trish laughs. "Aren't you going to pay for those?" She peeks across the register at the package of fireballs nested in Rowan's open palm. "You been holding them there like they're going to explode."

Rowan drops her head and examines the shiny red candies. She forgot all about them. "Sure," she says. "Yup. Just had to make sure they were the right kind. I'll take a Rocket Bar too."

She buries her fluster in busywork—hand in pocket, emerging with change, paying Trish, a noisy goodbye, a boisterous walk out the door. All the while glossing over the interaction with vague generalities—acknowledgment of a classmate coming into her own, regret for past mistreatment of said classmate, appreciation of the angles and planes of skin on red.

And what was Ben's room number again? Room 232, was it? Yes, two-thirty-two. She sticks with the simplicity of these figures—their ease, their weight, their certainty. This is what gets her through, not fantasies about Trish and her paramedic heroics. She passes on the elevator and goes for the stairs instead. Part of her plan of practicality and sticking with the visible. She'll be fine as long as she stays the course.

The second floor is virtually empty and Rowan wonders for a minute if she's in the right place. Her father has worked in this hospital for as long as she can remember, but she hardly ever comes here—hates the smell of clean and sick, the narrow caged-in hallways and the lack of windows. Two-thirty-two, there it is. Says so on a silver plaque above the door. It's slightly ajar, and she walks on in.

Her brother's eyes are open and his head is covered with bandages. There are more bandages around his arms, and the sheet on top of him is crumpled, shoved this way and that. He looks like a mummy escaping his wrapping.

"Whoah." It's all she can say. He looks awful. Gray and flattened and exhausted. She sinks into the chair next to his bedside table. Luckily, it's a private room and no one else is here. She doesn't have to gauge her reaction for anyone but Ben.

"Like my new digs?" he says. Nothing moves except his mouth. She images it must hurt to move anything, even that.

"I guess." Her tone trips above the bandages, keeping it light. "The price of admission was pretty high, though. What did you—what happened?"

"Doesn't matter."

The chair she's sitting on is pure wood, hard and curved for where the human form is supposed to go. She sits on the front edge. "What do you mean 'Doesn't matter'? Of course it matters."

Ben winces. "They won't let me eat real food. Just this plastic crap." He scowls at a bowl of lime green jello on a tray. "What do they think? I thrashed my outsides, so now they're going to torture the inside of me too?"

"Maybe. It's probably in the manual somewhere. 'Jello. The Silent Killer.'"

"That's what I'm talking about. It's the stuff that looks all copacetic on the outside that's rotten in the middle. You never know."

"You never do." Rowan yawns, a face full of tired, and runs her thumb along the rim of the table next to her. Clean and tidy. A full glass of water sits next to a metal box with a black button. The button must be for the nurse. Though not currently a necessity, Rowan is glad to know this option exists, in the larger scheme of things.

Ben shudders. "Dad and I had a huge blowout," he says. "I confronted him on all his crap. There's stuff I've been suspecting for a long time. Ever since I went back East. I finally let him have it. Everything."

"Oh?" Rowan teeters on her chair. "What did you talk about?"

"Mom didn't die in a car accident."

"What?" Rowan yelps. "She's alive?" All those back pockets of her mother's presence, guiding her through her days. It always seemed more than real, an engine of more than just hope. "Where is she?" she says.

"She's not here." Ben wipes his hand against the tousled sheet. His knuckles are scraped and swollen. "She's dead. She killed herself."

"No, she didn't." Rowan stares at the black button. Now? Do they need a nurse now?

Ben blinks as if to push away tears, but his eyes are dry. "Yes," he says. "She did. I talked on the phone last year with mom's sister. When I was at college. She said there was more to it than a car accident. She didn't say what, though. She just said the story Dad told her never seemed right. I finally put it to him last night and

173

he couldn't deny it. The whole car accident thing was total bullshit. Total fabrication."

"No. That's not true. Dad said she was—"

"She offed herself in the garage with the motor running." Ben's forehead twitches and his bandages shift in kind. "Jane found her and told Dad and they took her to the hospital. That's what happened, Ro. They didn't tell us because they thought we couldn't handle it." He looks her straight in the eye but it's more like through. "Like we were babies."

"I was a baby." Her speech is scratchy and weak.

"You were," Ben says. He burrows his beat-up body backwards, into the empty white of his pillow.

Rowan studies everything that outlines the bed—the jagged corners of the sheets, the wheels at the end of the bedposts, the metal bar that holds it all together. Ben is in the middle of chaos—so is she—but if she only studies its exterior, she'll be okay.

They sit like this, frozen and focused, until it is only that. Only the perimeter. Only the outside edge.

       ॐ   ॐ   ॐ

She remembers the name from that afternoon a few weeks back. The Golden Lion Inn. What she doesn't remember is the room number, but that's easily solved by a quick inquiry at the desk. Room 15. By the pop machines.

Rowan knocks below the number on the door, not really expecting a response. It's almost eleven in the morning. Catherine and her father are probably gone for the day, conducting their business. She can hear noise in the room, though—water running and a man's voice—so she knocks again, a little louder this time. She's not sure what she's doing here, or who she is, but she stands inside herself anyway, watching the door.

The number lurches into the room as the door opens quickly, leaving Mr. Mike Lowell filling the entryway.

"Well, hello there," he says. He's squinting at her and she can practically hear his memory ticking, sifting through all the girls in all the towns, to bring up the girl that she is.

"Hey." Rowan shrinks.

"It's Rowan, right?" He grins, jabbing a finger in the air. "You're the naughty one. The little thief. How have you been?"

Rowan freezes. "Fine."

Mike chortles. "I'll bet you are. You wanna come in? We're about to get going, but you're welcome to stay for a second." He opens the door wider, motioning her into the room.

Rowan peers inside. Catherine is over by the sink, washing a cup in the basin. Instead of turning around, which is something she could do, she finds Rowan in the mirror, taking her in with settled eyes. Then a word.

"Hi."

"Hi." Rowan says. Catherine must have heard, right? Her father's voice is too loud to ignore. Though she was washing her little cup, maybe the water drowned out the words. *Naughty. Thief.*

Mike coughs. "We don't have all day. You coming in or not?"

"Not," Rowan says. "I mean, am. I'm . . ." She stumbles inside, secures a chair by the table in the corner. All that just happened with Ben is outside these walls; everything else is inside them. Including Catherine. And her loud-mouthed father. And Rowan's transgressions. Rowan gulps. What is she doing here? What was she thinking?

"What's the latest out of Wakefield?" Mike says. He straightens his tie, a bright yellow number with blue boats and mud-orange fish.

Rowan blinks. "Oh, you know. We're all—"

"How's Sherry doing? She okay with how things turned out?"

"I think so. Yes. She's doing—"

"Great. Glad to hear it." Mike taps his tie with his fingers. He cocks his head toward his daughter. "Cath?"

"Yes?" Catherine turns from the sink, her head tilted sideways while she attaches her earring. Her face is different today, cooler. Is it because she's with her father? Or because of what he said

175

about Rowan? Or is her face the same as always and Rowan's just imagining the temperature drop, the frosting of features that are actually fine, regular.

"Big meeting today, huh?" Rowan says.

Mike Lowell beams back, his cheeks swelling above his mouth. "Yes, indeed. We're meeting with the Northern Regions District Manager for lunch in Cleveland. We've got good news for him—better than expected considering the crappy economy. And Cath will get a chance to meet some of the higher-ups. You almost ready, hon?"

"Almost." Catherine tugs on one sleeve of her jacket, then the other. Though she looks wonderful—serious and composed in her little business suit—Rowan can tell she's profoundly uncomfortable in the thing. There are many facets of Catherine that remain inscrutable, but as far as clothes go, Rowan knows that Catherine prefers them off.

"How about I meet you in the car?" Catherine says. She continues to fuss with her outfit—her shoes now, and the way they are interacting with her pantyhose. "Give me five more minutes?"

Mike plucks a briefcase off an impeccably made bed. "We don't have five minutes. We need to get—"

"Then give me three. I just want—I have to check in with Rowan about something real quick. I promise. I'll be out in no time."

He passes Rowan, the weight and energy of him cutting a trail through the dense hotel-room air. "Good to see you again, Rowan. Stay out of trouble, will ya? If you can. And say 'hi' to Sherry for me." He winks as he speaks, adding a smile soaked in delight.

Rowan shivers. "I'll do that." She lifts her fingers from the table, the most she can manage, and nods at the pants that swish back and forth out the door.

"Three minutes, missy," Mike bellows. "I'll be timing you."

The room is extra quiet without Mike involved and Rowan exhales, relieved. She scans the area—the two double beds, the minikitchen, the silent TV, newspapers and magazines filling the empty spaces. It seems so different than the last time she was here, that afternoon when even the doorknobs looked like sex. Now it's just a room, isolated and depressing, with pictures on the walls that might be interesting anywhere else, but seem bland and ugly by virtue of being here.

"Why is one bed so messy and the other so neat?" Rowan's face is expressionless, she can tell. She's too drained to do anything but hold still.

"The unmade bed belongs to my dad." Catherine, finally dressed, perches on the end of the messy one. "He didn't sleep here last night. He stayed," her shoes tap the shag carpet, "out of town. With a friend."

"Ahhh. That's good." Mike's flashy smile creeps back into Rowan's head, roams around inside. "It's good to have friends."

"I tried calling you." Catherine's feet come to a rest, dark brown leather against bright orange shag. "A bunch of times. But no one answered. Is Ben okay?"

Rowan jerks forward. *Ben.* "He's okay. I mean, he will be. He smashed into a tree but nothing really bad happened. To his body or anything. He's at the hospital. I was just there." The sheets, the bedpost, the corners of all that happened, they whir outside the hotel room, rapping at the window. "He had a bad night."

"I'm sorry." One of Catherine's hands shrinks into a fist and Rowan thinks for a second she must be holding something inside it. But she's not—the fist opens to empty.

"Look," Catherine says. "I know we don't have much time to talk, but there's something I need to say. To tell you. We can't keep going, you and I. We need to stop."

"What?" Rowan stares at Catherine's empty hand. "What do you mean?"

"I mean we have to end it. That's what I mean."

"What are you talking about? Is this because of what your dad said?"

"My dad? What did he say?"

"Nothing. It's not ..." Rowan flushes. "Is it Jane? Is it because Jane saw us? Because that's not—"

"No. It's not about Jane. It's—"

"Yes, it is." Rowan punches her words into the room, into the stupid hotel with its stupid boring pictures. "You're freaked out and you're worried what she'll say. That's dumb. Jane is nothing to worry about."

"I'm not worried about Jane." Catherine's toes resume their tapping. "It's more complicated than that. Or, no—no, it's not. It's simple. The summer is almost over and we'll be going our separate directions and it's easier just to finish up now."

Catherine's hands come together, palm to palm, fingers intertwined. She studies them intently and Rowan sees through to why. If she looks up, if she looks at Rowan, Catherine will have to reveal the hundred percent portion of bullshit her statements are based upon.

"Finish up?" Rowan balks. "You make it sound like an art project. We don't just put away our paste and throw our scraps of paper in the trash, Catherine. We still have a few more weeks."

"Barely. And that's nothing. It's not—it's the same as nothing. It's better to just—"

"We still have a few more weeks. And then we'll both be on the East Coast." Panic, like a creature, strains inside Rowan's chest, vying for a chance to enter the room. She stops it with will, with confidence, with an alternative to what Catherine is telling her, what Catherine is trying to make true. "Don't tell me you didn't think of it. That we could keep going. I know you did."

"No." The blue suit rises from the bed, small hands pressing the color into the cloth. "I didn't. It's not an option."

"It totally is. Why are you saying all this? What's going on?"

"Nothing. Nothing's going on. That's what I'm saying." Catherine stares straight ahead, at the painting above the TV—a brook with an old shed on a steep hill—and Rowan stares at it too, at the tired grays and the crappy old shed and the way the water looks real, even though it's not.

"I have to go," Catherine says. "I'm sorry."

"There's nothing to be sorry for." Rowan's eyes fall off the fake water, onto Catherine. "There's nothing wrong."

"I have to go," Catherine says it again as she snatches a set of keys from the dresser, clenches them in her hand. "I can't leave my father waiting."

Rowan's arms squeeze against her chest and she smashes back into the painting. She dives into the fake water, its artificial wetness scouring her skin.

"No," she says. "You certainly can't keep you father waiting."

"Thanks for understanding. I know this is difficult. I'm not saying it's not."

"Difficult. Yeah." Rowan takes one last plunge into the painting. Splashing, kicking, breathing in the phony mist.

"Go," she says.

        ૐ   ૐ   ૐ

It's in the car, twenty minutes later, that it hits her. The full force of being smacked with two voluntary withdrawals in one morning. The fact that it's too much to bear.

Rowan pounds her hand against the steering wheel, slams her shoe against the gas pedal, cranks up the window, and screams into the long black thread of approaching road, leading nowhere. She's headed toward Wakefield, which is technically somewhere, but the thought of going back there breaks her apart, leaves her desperate and rangy and turning west on Route113, toward somewhere else. Anywhere else.

It's cool for late morning, clouds plump and low on the horizon. Rowan rolls up the car window to keep things simple. It's like she's sealing in the misery, containing it to just one vehicle rolling down the road. Maybe this way her sorrow can drift through her, penetrate her core, let her go. The road and the hours pour through the endless flat of northern Ohio—corn and beans and ratty gas stations—and she keeps her head fixed forward, eyes on a new project. There are innumerable ways she could do it, an infinite variety of techniques she could try. She catalogs them effortlessly, one at a time, like recipe cards of items she could bake. Each one an option, a consideration.

Crashing the car is too easy, too risky. Look at Ben for example, painfully alive. And her mother, in an unmoving car. A different sort of crash altogether.

And then there are knives. Cutting open all sorts of places, blood transitioning from inside to out. But where would that be? And who would see it? That's the real trick—the people who would see it. It's probably best not to involve them. That is the point, after all—the noninvolvement of others. Right?

Another possibility, slinging from the sidelines, jumping off an old barn that whips by at cruising speed of seventy miles per hour, is sheer willpower. The act of wishing it to be so—death—with such force, such intensity, that it would have no choice but to bombard her with its grace. A halfhearted gesture in this direction leads nowhere, though, and Rowan is back to actual scenes involving actual things.

Like drugs. Of course! Drugs. She scans the sky and finds the cloud that's harboring the sun, a bleary patch that mocks her with its dimness, its lack of full responsibility for the day. Why didn't she think of this sooner? Drugs. It's such a wide highway, such a popular way to go. Though it's usually pills, isn't it? Hardcore stuff she could never get her hands on. Booze might work, if she swallowed enough of it. But that would involve a trip to her family's house, which is not only in the opposite direction but, again, like the blood, involves others.

Rowan slows the car and swerves off the road, stopping just past the forty-five-miles-an-hour speed limit sign. Drowning. That's one that's always baffled her. Do you drink in the water willingly, like thirst? Or does it drink you instead, weaving you inside its liquid wall, clinging until it's had enough? It's been done before. Other women have done it. Why shouldn't she?

Rowan revs up the engine and yanks the steering wheel to the left, in the direction of Wakefield. She'll pick up a boulder on the way.

It takes much longer to get to the creek than she would have imagined, mostly on account of her being so far outside of Wakefield to begin with. She manages to find a substantial chunk of rock on her way from the car to the creek, but realizes—once its weight has pinned her to a spot close to, but not exactly the same as, the one she and Catherine used to frequent—that she doesn't have a rope. It probably won't work without a rope. She could clutch the rock to her breast, maybe even shove it down her pants, but it's not likely she'll be able to stick to a task as radical as drowning without a line of some sort. Without that certain tug.

Rowan blinks. She calls up her mother's face, the one that usually brings her solace. What did her mother look like, that last day? What was she thinking? Was she remembering she had a daughter, a little baby who barely knew her? How could she leave when Rowan was just getting started?

Rowan strains to see through to the other side of the bank and discovers, when the picture in front of her is too blurry and remote to permit this, that she is crying. She never cries. She thought she didn't know how. Her eyes well over, swollen and disoriented, and she drops her head toward the stone. How pathetic is this—that she attempts a drowning without one of the main ingredients? That she's sitting here alone in the woods with a boulder between her legs, paralyzed with incompetence. That her mother left her as an infant and Catherine just left.

It's nothing Rowan's ever been able to prove, just suspected from time to time. Her lack of worth, her lack of importance. Every time the fucked-up feeling washes into her awareness, that's when she remembers. And then there's her inability to fit in with other kids or even—let's face it—her own fucking family. There's not much more proof she needs, though Catherine's departure certainly solidifies the notion that Rowan's worthiness is up for serious consideration.

Yet even this is too much to manage. Rowan holds it for an

instant—a deep coil of empty, splitting her apart, hoisting her under—and then it slips away, like the turn of a fist into an open hand, fingers gaping with air. It occurs to her, like a breeze, that maybe it's Catherine who's fucked in the head, not her. That Catherine is fleeing and Rowan is standing still, hanging in. It's not much of a comfort, though, as the place she inhabits is swollen with ugliness and desperation. Like the center of her body has decided to turn inward and chew itself raw, a wad of blood and bones and undigested joy. It's not here, happiness as others seem to experience it—Jane with the baby, Catherine with her career, Hank with the prospect of an unblemished tooth, her father with time alone in his mind. All she's got is this random chaos inside her belly, paring down her soul, leaving her alone in her body by this creek in these woods, with birds who can't stop singing because they don't know everything has gone so completely wrong.

Rowan shakes her head. She can't stay here. Not anymore. She can't stay at the creek and she can't stay in this chaotic place inside her. She needs to escape. Now.

She stands, shaking her legs. She's got an idea. It's not a good one, but it's an idea nonetheless. She thinks of her mom, or the version of her mom that lives inside her. The one that's been irrevocably changed.

"Here we go," she says.

ॐ ॐ ॐ

Henny Penny Market is not a place Rowan usually frequents. It's too far outside Wakefield, for one. And cheap—or at least that's what Jane would say. Bright, fluorescent lights, floors in need of cleaning, staff who look like they're not paid enough. It's the kind of store people go to, to save money, though Rowan can see why Jane doesn't like to come here. It's depressing. Sad and lonely and tired.

Rowan trots down the canned goods aisle, then turns the corner into the candy section. She didn't even know where it was, she's just following her instincts. The candy aisle is packed with options—chocolates and mints and fruity candies of all kinds. Who knew that so many different choices could exist in one place? And so cheap too.

Rowan shudders. She shoves her hands in her pockets. This is stupid. What is she doing here? She should go home. But she can't. It's like she's on a mission. One that's going to make everything right. And even though she knows that's not true, even though she understands that this is the exact opposite of making everything right, she reaches into the bin of Rocket Bars and plucks not one, but two candy bars into her pocket. Then sighs. Because she feels better, she does. As crazy as that seems.

"What do we have here?"

The voice is high and chipper. Like Jane's, but with more enthusiasm added.

Rowan turns. A Henny Penny employee named Karla—says so on her badge—stands with her arms folded across her chest. She's wearing a hairnet and black orthopedic shoes.

"That's not how it works," Karla says. "You don't just shove stuff in your pockets and leave. You pay for it. You know that, right?"

Rowan squints. She's not sure how to answer. Should she pretend she didn't do it? It's probably too late for that, but for whatever reason, playing dumb seems like a good idea. "I don't know what you're talking about," she says.

"Wrong answer," Karla huffs. "I would have let you go," she says. "If you'd copped to it. Now you got a lot more trouble on your hands."

Rowan blanches. This wasn't how it was supposed to go. "But—"

"Like I said. Too late. Let's go, little missy."

❧   ❧   ❧

The back office of Henny Penny is even more depressing than the store. Cramped and dirty and smelly, too. Rowan sits on a chair next to a desk in the corner of the office. The desk belongs

183

to a guy named Randy. Randy's already made a few calls—first to the cops, then to a person of Rowan's choice. Rowan wasn't going to pick anyone, but her nerves got the better of her, and she had Randy call Jane. Now he's sitting, eating a sandwich and staring at Rowan. Like she might escape any minute.

Randy's desk is piled high with papers. There are other things on the desk as well, but it's the papers that really get Rowan's attention. They look like they could fall over. Maybe they will. That wouldn't be such a bad thing, really. Rowan swallows. She can't remember ever feeling this scared, this lonely. Her knees are shaking and her stomach feels like it might collapse inside her body. She keeps trying to think of something to do, some tactic to get her out of this mess, but there's nothing. Just sitting here and watching Randy chomp on his baloney sub. There's mayo on the corner of his mouth and he's eating so fast, Rowan thinks maybe he'll pass out. Is that possible? To faint from eating too fast?

"Rowan." Jane rushes into the office and runs to Rowan's chair. "What's happened? What's going on?"

Rowan stands and Jane crushes her in an embrace. Rowan can feel the baby portion of Jane poke against her, just below her ribs. Rowan falls back onto the chair. "This is Randy," she says, pointing at the baloney sub. "He can tell you."

Randy swallows his latest bite and wipes his mouth with a napkin. He's not too old, maybe early thirties, but he looks like a much older guy on account of his big belly and the beginning of a receding hairline. Rowan suddenly feels sorry for him. Not just because he works here, at Henny Penny, but because of what he has to tell Jane.

"We caught her stealing," he says. He nods at Rowan. "We called the cops. They should be here soon."

Jane flushes. "I don't understand," she says. "What did she steal?"

"These." Randy points to the desk. The Rocket Bars are sitting next to the pile of papers.

"Those?" Jane wrinkles her brow. "Why did you have to call the cops for that?"

"It's policy, ma'am. She denied it and we saw her do it. Plus she had the evidence on her person. We had to call them." Randy suppresses a burp.

Jane turns to Rowan, studies her face. "What did you . . . ? Why did you . . . ?"

Rowan gulps and tries to pull up an answer. There is one; she's just not sure she can find it. Should she start from the beginning, the first time she stole something? She was twelve and she and Ben were at Art's. They'd just finished a game of ball and Ben and Lyle were in the back of the store with Art, getting ice. Rowan swiped a candy bar from the front counter and felt a surge of power filter through her fingers. And guilt, there was that too. But now? There's no rush, not unless fear counts as a rush. And the guilt is so much different now, so much darker and fatter. How is Rowan supposed to explain all that?

Luckily, she doesn't have to. Officer McElroy struts into the room, shaking his head. "Well, look what we have here," he says. "Not the sort of call I wanted to make on a Thursday afternoon."

The officer is in uniform, with his shiny badge and the gun in his holster. Officer McElroy is the one who arrested Sherry's son Jerry a few weeks back. Rowan knows him only from a distance, a small-town cop who always looks serious and stern. It is a serious job, after all. Why wouldn't he look the part?

"Rowan?" he says. "That's your name, right? I know your dad. It seems the store caught you stealing. Is that true?"

Rowan nods. Her knees are shaking so badly now, she's worried they might knock together. She's also worried that Officer McElroy will see this and laugh at her. Though why would he do that? He probably never laughs.

The officer nods at Jane. "And this is your sister?"

Jane stands up straight, catches her breath. "Yes," she says. "I'm here for Rowan."

The officer pulls out a pad of paper and starts to write. "Here's how this works," he says. "You get a warning and a court date. Standard procedure. If you have any questions, have your dad call me. Okay?"

"Okay," Rowan says. She watches as Officer McElroy's pen puts words on the pad, words about Rowan and what she did wrong. She thinks back to the beginning of the day, to Ben in the hospital bed. And their mother in the car. And Catherine in the motel room. And now she's here. It doesn't make any sense. And yet it does.

When the officer is done with his papers, he hands them to Jane. "The court date is on the ticket," he says. "Make sure you're there early. Judge Williams doesn't like to wait."

"Of course," Jane says. Her voice sounds thin, brittle. "We'll make sure we're there early." She grabs Rowan by the sleeve, pulls her out of the chair. Then holds her hand.

"Let's go," she says.

⇛ ⇛ ⇛

"Why?" Jane says. "That's all I want to know. Why did you do it?"

"I don't know," Rowan says. She's sitting on one of the old kitchen chairs. She and Jane drove home in their separate cars, and when they got here, Hank and her father were waiting for them in the kitchen. Rowan peers up through the too-bright light at Jane, Hank, and her father, all standing around her. They look huge and wild and fractured, like the ogres in fairy tales who do worrisome things to children if left alone with them too long.

"There has to be some reason," Jane says. "Do we not pay enough attention to you? Is that it? Or was it Ben, did he set you off?"

"No. Jeez. Why do you think it's about Ben? Why do you think it's about anything?" Rowan swallows. It might be easier if she could explain it, but she can't. Her knees stopped shaking when they left the Henny Penny office, but she's still weak all over. It feels hard to breathe, hard to think.

Jane winces. "This isn't how we act, Rowan. I can't believe you would do this. What were you thinking?"

Rowan waits. Jane and Hank and her father still look like

186

ogres, but some of the malice is wearing off. The bright kitchen light is blurring their edges, making them appear softer, nicer. They deserve an answer, don't they?

"I don't know," Rowan tries again. "It was stupid. I guess I was just mad. I guess I just wanted someone to—" Rowan stops. There are pictures in her head. Pictures of her and her mom. Her mom coming to rescue her. Her mom taking her by the hand in the Henny Penny and telling her everything's going to be okay. Is that why she's been doing this? So her mom will come find her?

Rowan starts to cry. She never cries, but here she is, crying twice in one day. She shakes her head to try and stop, but it doesn't work. In fact, moving her head makes it worse. Big, fat tears falling down her face and onto her lap. "I know," she says between gulps. "I know about mom. I know what happened." She looks up. Jane and Hank and her father are back to normal. No ogres, no fractured faces. Just regular people who can't stop staring at her.

"Of course you do." Dr. Marks's eyes are dark, muddy. "I figured Ben would tell you."

Rowan shivers. "Why did Ben have to tell me?" she says. "Why wasn't it you? Or Jane? Like anybody ever talks about *anything* in this stupid family. It's so fucked up." She wipes her eyes with the back of her hand. "Everything is so fucked up."

Jane blanches. "That's not right. It's not right to say that. You have no idea what we've—"

"Yes, I do. I've been here all along, haven't I? Taking it in whether anybody talked about it or not. Because it's still there. You can't hide shit like this."

"Rowan." Jane's voice tightens. "You're not—you don't have all the facts. You can't—"

"You kids should get some rest." Dr. Marks folds into the chair across from Rowan. "Jane needs her rest."

Hank nods. "She sure does," he says. "It's been a long, long day." He picks up Jane's jacket and drapes it over her shoulders.

Rowan watches his wide forehead, his face coated with fatigue. Why is she always so hard on him? "Night, Hank," she says. It's as close to an apology as she can manage. "Night, Jane."

Her sister's jacket inches by, a muffled "goodnight" emerging from within its stiff folds. Rowan plays with her thumbs, pushing them together until it hurts. The pain feels good, clarifying.

The door latches shut, sealing Jane and Hank on the other side. Dr. Marks, instead of speaking, nudges the napkin holder to the center of the kitchen table. Then tidies up the salt and pepper shakers (two miniature ceramic figures, a man for salt, a woman for pepper), wiping them free of stray particles, tapping them against the empty table, positioning them, just so, next to the napkin holder. Even when he's finished he stays there, one hand on each, fingertips brushing the heads of the figures.

"I wanted to tell you," he says finally. "I always did. I thought it would be when you and Ben were a little older, a little more ready, but you never were. Or I never was."

He stops and Rowan can see him implode, reconfigure, whatever he's doing. She's not sure of the contents, what he's harboring, so she can't be sure where he stands in relation to it all. The surface of his face flexes, then sets itself still. It's his usual dance, adjusting himself, inside and out, before he can transmit any information to the outside world.

"Your mother was depressed," he says. "Always. We haven't really talked about it, but she was."

Rowan shrinks. She can feel her image of her mother shifting, transforming inside her. What has she been holding onto all these years? Was it all made-up?

"Always?" she says. "She was never happy?"

"She was happy sometimes," her father says. He shrugs. "But she was blue a lot. I didn't understand it when I first met her. As the years went by, it became increasingly clear. She wasn't just sad, she was clinically depressed. After my residency was over and Ben was born, we moved back here, hoping it would help. Or," he pauses, flips the salt man a quarter turn, "*I* thought it would help."

Rowan watches him struggling. Was that what it was like, being her husband? Was it always a struggle? And what would it have been like to have been her daughter? Would that have been a struggle too?

"The situation only got worse after we moved back to Wakefield," he says. "Helen was an outsider, with her accent, her city clothes. When she got pregnant again, it was our last hope. A chance. But her hormones. The fatigue. She couldn't handle it. She had to . . ." His fingers are trembling, the pepper shaker clinking against the salt. He pulls them apart.

"She had to leave," Rowan says. The words float into the room, hang in the air around her.

Dr. Marks's hands leave the condiments and fall into his lap. He studies Rowan for a moment, a few seconds of found, then looks away. "I'm sorry I never told you," he says. "I am. I hope you can forgive me."

"I still don't understand," Rowan says. "Why was she so unhappy? What happened to make her so sad?"

Her father shakes his head. "I don't know," he says. "Some people are just depressed. There isn't always a reason. It was like a place she would go, a place where she'd get stuck and couldn't get out. It's different for the rest of us. We can move out of it. She couldn't."

"But what if I'm like her? What if I . . ." Rowan waits. "I don't know."

"You're not like her, Rowan. She was depressed all her life. Even as a child. I know you're not always happy, but your lows are not like her lows. Believe me."

Rowan waits. If there was ever a time she wished her mother could come back to life, it's now. There are so many questions, so much to sort through. How is Rowan supposed to do it without her?

"But what about us?" she says at last. "What about me and Ben and Jane? How could she . . . ?" Rowan stops, her throat closing with tears. She takes a breath, swallows them down.

"It wasn't about you kids. It was about her. That's why we didn't tell you. Though I know it wasn't right. I didn't . . ." Her father sighs. "I'm sorry, Rowan."

Rowan fights off an urge to play with the salt and pepper, abandoned and alone in the center of the table, and settles into the facts. A dead mother, a living father, two lives ultimately unavailable to her. The fucked-up feeling makes an entrance, tugging at the bottom of her pants, burning the shine off her mother's memory, flattening her father's face into a gray slate with tired eyes.

"And how about you?" The slate is talking, eyebrows forging a crease in the uppermost part, the forehead.

"What about me?" she says.

"A couple of candy bars isn't exactly grand larceny. But you're in the system. We're going to have to deal with it."

"I guess."

Her father's forehead relaxes, the crease disappearing. "We'll figure it out," he says. "We'll think of something."

"Just like you thought of something when Mom died?" Rowan gulps. "Sorry," she says. "I don't know what I'm . . ."

"That's okay," her father says. "None of this is easy."

Rowan nods.

"Would you like to see someone?" her father says. "Talk to someone about it?"

"About what?"

"About your mom. About the shoplifting."

Rowan frowns. "What do you mean? Like, a counselor or a therapist or something?"

"Yes. There's a woman who works at the hospital. Liz Garrison. Maybe you'd like to—"

"Sure." Rowan surprises herself. What is she agreeing to? "Sure," she says again.

"Good." Her father smiles, or almost does. His shoulders soften and his face relaxes. He lifts his hands from his lap and places them on the table. Then folds them together. He looks like he's about to say something, but he doesn't. Or not at first. Finally, he clears his throat.

"Jane said you were upset about something when she found

190

you last night," he says. "She said you were with your friend and you were upset."

Rowan catches her breath. *Catherine.* She feels the pull to tears again, but she takes another breath to fend against it. "I wasn't upset," she says. And then, because she says this, because she asserts this to be true, it is. A buoyancy blooms inside her and she is weightless, headed for the ceiling.

Her father nods gently. "Perhaps Jane was wrong," he says.

"Perhaps." Rowan, what's left of her, mimics his serious tone. Up above, her knees scrape a layer of dust off the pale yellow ceiling, her toes flapping with freedom and relief.

Everything from the day—every emotion, every thought—is falling away. The shock and grief from the hospital room with Ben. The anger and disbelief from the hotel room with Catherine. The anxiety and ineptitude from her visit to the creek. The fear and mortification from the office at the Henny Penny. All of these feelings and scenarios float from Rowan like so must dust, so much unwanted debris. It's so much easier to drift above it all, traipse around the ceiling.

When Rowan was five years old, she saw *Mary Poppins* at the Roxy. It was her first movie. She doesn't remember much about it, just that her father turned to her in the dark, next to the excitement and the smell of butter, and said, "Rowan? This is your very first movie." She'll always remember that. The rest of the film, that installment of it at least, is pretty much gone, lost in the recesses of her beginning brain. The movie came on TV again later, though, when she was about ten, and the part Rowan liked the best was when Mary and the kids went to visit Uncle Albert and laughed so hard they ended up on the ceiling. Like now. She's not laughing, of course, but still.

"Jane was really worried about you. Yesterday and today."

Rowan kicks into the air, somersaulting backwards. It smells damp up here, musty. "No need to worry," she says.

"You've been through a lot, Rowan. We all have." Her father's voice is solid, packed with logic. The hem of her pants begins to feel heavy, like someone stuck a bunch of pennies inside.

"We want to make sure you're all right," he says. "It's not easy. Ben's troubles. This business with your mother. We didn't want you to be hurt."

"I'm fine."

What a worthless expression that is—"fine." It says absolutely nothing. The pennies in her pants turn to quarters and nickels and dimes. Fully weighted, Rowan thuds back in her chair.

"I'm fine," she says.

Stalk

Rowan sits in her car, waiting for Catherine. She tries to pretend she's waiting for Catherine like she used to wait for Catherine, like they planned a rendezvous at a certain time and place, and Rowan is waiting for the fulfillment of the plan. But that's not what this is. Instead, Rowan is sitting in her Chevy late at night, an empty candy bar wrapper in her lap and a feeling of dread in her throat.

She's watching the pop machines at the Golden Lion Inn, watching as a guy in a baseball cap and sweatpants drops his dime in the machine and emerges with a cold can of pop. Rowan did the same thing an hour ago and is considering doing it again, given that the cold pop is such a perfect companion for her waiting.

Though Rowan knows she's not waiting. She's pining. She's desperate. She has no clue what to do.

She tried calling a bunch of times, but Catherine won't talk to her. At first the phone just rang and rang. Rowan tried all different times of day, knowing that eventually she'd find a time when someone was there. Finally, after a week of no answer, Mike picked up the phone. It was Thursday evening, a week after the breakup. Mike said Catherine wasn't there, even though Rowan heard Catherine in the background telling him to say that. The next time, Mike picked up and told Rowan that she shouldn't call anymore. That she needed to leave Catherine alone.

That's when Rowan resorted to stalking. She knows that's what it is. She's been doing it for five days now and there's nothing else to call it. The lamest part is that she can come here only between shifts at the hospital and the Sugar Shack, which means the middle of the day or late at night. Times that Catherine will either be absent, or present but unavailable for conversation. Though Rowan did try knocking on the door last night. There was no answer.

Rowan shudders, pulls the letter from the passenger seat. It's been sealed in an envelope so she can't reread it, can't make any changes on what is now a complete and thorough plea. Given that Catherine is currently unavailable, Rowan decided that another approach was necessary. This approach took the form of a letter, a letter in which Rowan outlined all the reasons why Catherine should not have dumped her. Rowan is pretty sure that Catherine will read this and take her back. Maybe not right away, but pretty soon after. Rowan's heart is on these pages, poured all over them. And now it's contained in the crisp, white envelope she holds in her hands.

If Rowan had no clue what love was until Catherine came along, she had even less of a clue what it was like to have that love yanked away. This last week-and-a-half has been the worst of Rowan's life. She can't sleep, she can't eat—except for pop and candy bars—and there's no one to talk to about it.

Danny's out of the question—they're still in the middle of their feud, or fight, or whatever it is. Ben is home from the hospital, but he's perpetually drugged up on meds—prescription and otherwise. And then there's Sherry. Rowan tried a few times to talk with Sherry about Catherine, but Sherry seems to have no interest in the young Miss Lowell. Rowan's mother, Sherry's fine to talk about that. She greeted the news of the suicide with shock and sadness and sympathy. Turns out there was a suicide a while back in the Howard family—an uncle and a gun and a life yanked in the wrong direction. Everything Sherry has had to say about Rowan's mom has been perfect, as though sculpted from a plane of knowing beyond Rowan's grasp, one that Sherry has relayed to her with care, concern, and irreverence.

Sherry was even surprisingly cool about the shoplifting charges, even though it meant that Rowan has to do a bunch of community service at the hospital and can't put in nearly as much time at the Shack. Given what Sherry's been through with her boys, she said Rowan's little misdeed was "damn close to nothing" and didn't change her view of Rowan one bit.

Rowan's glad for the comfort, but it's done nothing to help the worst of the pain. She flips the letter over, traces her fingers over the handwritten "Catherine" on the front of the envelope. So much love went into those letters, the penning of that name. Or if not love, then passion. And hope. And desperation.

Rowan stares at the letter, tries to pour into it any last ounce of intention, or mojo, or whatever it is you use to make people do what you want. It has to work. It has to. She pops open the door of the Chevy and saunters over to Room 15. She considers whistling to show how nonchalant she is, but realizes, halfway there, that this is way too dumb.

The door itself is quiet and steady, giving no indication of the beautiful, incredible girl—or woman, or whatever she is—who lives behind it. Rowan slips the letter under the door, watches as it slides into the room. And then it's gone. She feels a pang in her stomach and a lightness in her heart.

No matter what happens, at least she tried.

ॐ   ॐ   ॐ

"That'll be five dollars and fifty-three cents. Would you like a bag with that?" Rowan reaches into the bin next to the cash register, grabbing the bag she's sure her customer is going to want.

The customer, an elderly woman with pale blue hair and a sweater to match, shakes her head. "No bag, dear. I'll be wrapping it at home."

"Um." Rowan holds the bag in front of her chest. She wanted to use it. What's she supposed to do now?

"Thank you, ma'am." Trish scoots next to Rowan, easing the bag out of her fingers. "Come back again."

"Thank you, dear." The woman takes her purchase—a paper-weight with the logo of the Erie County Hospital—and glides off. She's moving surprisingly fast for a senior citizen.

Rowan is intrigued by the way her hair bounces on top of her body, like it's an entity unto itself. Maybe it can talk, or even—

"I can't believe it's not even noon yet. This has been a slow one, eh?" Trish collapses onto the chair behind the counter. "You got plans for later?"

Rowan shakes her head. She used to have plans. She used to do a lot of things. "My sister and I are going to the reservoir. Bringin' some beers." Trish shrugs. "You can come with us, if you want."

Rowan shakes her head. She's been working in the gift shop for a week-and-a-half. Her dad spoke to the judge and asked what they should do. The judge recommended community service hours—a hundred of them. He said that if Rowan can complete those before her court date, she'd have a decent chance of clearing her obligation to the court. Knocking off the hours doesn't erase the dread, though. Or the shame. Or the paranoia that everyone in town knows and is judging her. That's an inside job, one she's made little progress on so far. As for the community service hours, she's got forty-eight so far, and after today's over, it will be fifty-four. She wanted to do something more adventurous, like work with patients or ride in the ambulance, but the hospital administrator decided that assisting Trish in the gift shop was more Rowan's speed. Trish is nice enough, but she has a bad habit of asking Rowan to do things. Things Rowan can't do. Like hang out and have fun. Rowan's in no mood for fun.

"Did I tell you about the moose?" Trish is scratching her arm. "My sister's boyfriend saw it on the highway."

Rowan scoffs. "No, he didn't. There aren't any moose around here. That's Canada. Moose live in Canada."

"No. He swore he saw a moose. He said he was mad he didn't have his gun. He would have—"

"Can we talk?" A new voice enters the conversation, one that's clear and concise and filters into Rowan's ears like a memory.

Rowan startles, turns to identify the speaker. Though even after she's turned around, she still can't make sense of it. She holds onto the edge of the counter to steady herself. "Catherine?" she says. "What are you . . . Catherine?"

Catherine nods at Trish, then locks her eyes into Rowan's. She's wearing her business suit, the exact same suit she was wearing the last time Rowan saw her. She looks older, like more than a week-and-a-half has passed since they last saw each other. Or maybe it's not older, maybe she's weary. Or angry. Her breathing is fast, rushed. Did she run to get here?

"Can we talk?" she says again.

Rowan blinks. "I don't know," she says.

"I got it." Trish rises from her chair, posts herself at the cash register. "I'll say you went to the bathroom."

"Really?" Rowan's still clutching the counter. Will she fall if she lets go? It feels like she might. A week-and-a-half of wanting to talk to Catherine, and now that she's here, Rowan's afraid to speak.

"Go on," Trish says. "But hurry. Lunch is in twenty minutes and you got to be here to punch out."

"Right." Rowan pulls her fingers from the counter, takes a breath. "We can . . . we can talk outside."

And then it's Rowan who's rushed, hurried. She clips down the hall like she's a doctor running to resuscitate a patient. Catherine is following, so Rowan can't see her. Which is good. They arrive at the glass front door and it splits in two, allowing them into the bright day. Rowan scans the front area for somewhere to go, somewhere they won't be seen. Or heard. But there's nowhere. Nowhere good, at least. She finally settles on a bench to the side of the entrance, under a buckeye tree. The bench is covered with buckeyes, so it's a less popular option. Which is a good thing, in this case.

Rowan sweeps the bench clean and plops herself down. Catherine joins her, but on the other end of the bench. As far away as possible. They sit in silence for what seems like a year. A young couple enters the hospital. A mother and teenage girl exit. Then it's quiet. No one coming, no one going.

"I got your letter," Catherine says at last. "I woke up this morning and there it was. I went to your house, but they said you were here."

"Yup." Rowan says. Her toes curl in her tennis shoes.

"It was a nice letter, Rowan. I'm sorry I didn't . . . I'm sorry I haven't been able to talk to you in this last week. It's been a . . . nothing's the same. This is a lot harder than I thought it would be."

"Yeah."

Catherine sighs. "We're leaving today," she says. "Back to Chicago. I thought you should know."

Rowan catches her breath. "What? It's only the middle of August. I thought you weren't leaving till later. Why are you going now?"

"Because."

"But you can't. You can't go."

Catherine doesn't answer. Just sits on the far side of the bench, tapping her shoes on the sidewalk. Not only is she wearing the same outfit she was wearing on that crappy day in the hotel, she's tapping her shoes just like she did then. Except instead of ugly shag carpet, it's a damp sidewalk strewn with buckeyes. Rowan stares at the tapping shoes and the buckeyes. What's she supposed to do now? She poured out her heart in that letter, and Catherine's still leaving. Though she didn't say they were still broken up. And she did come to the hospital. Maybe there's still a chance.

"So you read my letter?" Rowan says. "Really read it?"

Catherine nods.

"And did you understand? About why it was a bad idea? About why we should still be together?"

Catherine is still. No nod, no movement of any kind. Even her shoes have stopped moving.

Rowan scoots forward. The bench is damp from the latest rain, and she can feel the cool wetness against the legs of her jeans. It seems as though what she's about to say will be the most important thing she's ever said. And if she can just figure out the right words—the right combination of sentences and phrases, then Catherine will stay. Everything will go back to how it was and Catherine will stay.

Rowan sits up straight. "I love you," she says. "I know I never said that before, when we were together. But I do. That's what I was trying to tell you in that letter, even if I didn't say it directly. I love you, and I know you love me too. That's why we can't be broken up. That's why we still—"

"Rowan." Catherine speaks slowly. Her voice is low and soft. "That's not the point."

"Not the point?" Rowan bounces in place. "What do you mean, not the point? That's *everything*. You can't . . . Why are you here, then? If that's not the point, why are you here?"

"Listen, I know this probably doesn't make any sense to you, but there is sense in it. Somewhere. You have to trust me on this." Catherine stops, rearranging her curls into something wilder, more chaotic than what she came with. "I thought if I saw you, maybe I could bring the sense with me. Or I could try."

Rowan grabs her legs. There's a hole in her jeans, on the right knee. Even though the hole is small, she can see through to the old scar on her kneecap. She studies the scar, trying to remember how she felt when Lyle grabbed her from behind during a game of football and sent her eight-year-old body whomping onto the pavement, knee first. It hurt like murder, she remembers that much. But was it as bad as this? As bad as sitting here waiting for Catherine to explain exactly why, in more detail than Rowan ever would have expected, exactly why she broke her heart? Rowan pinches the skin around the scar for perspective, for a coded comparison, but comes up short. It's numb.

"I've decided to take a year off," Catherine says. "In Africa. I'm going next week. I got this chance to travel and I'm taking it. I'm sorry I didn't tell you sooner. I should have. But it's one thing I wanted to say. Now."

Rowan pinches her knee again. When she first hit, she thought she'd lost it, like her knee had blown open and landed over in someone's yard, where it would take forever to find. But, no, it was still there. Shining through broken-open sweatpants, matted with gravel and blood. It's all tidy now in comparison, a thin slice that looks like a knife.

"Why didn't you tell me?" she says. "You could have just told me."

"It's complicated."

"What's complicated?" Rowan's finger traces her scar—smooth flesh first, then a blip, then smooth again.

"It's just complicated."

What was it Lyle said, after he tackled her? *You never had a chance.* The tones mixing with the torn flesh and gravel, making her cry.

"Why Africa?" she says. "Where did that come from? Like, whose idea was that?" Just a guess, a stab at what's "complicated."

No answer from the girl on the other side of the bench. Rowan turns to look but can only stand a few seconds. She can't stay mad, can't stay bloody and injured, if she looks.

"Just tell me," she says.

"It was Larry's idea. I'm going with Larry."

With focused attention, the slice on Rowan's knee grows darker, more precise. She remains without motion, hoarding all words inside herself. There was pain a long time ago and there is pain now. It's all relative.

"I thought there was no more Larry," she says finally. "You said there was no more Larry."

More silence from the opposite end of the bench. Just the regular sounds of the outdoors and—because the wind is blowing at them in a specialized combination of force and direction—the faint whir of the freeway to Cleveland.

"What's going on, Catherine?"

"Yes, Larry and I are still together. I'm sorry."

"Sorry?" Rowan pulls her eyes from her knee and lights on Catherine, calm and composed on her side of the bench. "'Sorry' is so pathetic. Why didn't you tell me? What the hell were you doing with me?"

"If I had told you about Larry, would you still have been with me?"

"No." This leaves Rowan quickly, without deliberation. The echo, still inside her mouth, says something else.

"That's my point. I wanted this and I wanted you. I knew it wouldn't happen if you knew about Larry, so I didn't tell you. I know that sounds screwed-up, but it felt like the only option. You know?"

"No, I don't know. That's dumb." Rowan gulps. "You're a liar. You were lying the whole time. What did I—"

"So were you. My dad told me, you know. He saw you at that store and he told me. Your little stealing habit."

Rowan stares at the ground. Her heart is thumping like a drum. "That's different," she says. "What does that have to do with this?"

Catherine huffs. "It's the same thing. We had stuff we didn't talk about. We both had our reasons. But that doesn't mean this shouldn't have happened."

"Yes, it does." Rowan's throat feels tight, like a choke. "This is stupid," she says. "The whole thing is stupid. You, me, everything. It was a waste. The whole thing was a waste."

"No, that's not true. I couldn't *not* do this." There's a kink in Catherine's voice, like the fabric of what she's saying is all bunched up and she's trying to smooth it out. "There's no way I was going to miss this, even though I knew it would end. It was worth it. That's the part I hope you remember, the part I hope you play back later when you review this in your mind. Because I *know* you'll do that. So get it right, okay?"

Catherine's voice unravels and releases itself to tears. Rowan won't look, though, as then they might both be crying, and what good would that do? She addresses the buckeyes at her feet. Objects without tears.

"I don't understand you at all," she says. "I really don't. How can you just leave? If this is so great and wonderful and all that, why are you walking away? What the hell are you doing?"

The sniffles on Catherine's end of the bench indicate she is still crying. After a few minutes of this, muffled tears and the distant freeway and Rowan's thorough inspection of the five buckeyes at her left foot, Catherine tries again.

"I don't expect you to understand. Maybe it's that I'm older, that I've done this more often than you. I'm not saying it's easy to walk away. Just that I have to."

"That is such bullshit." Rowan kicks a buckeye and watches it roll off the sidewalk and onto the hospital driveway. "I'm sorry, but it is. I think you're scared. Jane found us and you freaked out. And now you're running away. Because it's convenient. Because you can. And it's total bullshit."

"No, it's not."

"Yes, it is." Rowan holds her stomach. Red-orange sparks fly around inside her, igniting her cells, her thoughts. While she sits in the middle, restraining and unleashing herself at the same time.

"You wouldn't be here if you really wanted to walk away," she says. "You would have done it. You'd be gone. But how gone is this?" She throws an arm toward Catherine, toward the tears. "Looks like *here* to me."

"It's not, though. Not really." Catherine stops crying. She sits quietly, bathed in an aura of patience and composure. "You don't get it."

"I get it, all right. I get that you're the type of person who likes to have her ducks all in a row. Where you can see them. Where they fit into the stupid formulas inside your head. But that's not how this is. The ducks are all over the fucking field."

"It's not up for debate, Rowan. You're not—"

"I know stuff. Stuff you're too scared to say. Or too ashamed." Rowan stops. It's her turn for a dramatic pause, her turn to pull the string taut, then snap it. "How does this compare to you and Larry? You and me, how does it compare?"

The sound that emerges from Catherine's mouth is an odd one, a mix of anguish and pleasure and relief. "I can't. I can't compare them."

"Try."

Catherine shudders. Rowan can feel the shift, can feel her stepping into that space, that place of connection between them. For a second, everything is like it was—simple and worthwhile. Existing as an object with its own logic, floating outside of all that's happened since. Until Catherine stops it; Rowan can feel this as well. Catherine clears her throat and straightens her spine and covers everything with thick black paint. With silence.

"Okay, then," Rowan says. "I'll tell you. This isn't like anything that's ever happened to me. And say whatever you want, but I think it's so intense, so uncomplicated, yes," she speaks to the protest splashed across Catherine's face, "because you're a girl, or a woman or whatever you are. *That's* what this is about. And it's scaring the shit out of you, and me too, but that's not a call to run. It's a call to stand still. To stay."

Rowan expands her lungs, contacting the memory of expanse she felt after their first night together. When the perimeter around her body relaxed outward by feet and inches, making room for everything. "Maybe there's stuff we didn't tell each other," she says. "But that's just because we were scared. We don't have to be. Not anymore. We can do this." She flushes. "We can."

Catherine draws her arms to her chest. "I'm sorry," she says. "But that's not how it is. I'm not—this isn't about being scared. It's about doing what's right."

"Right?" Rowan flinches. She squints at the top of her leg, at the scar. It looks like a body now, a dead one. Vacant and bloated and waiting for a funeral. "You're not who I thought you were," she says.

"You are." Catherine nods. Clean, sure. "You always were."

Rowan takes another breath. Damn her. Could she make this any harder? What? It's too much. How do people do this?

"It will probably all make more sense later. In time." Catherine is moving and shifting, changing her position. Now standing. "We'll each get married and have kids and look back on this and understand why it had to happen. Why there wasn't a choice. I have to go, though. I still have to go now."

Rowan shrugs, stares at the buckeyes.

"Goodbye?" Catherine pronounces it like she's asking for permission. Fat chance. Rowan is one with the buckeyes, and the damp bench, and the wide expanse of pavement in front of her. Permission to leave will not be granted.

"You take care of yourself, okay?" Catherine says. "You'll have a great time in Massachusetts, I know you will." She scatters the syllables onto the bench, onto Rowan's stone of a face, onto the buckeyes littering Rowan's feet. "College changes everything. Lots to learn, lots to see. You know?"

She waits, cocks her head as though registering Rowan's reply. Then strolls down the sidewalk, past the hospital entrance, around the walkway, and into the parking lot.

Rowan doesn't watch any of this. Or rather, she does, but it's like she's watching someone else's life. One that's battered and complete and bursting at the seams and has nothing whatsoever to do with her. It's funny, how easy it is to walk away, even when you're sitting right there, not moving so much as a muscle.

She can hear the T-bird from the parking lot, even though she can't see it. The engine revs and the car roars away. Just like that. Rowan's tempted to jump up and run after it, but her body is frozen. Everything is frozen. She stares at her feet, kicks a few more buckeyes away from the bench. She tells herself she'll get up in a minute, but it doesn't happen. She tries again, but it doesn't happen then, either. Finally, just as she's telling herself she's *really* going to get up, she notices someone watching her.

It's Trish. She's standing outside the entrance, her arms crossed. She's watching Rowan like she's afraid of her.

"What?" Rowan yells from the bench. "What's wrong?"

Trish shrugs. "Nothing," she says. She ambles to the bench, plops down next to Rowan. "I punched your card. I told them you had an emergency. A female emergency. You know how Mrs. Hamilton is. You mention cramps and periods and shit like that and she gets all sympathetic."

"Sure," Rowan says. As hard as it is to have Trish here, it feels good to have Trish here.

"Is everything okay?" Trish says.

Rowan blinks. "Everything's fine," she says.

"Yeah, right." Trish chortles. "You look just peachy. You and your friend get in a fight or something?"

"You could say that."

"She looked kinda uptight. And kinda old. Is she old or something?"

"Yeah," Rowan says. "Kinda old."

"I thought so." Trish sighs. "You sure you don't want to come to the reservoir later?"

Rowan peers at Trish. She remembers the first day she saw her again, the day after Ben's accident. It was hard to look at her then, hard to manage the fantasies that sprang up around Trish's red shirt and the sun-bleached hairs on her arms. The fantasies receded after that, and it's been easy to be with Trish in the gift shop, working side by side, chatting about nothing. It's still easy to be with her, like now, sitting on the bench. Except some of that first day in the gift shop is leaking back into Rowan's awareness. It's something about Trish's presence, how she's sitting so close and Rowan can feel the way Trish's breathing is affecting her own. Maybe it's because they're outside. Maybe it's because Catherine just left. Maybe it's because the midday sun on Trish's face makes her look sweet and soft and mysterious all at once.

But that's beside the point. Rowan looks away. Investigating the Trish factor is not something she can do. Not now. Though she knows that there are questions raised by Trish's presence, questions Rowan will need to answer. Soon. She kicks another buckeye over to the curb, but this one doesn't fall in the street. Instead, it stays right at the edge of the curb, poised to fall.

"I can't go with you," Rowan says. "Maybe some other time."

"Have it your way." Trish hoists herself off the bench. The sun is still playing with her face, making her eyes shine and her skin glow. "Catch you later."

Rowan closes her eyes. "Later," she says.

Home

"Is Danny around?"

Betty Thompson looks up from her project—sorting seemingly identical screws into two seemingly identical piles—and nods her head. "He better be," she says.

Rowan smiles, or tries to. "I was going to—"

"In the back. He's reorganizing the Lawn and Garden section." Betty gathers up a pile of screws and pours it into the glass jar beside her. Next comes a sigh, presumably for a job well done, though Rowan is not so sure about this. There might be something else in there as well. Suspicion, perhaps. Judgment, maybe. Betty pokes a finger in the direction of Aisle 3. "Down there," she says, tacking on a smile at the end.

"Thanks." Rowan's head jerks in response. She's imagining things again, that must be it. Betty is clearly benign.

Rowan's stroll down Aisle 3 is framed by painting supplies to the left of her, plumbing fixtures to the right. A bin of washers catches her attention and she stops to inspect them. Small metal circles with holes in the middle, all hanging out together in this bin. She picks one up and rolls it between her fingers. The compulsion to steal is still there, she can feel it. But she holds back the urge, leans on it like she's stuffing it behind a door. She can't afford to get into any more trouble before she leaves town, for one thing. But it's also about her mom, the pictures of her mom that arise in her head when she thinks about stealing now. She's still not sure what it means. Like, if she lifted enough stuff, her mom would come back to life? How crazy is that?

Rowan drops the washer into the bin and pads to the back of the store. Danny's back is to her, dark blue T-shirt hanging off his shoulders. He's standing in front of a display of rakes, pushing them into place with his foot. His hands are in his back pockets, and if Rowan didn't already know he worked here, she'd think he was just some kid, fiddling with the merchandise.

"Is this a bad time?" she says.

Danny turns, blinks. "Rowan," he says. "What are you . . . ? What's up?"

"Not much." She shrugs.

"Mmm," Danny says. He turns back to tidy the stack of rakes and Rowan is struck by his essential Danny-ness: the slowness, the busying. She knows—in the way you suddenly know a thing you've known all along—that she'd have to try really hard to keep up a charge of hate for this boy, and even then it probably wouldn't work.

She takes a breath. "Can you take a break, maybe? A short one?"

"I don't know," he says.

"Well, can you find out?"

The lawn ornaments, the ones Danny was sorting on Corn Day, stand in a line on the shelf behind his head. They're serious, all of them, including Danny. "Okay," he says. "I'll go check."

He marches toward the front of the store, and Rowan, who knows he'll get his break and that they'll sit on the loading dock in the back, heads there now.

She plunks down on the edge of the platform, lined with a metal strip for where the truck hits when it's backing up to unload fertilizer and grass seed and boxes of hardware supplies. She takes in the limited landscape: a driveway that curls toward the street and a few parked cars, empty and loitering. Not much to look at—or slip into, as far as alternate realms. She supposes this is for the best. The straight and narrow, as it were.

The screen door thumps behind him and Danny takes a seat beside her. He sits closer than she might have expected given their current estranged-friends status, but far enough away that she remembers how long it's been, since they sat together like this.

"I guess . . ." She waits. "I guess it's been too long. Since I've seen you. You know?" A fly swoops around his head and Danny waves it away. "Yup," he says.

"Yeah." Rowan nods but gets caught in the downward motion. Her hair falls in her face and she leaves it there, a large and unruly hat. "So. Yeah. I was thinking that . . ." She lifts a strand of hair out of her eyes. "I was thinking what an idiot I was. Or am. I messed up, with you. I'm sorry."

Danny's foot jabs upward, then bounces toward the platform. "Okay," he says.

"Okay." Rowan's tongue digs into her back molar. What else? What else is she supposed to say?

"Me too." Danny scratches his chin, then places a hand in his lap. "Sorry, that is. I mean, I'm sorry about everything that happened. It was stupid."

Rowan removes her tongue from her tooth. "It was. Totally."

"I guess," he says, "I guess I was kinda full of shit that day."

"Maybe." Rowan's legs peel off the platform and press against her stomach. "I was too, though. All the crap I said. I didn't mean it. I didn't. I was just pissed off, trying to drive you away or something."

"Or something."

"Yeah."

Danny leans back, onto his elbows. "Look, Rowan. I know about you and the shoplifting. Lyle told me. Word gets out about stuff like that. I'm sorry."

Rowan is thankful her legs are already jammed against her torso, against the jolt of dread that greets her neck from her belly and grips it tight. "Oh," she sputters. Her throat closes like a clot of blood.

"What's going to happen? Are you still going to college?"

"Yeah. I mean, I hope so. If the judge clears me. I'm doing a bunch of community service. And my dad says I have to talk to a counselor."

"Really?"

"Yup. It's pretty dumb. The whole thing."

208

"Right." Danny sits up, sweeps a batch of hair out of his eyes. He stares at the objects in front of them—the cars, the smattering of bushes beyond. "You know, Lyle told me about your mom too. About what happened there."

Rowan grunts. "What is he?—like, the Lyle Information Network? Jeez."

"I guess." Danny's face smoothes out, relaxing into the sun. "I'm glad I know, though. That's a pretty big deal."

Rowan can feel her insides drop through her body, like a sack of wheat, pinning her in place. "Sort of."

"What do you mean 'sort of'? It's more than that, isn't it?"

The sack of wheat gets heavier. "You mean, like my whole life has been based on a lie and I just now found out? Is that what you mean?"

"Is that what it's like?"

"No. That's not what I . . ." Rowan imagines she's losing key parts of herself, being replaced, bit by bit, with meaningless grain. "It's not like anything's different. She's still dead."

"It is different, though. Isn't it?" Danny peels away a portion of metal casing from the platform, holding it between thumb and forefinger. "Doesn't it change everything?"

"Maybe." Rowan studies Danny's thumb pressing against the metal, but it's attracting too much sun, too much light. She looks away.

"I don't know," she says. "I guess I worry that I'm going to turn out like that. That I'm going to get all messed up and sad and everything."

"You?" Danny suppresses a smile.

"What?" Rowan baps him in the arm. "Are you laughing at me?"

"Not laughing. I just don't think that's you. Mrs. Glum. It's not . . . that's not who you are."

"Maybe." Rowan's voice is close to silent, suspended above the pavement, the unmoving cars. She waits, reveling in the silence and the proximity to her old friend.

"Hey," she says at last. "What's this I hear about you and Sarah Scarpetti? You're not the only one who hears stuff, you know. You two are, like, married now?"

Danny coughs, his hair flapping against the fist that covers his mouth.

"Oh, I see." Rowan lifts herself a few inches off the platform and plops down in a new position. One of inquisition. "Not talking, are we?"

Danny shakes his head. "We're just friends."

"Yeah, right. I've heard that before." Rowan saunters into a smile. Under the surface, there's a clicking in her chest, like relief.

"Really. That's all it is." Danny drags a hand over his face, as if he's readjusting his expression, neutralizing it. "At least for now."

"If you say so." Rowan chuckles. She knows not to take this any further. She lets the moment sit like a puzzle, somewhere inside her. All the pieces are different—there's awkward, there's familiar, there's difficult, there's comfortable—but they all make sense. She understands all of them.

"You were right, you know," she says.

Danny blinks. "About what?"

"About me and Catherine." Rowan swallows. "There was something going on. It was just like you said."

"I don't . . . umm . . ." Danny's face shifts to angular planes, clashing against each other. "I'm not . . ."

"You don't have to say anything." Rowan focuses on the soles of her feet, the only part of her body not sheltered by fear. "I just wanted you to know. You were right, and I didn't tell you because I thought you'd hate me. I didn't want you to hate me."

Danny coughs. "I couldn't . . ." He studies the cars in front of them, shakes his head. "So, wait. You and Catherine were . . . was it like how it is with a boyfriend and a girlfriend? Like that?"

It's such a simple question. It kills her, it's so simple. "Yeah," she says. "Like that."

"Oh." His face is still at war with itself—moving, shifting. "She was a looker, I'll give you that," he says. "I get that part of it."

"She was okay," Rowan says. "Except when she wasn't. She's gone now. It's over."

Danny brushes away a crop of staples onto the pavement below. They bounce and pling under his feet. "Sorry," he says.

"It's okay. She was kinda a jerk. A jerk I fell in love with."

Danny peeks over at her, then back at the cars and the bushes. "You'll always be my friend, Rowan. I don't think I can help that."

"You better not." Rowan catches her breath. The light in the air hangs around everything, magnifying what's ordinary.

"Danny?" Betty Thompson's voice sneaks through the screen door and out onto the platform. The hinges squeak as the door nudges open.

"Yup?" He squints.

"Can you give me a hand up front? We got swamped all of a sudden."

He hops up, quick and light. "Sure. Give me a sec." He peers down at Rowan. "Can you hang out for a bit?"

"I guess."

She glances up at him. He's so tall, his standing to her sitting. Like the Jolly Green Giant in those commercials on TV. Except he's wearing blue and his name is Danny and he's not attempting to sell her frozen vegetables of any kind.

"Wait right there," he says.

With Betty and the Giant gone, Rowan thinks she'll have a second to haul her thoughts in order, but it doesn't happen. Danny returns immediately, holding a stack of papers and looking how he always does—hopeful and steady, packed solidly inside himself.

"I thought you might want to see this," he says. "It's my latest stuff. For the strip. If you're interested."

"Of course." Rowan pats her lap. "Hand them over."

"Great." He smiles like a kid on a swing—open, cherished. "I'll be back soon. Ten minutes, tops."

One more squeak of the hinges and Rowan is alone with Hector and his world. She crosses her legs and props the papers against them, edging into the experience. It's been a while since she's been here.

She flips through the pages slowly at first, as if she's afraid of what she might find. It's pretty much the same, though; Hector is unchanged, as are Vince and his minions. Then there's a new guy—huge, with legs like trees, a friend of Hector's—who crops up in a few of the cells. Rowan gets trapped by the story at this point and realizes, a ways in, that this new guy is the one she gave Danny earlier this summer. Coltar. The jumper. Except Danny hasn't revealed Coltar's talent yet and he's renamed him Jeremy. Rowan traces a ring around Jeremy's head. Clearly, she and Danny will have to discuss this.

She suspects there's another reason Danny offered these drawings, though, one she hasn't found yet. Lifting herself away from the plotline, she searches the pictures until she finds her. Guinevere. In the final drawing on the final page. Looking not at all like the old Guinevere—last seen making a beeline out of Danny's room with Rowan in tow—but someone completely different. Higher cheekbones, a wider forehead, fuller mouth. Transformed. Pushing aside all traces of who she used to be.

"Damn." Rowan wipes away the wet splotch that falls out of her eye. Danny'll be pissed if she messes up his drawings. It's a dumb thing to cry over, anyway. She hasn't cried over a cartoon since *Bambi*, and that was more terror than sadness. This is just, what?

She turns over the last piece of paper and props the stack by her knees, away from her eyes. No big deal, really. Just the way it goes. She's no longer on the page.

Rise

"Rowan Marks?"

"Yes, sir."

"Please rise."

Rowan stands. The courtroom of Judge Williams is smaller than the courtrooms on television. It's like a big box, with the judge's bench and the jury chairs and some seats for people to watch. There aren't many watchers today, though, and no one Rowan knows. Jane wanted to come, but Rowan told her it wasn't necessary. Rowan's father had to work, and Ben is Ben—home in front of the tube, propped up on pillows and medication. No one else knew about the court date—not Sherry, not Danny. Rowan wanted to do this alone, though now that she's here, she's wondering what she was thinking.

"Let's see what we have here." The judge riffles through his papers. "Shoplifting. I see."

Judge Williams is a small man, though maybe it's just the hefty size of the judge's bench that makes him appear small. He's wearing a black robe, with black spectacles to match. They're the kind of glasses that prop halfway down the nose, so the judge can read the papers before him. Papers about Rowan and her transgressions. He studies them slowly, carefully.

"I see here that you've done over a hundred hours of community service," he says. "At the hospital?"

Rowan nods. She feels small and insubstantial. She feels like she could wet her pants.

"And the items in question . . ." The judge flips from one page to the next. "Two candy bars at the Henny Penny. You like your candy, Rowan?"

Rowan is unsure whether to agree or disagree. She waits. "Yes, sir," she says finally.

The judge takes his glasses off his face and holds them in his hand. He squints at Rowan. Without his glasses, he looks a little less scary. A little more like a regular person. "I see a lot of people in this courtroom," he says. "All kinds of people. And you, young lady, are what we call an aberration. Do you know what that means, Rowan?"

Rowan is tempted to tell him that she not only knows what it means, she can spell it too. She holds back from sharing this information and simply nods.

"There are two things that could happen," the judge says. "You remain true to your aberrant status and, once this matter is settled, you never see the inside of a courtroom again. The other route, one I do not recommend, is that you continue your little flirtation with thievery and land yourself in trouble again. While I neither predict nor recommend this second option, it is nevertheless one that exists. Do you understand me, Rowan?"

Rowan shrinks. "I do, sir."

The judge props his glasses back on his nose. "I also see that you've agreed to see a psychologist. Dr. Garrison at the hospital. But you have yet to complete this appointment?"

Rowan stands up straighter. "It's in two days, sir."

"Good enough." The judge gathers up his papers and taps them together on the desk. "Do me a favor, Rowan. Please. Do not grace me with your presence again. Can you do that?"

She nods. And though her head moves up and down, agreeing fully with the judge's command, she wonders if it's true. Will she stop? Can she? She folds her hands together in front of her torso to show how composed she is, how mature. The urge to pee in her pants has lessened slightly, but she still feels about five years old.

The judge bangs his gavel on the bench. "You're dismissed," he says.

Dodge

It's all there. Everything is in order. Rowan takes one last look at the columns of figures in front of her—a summer of red and black and vanilla and chocolate—and pounds the ledger closed, delineating the past. She uses her arms to liberate her chair from the desk, feet riding the wheels, then slumps in place, unable to complete the momentum of leaving.

As if on cue, perpetuating a reflex that started with the closing of the ledger, the doorknob clicks and Sherry enters the office, her cheeks flushed with the heat of the kitchen and a humid afternoon.

"Bud said you were back here. Trying to sneak out on me, eh?"

Rowan looks up. Sherry. White-blonde curls, shit-stirring grin, too-tight jeans. "Nah, Sher," she says. "I wouldn't skip town on you like that." She rides her thumb along the outside of the ledger, making a square.

"That's what they all say." Sherry winks and chomps on her gum, a new habit. "It might be easier that way, you know. Blow this town in the middle of the night. Take no prisoners."

"Yeah." Rowan rubs the tops of her knees, trying to erase a swell of self-consciousness. "Maybe surreptitious is the way to go."

"Surrepwhatis?" Sherry plants herself on the edge of the desk. She smells like sweat and roses. "Does that have anything to do with libraries? Because if it does, I ain't buying."

"No libraries. You're off the hook." Rowan takes a breath. For some reason, Sherry's proximity is making her uneasy. She taps the ledger and feels its certainty, its order.

"Your books look good," she says. "We did pretty well, considering the crappy economy and all. I still have to write down

215

what you'll have to do to close it up for the season. Shouldn't be bad, though. You can always write me, or call. If you have questions."

Sherry nods. She blows a monster bubble with her gum, pops it by sucking it into her mouth, then chaws viciously. "Did I tell you about Jer's latest scheme?" she says.

Rowan hops up and down on her chair, solidifying her position. "Nah. I thought he was joining the Marines."

"Not anymore." Sherry blows upward, repositioning a loop of hair on her forehead. "He's decided to be a chef. He already signed up for some class at Community. Pastries 101."

"No shit."

"Shit. I guess it was his gig here this summer. Bud turned him on to the art of Burger Presentation. He hasn't been the same since. I shoulda known. When he was little he would make mixtures—salad oil and Kool-Aid, like that. He'd make Little drink everything. Had to put a stop to it when I saw him headed for the household cleaners. But I guess he had it in him even then."

"I guess." Rowan attempts to bolster her end of the conversation by examining the ledger, but it doesn't do any good. It's all corners and closure; nothing she can use.

"I just hope he don't get all light in the loafers with them other chefs there." Sherry tugs on her gum, snaps it back into her mouth. "All them fruitcakes, swishing round the kitchen. Though knowing Jerry, he'd pound the first sucker who tried anything."

Under her forehead, where her vision lives, Rowan watches her options dwindle away. Is this how it will be from now on? People talk and she burrows in, all alone in the middle of company?

"I'm glad he ain't joining the service, though." Sherry snorts. "I can't see that boy in a crew cut to save his life."

"Sher?" Rowan fights her way out of confinement, words first. "There's something I need to tell you. About me and Catherine."

"No, you don't." Sherry looks directly at her, head wagging. "Believe me."

"But I do." Rowan says this, but is already taking it back. Her skin shrinks like paper peeling and she checks the floor beneath her. It's dark—scraped slabs with dust in the ridges.

"I had a girl come on to me once." Sherry folds her arms across her chest, propping her breasts between her elbows. "It was at a bar. Told her to stay the hell away from me. Told her I'd bust her ass into next month if she thought she was slipping her mitts into my britches." The flush in Sherry's cheeks spreads as the distant scene plays out across her features. "There's a reason we got women and men," she says. "Two to tango, like they say. Ain't right to try to make one side into the whole dance. Throws everything off, if you know what I mean."

Rowan's heart, which is about the size of a pea, dings inside her chest. She remembers to breathe, but that's all. "Yeah, I know what you mean."

"Look, I'm gonna go back to the grill. You want anything?"

"No." It comes out snappy. Mad.

"That's cool." Sherry stands with all the resources of oblivion available to her. "I'll come back to check on you in a bit."

"I'll be here," Rowan says, lying.

New

Dr. Liz Garrison's office is surprisingly homey for a hospital room. The walls are pale peach and the curtains are a gauzy white that softens the sun as it enters the room. There are paintings on the wall and lots of pillows on the couch. The room even smells like a house and not a hospital—a waft of cookies and cinnamon.

Rowan sits in the middle of it, trying to come up with a response. The doctor has asked her a question, one she can't answer. Or rather, one she doesn't want to answer. She likes Dr. Garrison, she does. The doctor is a lot like her room—warm and easy, with soft edges and the promise of something good. But that doesn't mean Rowan can answer her question.

"I'm not sure." Rowan stalls.

"Okay, then. Let's try this." Dr. Garrison puts down her pad. She said at the beginning of the session she'd be taking notes, but she hasn't taken very many. Now she's putting the pad in her lap and patting it with her hand. She looks like she's just finished a book, one she liked.

"Let's pretend you know why you took those candy bars at Henny Penny," she says. "It's like a game. Just take a guess."

"Uh," Rowan says. The couch is so comfortable, it's hard not to relax. Even though she wants to strain and stress, she can't. Even now. "I think maybe it was about my mom," she says. "I mean, I don't know. That's probably pretty stupid."

"Not stupid." Dr. Garrison's face matches her voice. Like everything Rowan says is valuable and important. "Why would it be about your mom?"

Rowan takes a breath. "The Henny Penny thing wasn't the first time," she says. "I've been shoplifting for a while."

"How long?"

"I don't know. Since I was a kid. I don't know why I did it. I guess because it was fun. But I also knew it was wrong. It's not like I didn't know it was wrong." Rowan picks up a pillow and puts it in her lap. It smells like the room, like hope and cookies. "And then, after I got caught, I saw these pictures in my head. Pictures of my mom. Like, I wanted her to come get me." Rowan flinches. "I told you it was stupid."

"Sorry," Dr. Garrison says. "I don't see it that way at all."

"Why not?"

"Because it makes a lot of sense to me. Your mom died when you were just a baby. And everyone told you she died in a car accident, only it wasn't true. There was a hole there, a key piece of information missing. Yes?"

Rowan nods.

"When you're little, it's hard to understand these things. And when the truth has been . . . masked, it makes everything even harder. I'm not surprised you developed a little secret of your own, one that was tied to your mom."

Rowan grimaces. "It sounds like you're making excuses. Like you're saying what I did was okay."

"No," Dr. Garrison says. "That's not what I'm saying. I'm just trying to make sense of it all. Sometimes we do things that don't serve us. But that doesn't mean there's not a reason beneath the behavior. You see?"

"I guess." Rowan clutches her pillow. "Maybe."

Dr. Garrison chuckles. "You don't believe me?"

Rowan gulps. "I didn't say that. It's just . . ."

"Just what?"

Rowan stares at the pillow, at the bumpy cream-colored fabric and the tassels on each corner. "I guess it feels good. I thought I was crazy. It feels good to think that maybe I'm not. That there was a reason for what I did. Though I still think it was bad."

"*It* was bad? Or *you* were bad? There's a difference."

Rowan shivers. Dr. Garrison is watching her, but not in a way that makes Rowan nervous. Actually, it's the exact opposite. It's like Dr. Garrison is sitting in this vast space, but not empty or lonely space. More like space that can hold anything, absolutely anything. And because she's there, because she's in this open, forgiving place, Rowan gets to be there too. It's a strange feeling. Rowan's never met anyone like Dr. Garrison before.

"It's me," Rowan says. "I'm the bad one. That's what I . . . that's what it feels like."

Dr. Garrison nods. "Yes. Sometimes we feel things because of what we tell ourselves. And sometimes what we tell ourselves is wrong. Even though it feels true. You see?"

Rowan shrugs.

"What I'm saying, Rowan, is that you're not bad. You did something that wasn't . . . ideal. But you're not bad."

"Mmmm." Rowan keeps her eyes down. Then peeks up at Dr. Garrison. The doctor has laugh lines in the corners of her eyes and cheeks that bloom with red. She looks like she spends a lot of time smiling, which seems strange for someone who has her job. Isn't she supposed to be sad and depressed after listening to people's troubles all day?

"We have a few minutes left," the doctor says. "I understand you're leaving for college in a couple days. Is that right?"

"Yes," Rowan says. She suddenly feels bereft, like the doctor just told her she has only a few hours to live. Rowan swallows hard, trying to stop the sadness that threatens to leave her crying. "Yes," she says again. "In a couple days, I'll be gone." She shakes her head. Why did she say that? The words only magnify the sadness, and the tears start to flow freely, streaming from her eyes and onto the cream-colored pillow.

"Ah yes," the doctor says. "That's good. It's good to cry."

For whatever reason, Rowan believes her, and the tears continue with enthusiasm. Crying alone is strange enough. Crying in front of someone else is even worse. And yet here she is, doing it. There are so many things to cry about—her mom, Ben, the shoplifting, Catherine. They all mix together in a soup of sadness, flowing from Rowan's brain and heart and down her face, plopping onto the plump little pillow in her lap. Until she remembers what the doctor said, about how it's almost time to go.

Rowan sniffles and wipes her eyes. "Thanks," she says. She picks up a tissue from the table next to her and blows her nose. "I mean, this was good."

"It's Boston, yes?" Dr. Garrison picks up her pen and writes something on her pad. "That's where you're going to college?"

"Yup. Wellington. Why?"

"This is just a thought, but would you be interested in continuing to talk to someone? I have a friend, a colleague, who works in Boston. Renee Olsen. I think you'd like her. It might be good to keep talking like this. It could help."

Rowan flushes. "Okay," she says. "That sounds ... good."

"Good." The doctor puts down her pen. "It was nice to meet you, Rowan. I'm glad you came to talk to me. I wish you all the best."

Rowan blinks. "I think maybe I'm gay," she says. "That's another reason I was at the Henny Penny. I was upset about a girl."

Dr. Garrison smiles. "Ah," she says. She clasps her hands together on top of her pad. "I'm glad you told me. That's a lot to deal with all at once." She smiles again, the laugh lines around her eyes rising.

"You don't think it's bad?"

"No. Not at all."

"Huh."

The doctor takes her pad off her lap and places it on the desk beside her. "You're a remarkable young woman, Rowan. Has anyone ever told you that?"

Rowan shakes her head. "Not really," she says.

"I wish we had more time to talk, but I have another client coming in a few minutes. Look up Renee Olsen in Boston. And if you ever want to talk to me again, I'm here. Okay?"

"Okay." Rowan pries the pillow off her lap and rises from the couch. She feels light, like her insides are made of air. "Thanks," she says. "I'm really . . . Thanks."

As the doctor escorts her to the door, Rowan continues to feel like she's floating. Like she's attached to her body, and to the earth, but worlds lighter than she used to be. She floats down the hall, down the stairs, and out the front door.

It's another muggy day, the air fat with humidity and the sun shining on everything. The sky is bluer than it was an hour ago, and the trees are greener, the leaves shaking and shimmering in the wet air. Everyone's nicer too—at least everyone Rowan passes on the sidewalk out of the hospital. They all smile at her like they know her, like it's her birthday and everyone is wishing her well. Maybe it's because she's smiling too, a smile so big it makes her face hurt.

Rowan walks over to the bench, the one with the buckeyes, the one where Catherine said goodbye. Even the bench looks better, not beat-up and lonely, but ripe with possibilities. Did everything always look like this, and she just couldn't see it? Rowan eases onto the bench, so as not to disturb the open, floating feeling inside her. She allows her arms to rest against her legs, and her legs to rest against the bench. She is held up, supported. It feels good. New.

There's a woman approaching, a nurse in uniform. She's clutching a purse and walking toward the hospital with a steady, determined pace. Is she back from a break? Starting her shift? Either way, she's ready—her eyes carrying everything she knows and everything she's about to see.

Rowan wants to keep watching her, but she doesn't want the woman to think she's staring. So she closes her eyes. She can still see the woman, though. And other things too. Ben in the hospital bed. Her dad at the kitchen table, talking about her mom. Trish in the gift shop, cracking up at something Rowan just said. Catherine in the hotel room, her feet tapping the shag carpet. And Dr. Garrison in her office, telling Rowan she's okay.